# The Child
# of
# 100 Years

By Cana Gauthier

HIGHVIEW PRESS

Rochester, NY

Published by Highview Press, LLC.

*This is a work of fiction. Names, characters, businesses, places, events and incidents are either the products of the author's imagination or used in a fictitious manner. Any resemblance to actual persons, living or dead, or actual events is purely coincidental.*

Cover Design by Highview Press, LLC.

Author Photo by Isabelle Nudd

The Child of 100 Years/Cana Gauthier

ISBN 978-1981749751

*To my husband —*
*For dreaming next to me each night*

# CHAPTER 1

"I can't believe they paired me with Meghan," Sophie said, almost slamming her tray down beside me. "She's probably the most judgmental, stuck up person on campus."

"That's only a first impression," Julie said. "Anyway, it's not as though she can disclose anything personal about you. There's the confidentiality clause and all."

Sophie huffed a dramatic sigh and smashed cream cheese on her bagel. "Yeah I guess. Who did they pair you with?" she asked, looking at me.

I reflected on the vague email I'd received earlier that morning.

*Dear Elena Gray,*

*See below for your lab partner assignment.*

*Lab 237*

*Row 17*

*Project Partner: Vincent Miller*

*Please remember to adhere to the program guidelines, including professionalism and confidentiality. Any violation of the program guidelines will be considered a breach of your research contract agreement with the Sleep Research Academy, and may result in disqualification from the Dreamscape Research Program.*

"Oh, I don't know him. Someone named Vincent Miller." I shrugged and took a sip of my coffee.

Julie cringed. "Oh no, not *that* guy."

"You know who he is?" I kept my tone casual and my expression blank, attempting to appear unmoved by her apparent disgust.

Julie rolled her eyes. "He's one of the tech nerds. He's an anti-social geek who needs a shower and a hair-cut. Probably a pervert too."

Sophie was listening with a frown. "How do you know him?"

"My friend Rachel hung out with him a few times, and let's just say...he's a confirmed weirdo," Julie disclosed.

"Wait, if he's anti-social, why was he hanging out with your friend?" Sophie inquired.

*Good question.*

Julie shrugged and replied, "Have you seen Rachel? She can have her pick on campus. Vincent probably saw an opportunity and took it." She dipped a small donut in her coffee and took a bite.

"Did they hook up?" Sophie asked.

Julie shook her head and swallowed before replying, "No, Rachel's too good for him. She decided not to waste her time."

I couldn't help but feel a twinge of disgust myself, but not for the same reason as Julie. First of all, I generally hate gossip and girl drama, but I also detest people who think they're better than someone based on their appearance. If what Julie said were true, it just caused me to think more ill of her friend Rachel.

Sophie spoke up. "Well, it's research anyway, right? It's not like Elena has to be friends with this guy."

I laughed. "A minute ago, you were complaining about being paired with Meghan."

"That's different. You're lucky to get paired with a guy. He won't judge you if you have a whacked-out dream. Guys are easier to work with," Sophie muttered.

Julie was texting someone. "I gotta go. I told Rachel I'd meet her in the library before class." She stood and gave us a wave. "Sorry you got stuck with the tech nerd," she said to me before walking away.

I gave her a half smile and shrugged again.

Sophie rolled her eyes once Julie was gone. "Don't pay any attention to what she said. Rachel isn't really anything special. I'll bet money this guy Vincent didn't want her hanging around, and Rachel just made up some story about him. Girls are the worst."

Sophie was the only girl in a family with four brothers. She was quite attractive, but not in a typical feminine way. She kept her dark hair short and rarely wore makeup. I was envious of her naturally tan skin and effortless beauty.

She tapped her phone. "We should get moving. It's almost time for lab to start."

We pushed our chairs away from the table and dumped the remaining contents of our trays in the garbage. I parted ways with Sophie to use the bathroom one more time before the lab session.

As the time drew nearer, I was more nervous than I would have liked to admit. The discussion I'd had with Sophie and Julie only increased my anxiety about working with Vincent. I tried to take comfort in the fact that if Vincent really were an anti-social person, he may be less inclined to report my nightmares to the Academy.

The nightmares had begun as soon as I logged into the Dreamscape Program. I kept them to myself, afraid to admit that perhaps I was adversely affected by the new technology. Anyway, the opportunity to be involved in dream research was too exciting, and I couldn't bear the thought of discontinuing my studies. Unfortunately, partnering with someone else in lab meant my nightmares wouldn't be a secret for much longer.

It wouldn't have been so bad if the nightmares occurred only while I was logged into the program. Perhaps my anxiety triggered an odd response to the Dreamscape Program, or a faint childhood memory resurfaced every time I used it. Maybe that part could be explained. But for the past several weeks, from the day I began using the program, the nightmares persisted – every night when I went to sleep.

They were terrifying. I would wake in a sweat, gasping, my pillow drenched from tears. The darkness in my room played tricks on my eyes, and every corner hid an ominous shape, so that I couldn't tell what was real and what was a part of the nightmare. The fear was paralyzing. If I needed to use the bathroom, I would hold it until it became painful, simply because I refused to walk the dark halls at night.

My weight dropped after a few weeks and I developed permanent dark circles beneath my eyes. I told my friends I was homesick for New York and stressed out from the workload at the Academy. California was a long way from home, and the program was rigorous at the Sleep Research Academy, so they accepted my excuse. At 22, I was unwilling to share my night terrors with anyone. Yet I was more worried that I would be exempt from using the Dreamscape Program. After working so hard to get into the Academy, that would have been even more of a nightmare.

The lab was humming with activity as students prepared for their first paired session with the Dreamscape Program. The lights overhead seemed brighter than usual, though it could have just been my lack of sleep that made them seem so.

The Sleep Research Academy specialized in dream research. Their Dreamscape Program was heralded as a "miracle of science," because it allowed dreamers to not only record their dreams and view them later, but to experience someone else's dream as well. The implications were unfathomable. At last, we could without limitations, explore the human psyche. We could unlock the deep mysteries of the subconscious, and understand the vulnerability we endure each night in our unconscious state.

There was a process to the Dreamscape Program. At first, we used it solo and reviewed our recorded dreams independently to evaluate our inner selves. This was also the adjustment period. Apparently, the program did indeed take a toll on the user, but after more regular use, our brains calibrated to it, and we were able to spend more time logged in. These longer stretches of REM created more dream data. Later, we could log in consciously and "re-watch" various dreams, making observations accordingly.

Phase two of the program we were assigned to a partner. But instead of watching a pre-recorded dream, we would log in at the same time and view our partner's dream as it happened. A more accurate way to describe it is that we would *experience* another person's dream, as if it were our own. There were some restrictions to the process, however. For example, we were unable to interact with our partner while logged in to the program, so although we would share their dream, they would be unaware of our presence.

I found row 17 and logged myself into the terminal. Then I reclined in my lab chair and waited for Vincent to appear. I was weary and anxious all at once, but pulled out my phone and pretended to be busy on it.

At last, someone came up beside me. Dropping his backpack on the floor next to a vacant lab chair, he logged into his terminal and sat down without so much as glancing in my direction. He wasn't very tall, but he was very pale, as if he seldom ventured outdoors, and his dark hair was sort of messy, like he was overdue for a haircut. He had his laptop out on his lap and was typing rapidly as we awaited further instructions.

*Vincent Miller, I presume.*

We were given a brief lecture on how to properly use the program in pairs. I listened as closely as I could, running on so little sleep. Vincent typed throughout the entire explanation. It may have been my current state of sleep deprivation, but I was already irritated by his disinterest in the research process.

Then it was time to begin the lab session. The room once again broke into a buzz as everyone readied for the first dream pairing. Vincent continued to type on his laptop, looking altogether more immersed in his current preoccupation than what we were about to do with the Dreamscape Program.

I placed the metal halo on my head that would read my brain waves, and readied the sleep mask in one hand. I waited.

"You're going first," Vincent said, without pausing to look in my direction.

"As the dreamer or observer?" I questioned.

"You're dreaming first." He folded his laptop down and returned it to his backpack.

I was silent.

"You still need to set your parameters," Vincent stated, his tone indifferent.

"Oh, right."

I punched the required criterion into the computer terminal and leaned back.

"That's not right." I heard him say. He got up and came to the arm of my chair. I watched him correct my error, and then sit back again.

"Thanks," I said. "I'm Elena, by the way."

He nodded. "I know."

His reply seemed to signal the end of any further conversation.

*I guess this is it.*

I placed the mask over my face and fell swiftly into darkness.

*

They won't find me here.

*I'd found that hiding was my best chance of escaping the shadows. They were ever lurking, wandering the halls and empty rooms of the mansion. I was alone but for them. Always alone. Sometimes they would cry out together, practically rending the structure of the building with their shrieks. I'd watched them feel along the walls and windows, as if longing to get out. They were imprisoned, and I with them.*

*But here, alone in the dark, perhaps I would be safe. If I could just be still long enough, I may have the chance to get out.*

*Maybe this time.*

*I put my eye to the crack in the door. The room was unusually still, and I feared they waited for me with baited breath. They were patient. If I moved too quickly, they would find me and smother me in the darkness. I needed to be patient too.*

*Then the creaking began. It was as if the mansion itself moaned and moved about. The room seemed to wave before my eyes and strange lines danced in my vision. Sometimes sitting in the dark can have that effect.*

*I grew tired of waiting. It was time to move; time to get out of there.*

*As I emerged from the closet, I felt as though I might make it after all. The creaking had ceased and the shadows were nowhere to be seen. Perhaps I would be free this time. I would step outside the mansion and never return. I would feel the sun on my face once more, and hear the laughter of my friends. I wouldn't be alone anymore.*

*This felt familiar somehow. I'd been here before — done this all before. Thoughts such as this swam to the surface of my mind and I felt a rush of panic as I realized I already knew what happened next.*

*The walls changed, strange images appearing and disappearing along them. The images were gruesome, deathlike faces, with haunting eyes. They were speaking to me, but I couldn't hear what they said.*

*Where the faces once were, the shadows began to come through the walls. They were massive and slow-moving creatures, with long arms and torsos, and* legs that almost dragged behind them. I was crippled with fear, until I realized they were nearly upon me. I turned and ran.

At that point, the mansion changed. It happened so suddenly, I didn't notice at first, but then I was in a structure with concrete walls, decrepit and dripping with some grotesque substance. The most frightening part was yet to come.

I slowed to a stop, panting and shaking from cold and terror. Damp, foul-smelling air filled my senses. To my right was an ancient elevator shaft, and to my left a doorway leading to a stairwell. I was in a basement, barely lit. I stood still for ages, until I forced myself to venture forth toward the elevator shaft.

The doors were open, revealing no elevator, but a cavern leading further down into the depths of the structure. I felt a frigid draft on my face and backed away.

With resolve, I moved toward the stairwell to my left, vaguely wondering how it was possible to descend any further, given the nature of the basement. Yet the elevator clearly led down, and the stairwell likely did the same.

Silence had smothered all other sensations. An unnatural pressure mounted in my head that made me feel somewhat dizzy, but I reached for the handle to the door nonetheless. It was rusted in places, and I thought that it might not open. I gave a firm pull and the door, without so much as a sound, gave way to my grasp, revealing a massive yaw of a stairwell.

I felt the air from below rush up to me, once again filling my nostrils with the vile smell from beneath and with it, hopelessness. I would never leave this place. I would succumb to the shadows and become nothing more than a gruesome face on the walls.

Then a small figure materialized before me, ascending the stairwell. With no discernable features, it beckoned to me to follow it to the darkness below. I wanted to follow, terrified as I was. I wanted to see what awful phantom produced such a putrid odor.

Wanted to look death in the face

An invisible hand seemed to gently press me, guiding me below. Before I knew it, I put one foot before me and was swallowed in blackness.

# CHAPTER 2

My ears were ringing. I lay still for a full five minutes before my sluggish brain pieced together where I was.

*I'm in the lab.*

Very slowly, I brought myself to a sitting position. Once the ringing had finally ceased, I heard a faint clicking noise beside me. Vincent still sat in his lab chair with his laptop. Otherwise, the lab was nearly empty, except for a few lingering students and technicians.

"Have I been sleeping long?" I asked quietly.

"Twenty minutes or so. You didn't wake up when the session ended, but I told them you'd taken a larger dose of the sleep gas by mistake." He spoke without taking his eyes from the computer screen.

"Oh. Well, thanks. I just didn't get any sleep last night. Guess I needed a longer nap," I replied, shifting my legs over the side of the chair and preparing to stand.

Vincent was quiet as he continued to type. Then he closed the laptop and packed it away.

I expected him to say something else. Maybe ask me how the dream ended, or if I were accustomed to having such nightmares. Anything. He remained cold and detached as we stood to leave the lab. In fact, we said not a word to each other, even at parting in the hall. I was confused, to say the least. Could he really have so little interest in my dreams? It was disappointing. I guess secretly I had some hope that sharing my dreamscape with another person would somehow lend itself to an explanation.

With lab over, I returned to my room before lunch and afternoon classes. I was more tired than I'd been before lab, and tempted to sleep forever – or at least through the afternoon. Instead I lay on my bed, eyes wide open, and reflected on my nightmares.

Research had produced no helpful solution to the recurring dreams. Everything I read merely confirmed what I had already known: a recurring dream may signal an unresolved issue the dreamer faces in real life. There were many case studies involving subjects who experienced night terrors or unexplained dreams of a repetitive nature, but nothing so pronounced as what I experienced each night in sleep.

I wavered between sleep and conscious thought for a while before my phone buzzed on my nightstand, snapping me out of my trance.

Sophie had texted me. Her message read: *Where are you? Come to lunch.*

In the cafeteria, I grabbed a tray and found where Sophie was sitting with Evan and Alex. They were laughing loudly as I placed my tray next to Sophie.

"There's the little sleeper," Alex said with a smirk.

I saw Evan eyeing my plate of food. "You're going to eat all of that?"

I looked down at my tray. I had grabbed a burger and fries, an orange, and two cookies. "I am, why?"

Evan shook his head in disbelief. "You're so tiny. Where do you store all that food?"

"At least she's not eating a salad," Alex said. "Why do girls always eat salad? There are much better things to eat."

"How was lab?" Sophie asked.

I shrugged. "Fine."

"What's Vincent like?" she probed, interestedly.

"He's quiet. We didn't really talk at all," I explained.

"She got paired with a tech nerd," Sophie told the guys.

Alex raised an eyebrow and smirked again. I could read his thoughts and rolled my eyes.

Evan chimed in, "Well that's good. He can help you out if you have a tech issue."

Sophie and Alex laughed. Evan looked confused. Then he turned a little red, but didn't say anything.

"All those tech nerds are closet perverts," Alex stated. "Look at them. They sit together and never talk to anyone else." He motioned to a table in the far corner of the room where several of the students in the tech program sat with their laptops. I'd noticed before how exclusive they tended to be, but now realized that I had never once seen Vincent sit with them. In fact, he rarely came to the cafeteria at all.

Later that day, I headed to the library to work on assignments. The Academy's massive library was full of both physical and online resource material. I spent a lot of time there in one of the reference rooms toward the back of the library. Perhaps part of the reason I frequented that room was that I hoped to have a chance to talk to Luke Phillips. Although he was in the medical research track and I didn't see him around very much, I made a point to visit the library often, if only just to talk to him for a while.

Luke and I had many things in common and enjoyed each other's company. Quite honestly, I was very attracted to Luke, but refused to seek him out aside from an occasional conversation in the library.

My stomach flipped over when I saw him seated in our usual room. He had spread before him several large textbooks and manuscripts. He was wearing glasses and his hair was slightly mussed, which only improved his overall appeal.

"How long have you been here?" I asked him quietly, sitting across the table.

Luke looked up at me, adjusting his glasses and swiping a piece of hair away from his face. He smiled, a bit embarrassed. "Oh hey. I've been here...um, I don't know how long." He checked his phone. "Four hours." He looked a little flustered. "It's this damn assignment they've given me. I think I'm obsessed Elena."

I laughed. "You do look rather absorbed. What are you working on anyway?"

Luke's blue eyes, though tired, gleamed as he said, "It's night terror research. Fascinating stuff. I can't stop reading these case studies."

I suddenly felt heavy. "Night terror research? What kind of research are you doing?"

"It's sort of complicated. Although we can use the Dreamscape Program to induce nightmares, the research isn't always so reliable. Some of these case studies are very interesting though."

I felt the color drain from my face. "You're inducing nightmares? Who are the test subjects?"

"Just other students in the medical track. They volunteer," he replied, nonchalantly. "It messes some of them up a little though. But how else can we study nightmares? They're unpredictable." He shrugged.

I was a bit taken aback by this information he'd shared. It seemed too closely connected to what I was experiencing.

"These students who have induced nightmares in the program...do they have any problems with nightmares afterward? I mean just on a regular basis?" I asked.

Luke glanced at me. "No, nothing like that. It's just a temporary state of terror. The program can affect the amygdala in such a way that it fools the dreamer into believing they're having a nightmare. But it's not ideal. It's not a natural nightmare, so the research isn't so reliable."

"I see." I frowned and opened my textbook slowly, fumbling for a page to read.

A moment of silence passed between us, until I realized Luke was watching me.

"What's wrong?" he asked.

I shrugged. "I don't know. It's an interesting assignment. But I guess I agree: if the nightmares aren't real, then what's the point?"

Luke sort of laughed. "The point is to research the brain's pattern during a nightmare."

"But if the program is what's affecting the amygdala, it's counterproductive, don't you think?" I argued.

Luke scratched his head. "You could say that I suppose. I didn't come up with the project, like I said. It's an assignment. The goal is to find a way to soothe people's fears through the program. I think they're considering using it as a treatment method for chronic nightmares."

I shook my head. "It's sort of a backward way to go about it," I grumbled.

Luke gave me a thoughtful look but said nothing.

As I pretended to study, thoughts of the first day I used the Dreamscape Program rushed into my head. The program not only recorded dreams for later viewing, it also enhanced the vividness of sleep, so that dreams seemed far more real and much easier to recall afterward. That first nightmare had been the most terrifying. It stayed with me for hours, until I fell into sleep again that night and discovered it wasn't over.

I can't explain why exactly I didn't share my problem with Luke then. It was too perfect an opportunity. I could have told him everything and offered to become a test subject. I'm sure somehow, he could have helped me make the nightmares stop. Later I realized that I didn't just want the nightmares to go away, and I certainly didn't want to share them with everyone else. At least, not until I understood them more first. In fact, it was in that small room in the library that I began to suspect my dreams really had a purpose. Perhaps I was meant to find out what it was.

That evening, I found myself standing outside the lab. It was only 6:30 pm, and the lab would be open until 8:00 pm. I had some time.

The lab was empty. I made my way to the far corner and logged into a vacant chair. I must have viewed my dreams a dozen times before, but it was possible I'd missed something.

Re-watching a dream in the program was like stepping into a 3-D movie. I could move the scene around and view it from different angles, and I could even zoom in and slow down the footage. The recording was slightly grainy, certainly not as clear as actually experiencing the dream inside the program. I regretted then that I couldn't leave my body and view my own dream.

I spent some time examining the first room, the one with the faces on the wall. I scanned the faces carefully, but found them to be rather nondescript. Viewing the dream this way lessened its intensity. I felt as though I were playing a video game, actually. Because the dream was recorded from my own brain waves, I watched it again in first person. Except for one part. I was surprised to find that when I reached the stairwell, at the end of the dream, I was watching myself. Somehow, I didn't remember that. I could clearly see my face, white and pale, and my eyes wide with fear. My mouth moved, and I guessed I might be screaming or yelling.

Then my face changed. In fact, my whole countenance now appeared as one dead. That scared me more than anything else. My palms began to sweat and I didn't want to watch anymore. I tore the visor from my face and sat staring blankly at the lab ceiling.

*Maybe I'm going to die.*

# CHAPTER 3

A week passed. Before I knew it, I was in the lab again, preparing to view Vincent's dreamscape. I arrived several minutes before he did. This time I had already inputted my parameters into the computer and prepared myself. Then I took out my tablet and read a research article to pass the time.

Vincent entered the lab several minutes later, but I kept my attention on the article, even when he had approached me and sat in the chair adjacent to mine.

I looked up briefly. "Hey," I greeted him.

He sort of gave me a nod as he set himself up for the procedure.

I had tried to think of something casual and intelligent to say to him beforehand, but had settled on remaining silent for the time being. Perhaps after I viewed his dreamscape, it would be easier to conjure up a conversation with this anti-social individual.

Vincent was leaning back in the chair with his eyes closed and brow furrowed in a troubled manner. He appeared exhausted.

"Are you feeling alright?" I asked in a low tone.

He nodded, eyes still closed.

Just then our instructor signaled for us to begin the lab session. I was nervous as I placed the visor on my face and readied myself to observe.

Becoming part of another person's dream was an altogether surreal experience. I was conscious, yet in a mixed-up kind of way, like I was floating somewhere unfamiliar, waiting for my feet to land. At last I felt myself begin to adjust to Vincent's dreamscape. Whereas initially I struggled to discern colors and sounds, I could now make them out and identify what it was I saw.

The scene became clear before me. Vincent, in what seemed to be his room at the Academy, sat at a desk typing on a blank keyboard. There were two monitors in front of him, each lit up and showing what looked like html code. He was working. I took my eyes off him and examined the rest of the room. Some of the details were rather vague, as if they made up part of a pre-rendered background. I could move. I walked around his room, attempting to touch various items, but could not actually connect with anything.

I came up behind Vincent and reached my hand out to him. It passed easily through him and his desk chair.

*I'm a ghost.*

Time was different in the dream. I couldn't say exactly how long Vincent worked, but at last the scene did change. His room vanished and he walked through the halls of the Academy. I found that I was connected to him somehow, and whether I moved was irrelevant. If *he* moved, I moved as well. My freedom to explore was limited to where he dreamt we were at present.

There were people with no faces, and sounds of voices, which made no actual words. Movement, color, sound all blended into an inconsequential scene. Vincent moved through it, paying little attention to any of the details.

We stopped in the cafeteria. There were many more chairs and tables than in reality, and so many people. It was like a labyrinth. I could feel Vincent's heaviness in that room. He moved more slowly, weaving through the tables and chairs filled with more nondescript faces. Someone spoke to Vincent. Maybe it was Rachel. It sort of *looked* like her, but when she moved her head, her features would change. I couldn't hear what she said because every sound in that room was suppressed, like being underwater.

Then something rather odd happened. Vincent jumped onto one of the tables and climbed up the wall. I glanced around, expecting some reaction from the people in the room. They had already begun to disappear. Vincent's movement pulled me with him. He opened the ceiling and we were in an air duct, so large we could easily stand. As Vincent moved, the duct morphed and the walls opened up until we were outside.

Vincent kept walking and we eventually stood on a beach at twilight. Several people sat around a large campfire and music played in the background. Vincent sat with the people there and they all laughed about something. I found myself fixated by the scene before me, taking in every small detail and savoring the sense of nostalgia, which flooded through me. This was a memory, not merely a dream. It was sharper and cleaner than the rest of what I'd seen in Vincent's dreamscape. The people's faces didn't blur or change, though their features were slightly unclear. Vincent laughed with them as they poked at the bonfire with sticks.

I could almost smell the burning logs from the campfire and the salt from the ocean. Even the wind gently blew, rifling Vincent's hair and clothes. Knowing I couldn't interact with anyone in the dream, I passed through their circle until I stood in the fire itself. There I sat and watched Vincent laugh and talk to his friends.

Then all at once, everything faded and I was left in the dark. The lab session was over. I removed the visor and breathed slowly, readjusting myself to the real world.

Beside me, Vincent remained motionless, with the halo and mask still in place. I reached over and removed the mask from his face. Then checked to be sure the program had ceased running. It wasn't unusual for the dreamer to remain asleep for at least a few moments after the session had ended. Around the room, others gradually awakened, and finally Vincent stirred. I sat back in my chair, waiting for him to fully rouse.

He sat up.

"How are you feeling?" I asked.

"Fine," he said, but he winced slightly, as though in pain.

We were given time that morning to debrief in one of the lounges not far from the lab. Students paired off, speaking quietly and taking notes on their laptops. Vincent and I found a small table by a window.

"What did you think?" he inquired. His hands were already busy with his laptop, his attention fixed on the screen.

I exhaled thoughtfully. "Well much of the dream was rather unclear. I couldn't tell who you were speaking to really or what was being said. You moved around a lot too." I laughed a little.

Vincent's gray eyes broke away from the screen and landed on my face. "I meant about the overall experience, as an observer. The dream itself was meaningless."

"Oh," I said, embarrassed. Vincent's tone and attitude made me very self-conscious. I wanted to crawl under the table. "Well, that part was quite intriguing. It was like...um, how do I describe it?"

"Playing a videogame?" he offered.

I paused. "Yes, exactly," I agreed. "But an older one with pre-rendered backgrounds."

Vincent raised an eyebrow. "So, you're a gamer."

"Sort of. I used to play videogames with my brother growing up," I explained.

Vincent nodded. "What else?"

"Huh?"

"About the dream pairing."

"Right. Well...I was tied to you. I couldn't move around much on my own."

Vincent nodded again.

"What about you?" I asked him.

"Hm?"

"When you were in my dream. Was it the same?"

He nodded but continued to type on his laptop.

While waiting for him to respond, I recorded my other observations from Vincent's dreamscape, and became rather engaged in transcribing his dream on my tablet. Every detail intrigued me. I even found myself attempting to sketch out Vincent's character based on his dream. It wasn't all that difficult. For example, he didn't like rooms full of people, which explained why he avoided the cafeteria. Rachel's obscure features told me he really didn't care much for her, despite Julie's story. Climbing into an air duct had been his escape, and he missed the people around the campfire on the beach. I was convinced that last part was a legitimate memory.

Vincent closed his laptop, interrupting my train of thought. "I have to go," he said.

I hadn't been aware of how much time we'd let pass in silence.

"Oh, sure. I'll see you around then," I said.

Vincent left without another word.

I sat back in my chair and sighed deeply, suddenly remembering Vincent hadn't really answered my question.

"How's it going?" Sophie asked. She slid into the chair Vincent had recently vacated.

I gave her a half smile and shrugged. "It's what you would expect. Observing was fun, but Vincent isn't too talkative. I'm kind of working things out on my own."

"That's too bad," Sophie sympathized. "Hopefully your research won't be inhibited in any way."

"I don't think so. He does talk, but it's just...he makes me feel so stupid when he does. He's kind of cold, you know?"

Sophie gave me a sorry look. "Yeah, he has that reputation around here."

"Right." I said. "How are things with Meghan going?"

"Not so bad, really," Sophie admitted. "I guess Julie was right — I did judge her a bit too soon. She's very dedicated to dream research and she's already helped me with some of my own research."

"Nice. I'm glad it's working out for you."

Sophie nodded. We glanced out the window for a moment without talking.

"Elena...I know we haven't known each other long, but...you can tell me things if you need to." Sophie looked at me carefully, her dark eyes expressing unspoken concern.

I studied her face. "Yeah, I know. Thanks. Maybe soon I will, I'm just working it out still," I told her.

She nodded. Then after another pause, changed the subject. "Hey, have you heard anything about this building? It has an interesting history."

"I know it was built in the mid 1930's. Some French scientist built it, right?" I said, with little interest.

"Yeah, I heard that too. But you know some of the building hasn't been renovated yet. There's a whole wing off the faculty hall that's closed up."

"Oh really?" I wondered what Sophie's point was in bringing this up.

"I heard some rumors that it may be haunted. Wouldn't it be fun to get in there and look around?" Sophie's eyes shone excitedly.

*Ah. I see.*

"Maybe it would," I replied with a short laugh. "You like haunted houses?"

Sophie nodded. "It would be nice to blow off some steam, don't you think? What do you say we get in there Friday night and look around?"

"Why not? I'm up for it."

"Want to see if Evan and Alex will come?" she asked.

"You don't think they'll make too much noise and get us caught?"

"I'll threaten them. They'll be quiet," she assured me.

The week passed rather slowly after that. I found myself looking forward to my upcoming adventure with Sophie and the guys, and as for my dreams, they were worse than ever. Since sharing Vincent's dreamscape, certain components of my own nightmares shifted somehow. The overall dream was the same, but flashes from Vincent's dream would occasionally appear. Sometimes I would even see his face, either in the wall or in the darkness of the elevator shaft. One time he appeared on the stairwell, beckoning me down into the black abyss. Seeing him there produced in me a stronger sense of urgency than I'd known beforehand, though I couldn't understand why.

I felt as though I saw Vincent more around campus as well. At times, we'd pass each other in the hall on the way to classes, or he would leave his room just as I happened to be walking by. I even saw him more often in the cafeteria. But we never spoke to each other. Vincent acted like he didn't know me, so I followed his lead and did the same.

At last, Friday came and Sophie knocked on my door.

I opened to find her dressed in black, armed with a small flashlight.

I laughed aloud. "What are you supposed to be: a thief or a ninja?"

She struck a comical martial arts pose. "A ninja thief of course." She came into my room and shut the door behind her. "You need to change. You're too conspicuous like that."

I gave an exaggerated sigh and rolled my eyes. "You're ridiculous. No one will care what I'm wearing. Everyone's either out or sleeping anyway."

"Come on, just do it," she pleaded.

"Fine. You're a nut," I muttered, as I pulled a pair of black pants and a black t-shirt out of my dresser.

Sophie giggled and threw herself on my bed. She took her phone out and scrolled through it while I changed.

"Where are we meeting the guys?" I asked.

"Aw, they chickened at the last minute. It's just me and you," she replied.

"'Chickened?'"

"They went to a movie with a group of people. Bunch of fun-suckers," she mumbled, still scrolling through her phone.

"Aw, too bad," I said, wryly.

Sophie looked up at me. "Just for that, you're taking a selfie with me."

I cringed dramatically.

"You deserve it," she exclaimed, hopping up and swinging her phone around so we were both in the frame. She glanced at the picture. "Oh, nice," she said, shoving her phone in my face so I could see the result. Sophie's dark eyes and tan skin had succeeded in turning me into a green-eyed ghost with limp, pale hair. The black t-shirt only washed me out even more.

"Yeah. You can delete that," I remarked.

"Nope. Already posting it," she said as her fingers moved rapidly across the screen.

After she'd finished torturing me with her phone, we emerged from my room and tiptoed through the halls. Though we heard faint voices behind closed doors now and then, we passed no one, and I began to feel a bit of a thrill about sneaking into the west wing, although it seemed to take forever to get there. Then at last, we were standing in an empty, darkened hall staring at an ornately carved wooden door. Even from outside the wing, a faint, musty smell seeped through the cracks in the door. Sophie turned a worn-out door knob to find that it opened easily.

"I was sure it would be locked," she whispered.

"If you thought it would be locked, why did we come?" I asked, whispering back.

"Well I had to at least try to get in. Ok. We're committed now. Ready?" she asked, turning to me.

I nodded.

Sophie appeared almost nervous. It made me nervous too.

The door swung open and we stepped across the threshold, closing the door gently behind us. We swept the hall with our lights. Beneath our feet was a well-worn carpet, deteriorating in places. As we moved forward, the floor creaked, announcing our entrance into a forgotten place.

We entered each room we passed. They were the same – empty of furniture and in the process of being ripped apart. Wallpaper hung, exposing plumbing and plaster. One room was covered in large, brown water stains.

"This is just depressing," Sophie muttered.

I was silent, overcome with a sadness I couldn't explain. A lump formed in my throat and I felt a little short of breath.

We moved on. The rooms grew colder and mustier the further in we went.

*So many rooms.*

"I wonder what they're going to do with all this?" Sophie mused.

After a while, we approached a set of double doors in much better condition than anything else we'd seen in that part of the mansion. They were heavy, expensive-looking doors with large, brass door knobs.

"This one's locked," Sophie stated. I sensed her frustration after she tried the knob several times with no success. "Guess we won't get in there tonight."

"There's one more room," I said, motioning with my light.

Across from the locked room was a smaller one that looked as though it could have been a guest room at one time. I was tired at this point, and a chill had spread over me. Then I saw it. My light shone on a closet in the corner of the room. I approached it carefully and crept inside, closing the door so I could peer through the crack at the rest of the room.

"Elena?" Sophie sounded confused. "Are you playing a game?" She laughed.

I closed my eyes and could see everything. Yes, I had been dreaming about this part of the mansion for weeks and I'd never even seen it before.

"Let's go back," I said to Sophie, jumping up out of the closet.

"What's wrong?"

I didn't reply. I almost bolted into the hall and back the way we'd come. I vaguely heard Sophie following behind, trying to ask me if I were ok.

When we exited the west wing, I closed the door behind us a little too forcefully. I would have been concerned someone had heard if I'd cared at that moment. All I wanted was to be away from that room. I didn't want the shadows to find me, if indeed they could when I wasn't lying prone on my bed, vulnerable to my subconscious.

I leaned against the door, panting slowly.

"Did you see something?"

"Let's go back to my room," I said quietly.

We said nothing as we made our way back to the safety of my room. I'd never been happier to open that door.

"So, it *is* haunted?" Sophie ventured, as we sat on my bed.

I didn't know what to say. I could lie and pretend that it was, but I was too exhausted to even try.

"I've seen that place before. This is going to sound really strange but...I've been dreaming about that part of the mansion...for weeks." I allowed my gaze to meet Sophie's and I searched her face for a reaction. Her brows were slightly furrowed, but she waited for me to continue.

I sat back on the pillows on my bed. "I've been having the same dream over and over. There are these black shadowy things coming after me, and I'm running through the Academy. Sometimes it's the dorm halls or labs, but I always end up in that room we saw. I always hide in that closet. Then the walls change." I sighed. "These faces appear. They look like dead people. Then I'm somewhere else, in a basement or something." I hugged my knees. "It always ends with me standing at a stairwell, but I can't see what's down there. I never make it down. I want to, even though I think I'll probably end up dying, or something horrible will happen." I stopped talking and rested my chin on my knees.

"When did the dreams start?" Sophie asked quietly.

"The day I logged into the Dreamscape Program," I told her.

"So, it's the program," she stated.

I shook my head. "They started that way, but now I dream about it no matter what — napping, logged in to the program, at night — it doesn't matter. My brain is stuck on that dream."

"Have you said anything?"

"No. I can't say anything. They'll make me stop using the program. I need to keep researching," I explained. "I'll figure out what's going on. I just need a little more time."

"What does Vincent think?"

I looked up at Sophie. "He doesn't know the dreams are recurring. Not yet anyway. He's going to find out very soon. I don't know what he'll say. Probably nothing. He doesn't seem to care."

Sophie was quiet. We both sat without a word for a while. Then she said, "This is what's been bothering you?"

I nodded. "It's not just that I don't sleep well...I'm afraid in these dreams. I don't think I've ever had nightmares like that before. I mean, I wake up and think something is going to happen to me."

"It sounds serious then, don't you think?"

"What do you mean?"

"I mean if you dreamt about that room and you've never seen it before, maybe you're dreaming about that feeling of danger for a reason," she said.

"What are you thinking?"

Sophie shifted so that she sat facing me on the bed. "Could there actually be a reason to fear? Maybe something weird is going on with the program. Or maybe this place has a strange history and you're just...dreaming about it. People have had premonitions in their dreams before. Actually, it would be a great research project."

*She's trying to cheer me up.*

I smiled at Sophie and nodded. She could be right in some way. It's possible that I'd read something about the mansion's history and I'd just forgotten about it. As for her first suggestion, it had already occurred to me that the Dreamscape Program may have produced a glitch of some kind the first time I used it. Though for that to be true, it meant that my *brain* was now glitching from having used the program. If that were the case, I needed to do something about it soon.

We were both tired after our adventure, so we said goodnight and Sophie left my room.

I slept restlessly that night. My mind kept mixing up thoughts of the west wing with my dream so that I couldn't tell if I were thinking or dreaming. I thought about Vincent a lot too. He would very soon find out that I kept having the exact same nightmare. I wondered whether I should tell him beforehand.

That weekend passed slowly. I stayed in my room most of the time, reading or watching shows on my laptop. Maybe I was a little depressed.

Sophie came by a couple of times to chat, but though we discussed the dreams and our exploration of the west wing, we were both at a loss to explain their connection. Then Sunday, at lunch, Sophie practically dragged me from my room to the cafeteria. She said I needed to be around people.

The cafeteria was usually less occupied on weekends. Many of the students and staff had families nearby or other commitments. Sophie and I found a table near one of the windows, at the far end of the cafeteria. Julie and Rachel joined us shortly after we sat down.

Honestly, I couldn't say what we talked about. It was the usual polite questions about how everyone's research was going and gossip about this teacher or that student. Before I knew it, Sophie had asked Rachel a personal question about her relationship with Vincent. I was surprised at Sophie's boldness, but intrigued by Rachel's response.

"Oh him." Rachel laughed and glanced at Julie. "He's not interested in girls I guess." She tossed a piece of long, highlighted hair behind her shoulder.

"You mean he's gay?" Sophie pressed.

Rachel shrugged. "Maybe. I don't think so. I know he doesn't like to be around people much. He's very techy, so maybe he'd just prefer to work on his computer."

"How did you meet him?" I asked.

"I was a beta tester for the program over the summer," she explained. "I met Vincent while we were testing. He wrote part of the Dreamscape Program you know."

I hadn't known.

Where their conversation turned next, I couldn't say. My thoughts wandered, processing the significance of this piece of information. If Vincent had written part of the program, he might be able to explain why I was having the recurring dreams. He might even know how to make them stop. A strange idea occurred to me then.

*I wonder if I can hack into my dream?*

Perhaps if I could intentionally prolong the dream and explore it lucidly, I would find something of significance – something that would reveal to me why the dreams began in the first place. As implausible as the idea was, I thought if there was a way to make it happen, I should at least try.

Sophie gave me a curious look. She mouthed to me, *"What's wrong?"* as Rachel and Julie chatted about something else.

I smiled tightly and shook my head. Sophie eyed me for another moment, but said nothing until we left the cafeteria. She walked with me in silence through the hall and we both said not a word until we were in my room with the door shut.

"What's wrong Elena? You suddenly turned pale when we were talking to Julie and Rachel." She sat on my bed cross-legged.

I sat opposite her in my desk chair. "I had an idea when we were talking," I began. "If Vincent wrote part of the Dreamscape Program, he might know why I've been having these dreams. I thought maybe I should talk to him about it." I shrugged and smiled ruefully. "He's going to find out about it tomorrow anyway."

Sophie was frowning. "What makes you think he'd be willing to help you? I guess I don't see why you won't talk to someone who really knows what they're doing."

"According to Rachel, Vincent *does* know what he's doing. Anyway, there's more to it." I paused. "I want to try hacking the program so I can explore the dream more. And I want to be lucid. It won't work otherwise."

Sophie's frown deepened. "I think you would get into a lot of trouble if you got caught. It may even be dangerous to try something like that, don't you think?" She shook her head.

I folded my arms on the back of the chair and rested my chin on them. "I'm tired of these nightmares Sophie, but I feel like I'm having them for a reason. I don't know. Nothing like this has ever happened to me before. In the end, it could be a real scientific breakthrough."

"What's the use if you don't tell anyone about it though? You won't be able to get approval for this, so you'll have to keep your plan a secret. I'm just concerned." She sighed and dropped her shoulders a little.

"Well, there's no guarantee Vincent will be willing to help me anyway. More than likely, he'll freeze me out or say something to make me feel dumb. Don't worry too much." As I endeavored to soothe Sophie's worry, I had already made up my mind to convince Vincent to help me somehow. I was set on carrying out this new plan.

Monday arrived and I was back in the lab preparing to dream. My gut had twisted into a knot of nerves by the time I sat in my lab chair. I could feel my pulse beating much quicker than usual and my hands wouldn't stop sweating. Waiting for Vincent to arrive was agonizing. I couldn't be sure whether I was more anxious about him finding out about my recurring dreams, or if I worried he would refuse to help me with my plan to hack into the program.

At last he did appear in the doorway. As seemed usual for him, he had his laptop backpack slung over one shoulder and looked as though he'd had a fight with his comb.

I took a few deep breaths. It was too late to worry any longer how he would respond to my situation. I was about to find out.

# CHAPTER 4

*"Elena"* I heard a voice say.

"Hmm? What?"

*What's going on?*

Everything was bright and loud. No, it was quiet. I heard the rushing sound of my own pulse pounding in my ears, but the room itself was practically silent. When I finally cracked my eyes open, an unfamiliar face peered down at me.

"Can you hear me?" he said.

I nodded.

"Are you feeling dizzy or short of breath?" he asked.

I shook my head. "It's just so bright," I murmured.

"Can you sit up? Slowly now," he encouraged.

Once I did, I started to figure out what was happening. The man attending to me was a medical lab technician. I must have responded poorly to the program somehow and he was trying to determine why I had stayed unconscious. "How long have I been out?" I asked him.

"You came to once, but you seem to have fainted. Have you eaten anything today?"

"I can't remember. No, I don't think I have," I admitted.

"Ok. You don't want to do that again. It's unwise to use the program on an empty stomach." He checked my eyes and took my pulse. "Do you feel like you can stand?"

"Yeah. I'm ok. Um, do you know where Vincent Miller went?" I gingerly stood to my feet.

"He had a class or something and had to leave. I told him I would take care of you."

"I see. Well thank you. I'll be more careful next time," I assured him. I left before he could say anything else.

The pounding in my ears had been replaced with the familiar, irritating ring that so often accompanied me once I woke from a nightmare. I rushed to my dorm room and collapsed on my bed. When I next stirred, it was late afternoon; I'd slept dreamlessly for several hours.

The first thought I had was that I needed to find Vincent and talk to him about the lab session. Honestly, I couldn't remember whether I'd actually dreamt in the program.

A glance at the clock informed me it was past 4:00 pm. My stomach growled in protest upon realizing I'd missed the lunch hour, so I scavenged in my room for a snack bar and bottle of water before leaving to find Vincent.

When I reached Vincent's door, I took a breath before knocking. The door opened a few moments later. Vincent stood in the doorway, appearing to have just woken up. He was barefoot and his hair was sticking out on one side.

"Hi," I said. "Is this a bad time?"

He looked at me for a moment. Then he ran a hand through his hair and stepped aside so I could come in. The room was dimly lit with a single bedside lamp. The curtains were drawn. He had two desks set up next to each other, upon which were two computer monitors and some other equipment. There was little else but a bed, night table, and dresser. Everything was kept very clean, which I found surprising for some reason. Otherwise, his room looked similar to what I had seen in his dreamscape.

Vincent had already sat on his bed and was leaning his head back against the headboard. His eyes were closed.

I hesitated.

He said nothing, so I sat on the edge of his desk chair.

"Um, I wanted to ask you about the lab session today," I started. "I can't really remember what happened."

After a brief pause he said, "You didn't wake up after the session ended, same as last time. The medical tech thought you had fainted or something." He stopped talking and opened his eyes to look at me.

"Yeah, he told me about that. I meant the dream part. I can't remember if I had any dreams this time," I explained.

Vincent stared at me. "You had a nightmare again."

A heaviness settled in my chest.

"What was it about?"

Vincent sighed very quietly and closed his eyes again. "You can re-watch it you know. That's what the program *does*."

"But you didn't notice anything unusual about the dream?" I urged.

He shrugged. "I don't know. I guess it was kind of like the last time."

"You don't find that odd?"

"People have recurring dreams. It's not that uncommon."

*Ok, here goes.*

"That's true, except, I've been having that same dream every night now for weeks, and...it started the first time I used the program." I paused to give Vincent a chance to react to what I'd just told him. He said nothing. In fact, his expression barely changed. I continued, "I just think I need to do something about it. It's not normal to dream the same exact dream over and over for weeks."

Maybe Vincent thought I was being dramatic, or he didn't believe me. He said, "Just stop using the program then."

"But I don't think it matters whether I use the program or not. Like I said, I have this dream no matter what. I have an idea though. I heard you wrote part of the program, so I thought maybe you could tell me how to hack into my dreamscape."

Vincent's expression finally changed. "Why would you want to do that?"

"I want to be able to look around lucidly. It's frustrating that the dream always ends at that stairwell. I want to go down it and see what I can find." I didn't tell him that the place I'd been dreaming about actually existed in the west wing. That could come later, if necessary. What mattered now was convincing him to help me find a way to explore my dream within the program.

He rubbed his forehead and sighed again. "Look, I was sleeping. I'd like to get back to that now."

29

"Oh, sure," I said. I was overwhelmingly disappointed.

"Please shut the door on your way out." It was less a request than an order. He had closed his eyes again, so I left.

I went back to my room. Disappointment soon turned to resentment. I couldn't figure out why he was so rude to me. I guess I had thought he might be curious enough to hear me out or offer some alternative to my plan, at the very least. But Vincent was like a mountain of ice. I would have to find another answer.

*Stupid Iceman.*

My encounter with Vincent left me with a frustrated, restless feeling. I couldn't focus on my studies that night, so I wandered the building, stopping in the lounge for a bit, but feeling too annoyed to speak to anyone. I had to finally force myself to go back to my room and go to bed.

I was exhausted most of the week. By Friday, I slept in and missed my morning classes. At lunch, I ate alone and very little. By that point, I felt on the verge of a mild depression. My body was suffering from the effects of frequent, interrupted sleep, I had trouble concentrating when I read or studied, and it was difficult to muster any sort of enthusiasm for my research.

Irrationally, I was angry with Vincent as well.

That afternoon, I made myself leave my room to study in the library. Although I'd skipped my classes for the day, I felt the need to at least get some sort of work done.

I was alone, reading in one of the library reference rooms with a pounding headache. Inwardly, I was replaying the encounter with Vincent again for the hundredth time, relishing a fictional scene I'd created in which I gave him a good piece of my mind in return for his rudeness. It was at that moment Vincent came in and stood near me. I looked up at him, making little effort to push down my irritation. He fidgeted very slightly, his eyes wandering the room and then meeting mine. After a moment's hesitation he said, "Um…I get pretty bad migraines sometimes."

I didn't understand why he would tell me this until it struck me he may be attempting to explain his behavior from earlier that week. I waited for him to continue.

"You can't hack into the Dreamscape Program. The security is designed to shut it down if anyone messes with the coding," he told me quietly.

My hopes were squashed. "But you *wrote* part of the program, didn't you? Can't you figure out how to get around that setting?"

He didn't answer at first. "That could get us into serious trouble you know," he finally said.

My mind grasped for something more to convince him. I had another idea. "What if when we were logged in *you* tried to go down the stairwell?"

Vincent shifted his weight and fingered his backpack shoulder strap. "I could try I guess. I thought you said the dream always ends at that point though."

"Yeah, it does, but you might see something I can't see," I insisted.

Vincent looked skeptical. "I don't think it will work like that, but I guess we could try it."

"Thanks. So, I suppose I'll be the dreamer again in lab Monday," I suggested.

"I can get us in to the lab sooner than that," Vincent offered. "They close it up early on Fridays. We can go during dinner. Meet me at my room later."

I wasn't sure whether that was a good idea, but he was willing to help me at least this much and I didn't want to refuse his offer.

I nodded. "Ok. Later then."

Vincent left without another word.

Reading was drudgery after that. I soon left the library and knocked on Sophie's door. She was on the phone, but motioned me inside. I waited impatiently for several minutes as she finished her conversation. Then she finally hung up the phone.

"What's up? I haven't seen you much lately. Are you feeling alright?" she asked.

"He's going to help me. Well, he's going to at least try to look around my dreamscape," I told her.

"Vincent? What did he say?"

I gave her a condensed version of my recent conversation with Vincent and finished by telling her, "I'm meeting him in the lab later so we can try it tonight."

Sophie smirked. "A date in the lab huh? He's probably got plans of his own."

I whacked Sophie's arm and laughed. "Gross. I just want to figure this thing out. This might at least be a start."

"Yeah, that's what *you're* thinking. You don't know this guy though. Just don't stay unconscious too long. Want me to come and keep an eye on him?" she said, lifting an eyebrow suggestively.

I rolled my eyes. "Can you please just stop? I'll be fine."

Sophie lifted her hands in concession. "Ok. Just don't come crying to me later if something happens."

I shook my head at her, suppressing a smile. "Unbelievable," I said.

Despite Sophie's playfully sardonic reaction to Vincent's offer, I looked forward to meeting Vincent that evening. I felt I had cracked open a door that would lead me to the answer I sought, whatever that was exactly. At that time, I had no explanation for how I could have dreamt about the west wing before seeing it, but I felt sure somehow that descending that dark stairwell in my dreamscape was the key to unlocking the puzzle of my recurring dreams.

At dinner, I headed to Vincent's room. He was just closing his door when I approached him.

"Come on," he said to me.

I followed him as he walked briskly down the hall to the research lab. We stopped outside the door and Vincent took a quick look inside. It was empty. He pulled a keycard out of his pocket.

"They ask me to run checks on the system sometimes," he explained.

As we went into the lab, I was feeling on edge. I looked around and noticed surveillance cameras in the corners of the room.

Vincent saw me eyeing the cameras. "I'll take care of that," he said.

His hands moved deftly over one of the keyboards. I could see he was clearly very familiar with the equipment. Then we each set our parameters in the computer terminal and sat in a lab chair.

"You know I won't be able to move very far away from you in the dream," he said. "It's likely I won't find anything down the stairwell, because you haven't dreamt it. Don't get your hopes up."

I nodded, pretending it didn't matter one way or the other, and tried to appear as calm as possible. Vincent offered no further advice, and before I knew it, I had begun to dream.

Everything progressed as it always did, except I saw Vincent from time to time. Somehow during the dream, I even became lucid and tried to move around more, but ultimately, the dream was in control and the shadows pursued me throughout the mansion.

At last, I found myself in that dark and foul smelling basement, unable to descend the cavernous stairwell. My frustration peaked when I glimpsed the small figure beckon me down. I couldn't move. Then something unusual happened: the figure lunged at me. I jerked awake just before it could grab hold of me. Gasping and trembling, I sat up and buried my face in my hands.

I heard Vincent move next to me as I struggled to regain my composure. He was on a computer terminal nearby typing something. I got up shakily and stood near him.

"I'm just erasing the data," he told me. "Go wait in the hall. I'll be out in a minute."

I obeyed silently. The trembling had ceased, but now I felt cold and weak.

It wasn't long before Vincent exited the lab. "Let's go," he said. I followed him back to his room.

We didn't speak until he'd shut the door. "Sit down," he ordered. I sat in his desk chair as he sat on his bed and pulled out his laptop. After he had typed for a moment, he looked at me seriously. "I'll help you," he said, "but...I have a condition: I want to be there when you hack in."

"You want to observe me?"

He shook his head. "No, I want to be in the dream too."

"But you just were," I argued.

"Not like that. I want to be part of the dream." He watched me calmly as I processed his request.

"Ok...I guess if that's what you want. How will that work though?"

"It will take a little time, but I can figure it out," he replied with confidence.

I nodded. "Can you tell me what you saw now?"

Vincent looked at the ceiling, as if searching for the words to describe his experience. "I saw a lot of shadows wandering around. You seemed very afraid of those things."

"What about the stairwell?" I asked impatiently.

Vincent looked at me. "There was something there. A person maybe, but it was small. When I tried to go down, it jumped at me"—

"It jumped at *you?*" I interrupted.

Vincent nodded. "I was standing in front of you, and somehow that thing could see me. The dream ended before I could see anything else though. It's going to be tricky to keep you dreaming once we hack in," he mused.

A flood of thoughts rushed through my mind. I wondered if the figure in my dream were more than a phantom created by my brain, and if perhaps the program had connected me to something else after all.

"Why was *I* in your dream?" Vincent suddenly asked.

*Right. I forgot about that part.*

I could feel myself grow warm as embarrassment threatened to steal my dignity, but I shrugged casually. "I was lucid during some of the dream and I knew you were there somewhere. I guess my brain fabricated a fake version of you."

Vincent seemed to ponder this.

"I really should get back to my room. I'm very tired," I told him. Inwardly, I chided myself for allowing Vincent's demeanor to intimidate me.

"Sure. Check your email. I'll send you a message when I need to see you."

"Ok."


I awoke Saturday morning more refreshed than I'd felt in weeks. Perhaps I'd even been filled with new courage, because one of the first thoughts I had that morning was that I wanted to find Luke Phillips.

After getting myself ready, I strode into the library and straight toward the small reference room in the back corner, determined to get to know Luke better than I did. As luck would have it, he was indeed seated in his usual place.

"Good morning," I said with a smile. I sat across from him and pulled out my laptop.

"Good morning," he returned, smiling back. "You seem to be in a good mood today. Have a date last night?"

I smiled. "No, not exactly," I replied, remembering Sophie's comment about my lab date with Vincent. "I guess I've just made a lot of progress on my work this week. How's the nightmare research going?"

Luke sighed and shook his head. "It's been slow. I'm actually taking a break from the project this week to work at the hospital in town."

"Oh really? I didn't know you worked there."

What followed between us that morning involved much more conversation than research, and I got the impression Luke had been waiting for an opportunity to get to know me as well. My suspicion proved accurate when he invited me to go out with him for lunch later that day. I was delighted, to say the least. We exchanged phone numbers and agreed to meet in the lobby at noon.

Although I wanted very much to fill Sophie in on the details of my login with Vincent the previous night, she was off campus that morning, and I thought it would be better to wait to tell her in person. Also, amidst my anticipation for my outing that afternoon, I forgot to check my email. Instead, I busied myself with laundry until the lunch hour. I hadn't been on a date since arriving to California. Thus far, the research program at the Academy had kept me so busy I could barely think about having a social life.

The lobby, as part of the original mansion, suggested expensive taste on the part of the former owner. The wood floors and columns were kept well-polished, and comfortable leather chairs were arranged near the floor-to-ceiling windows. I always felt as though I'd stepped onto the set of a movie from Hollywood's golden era when I walked through that part of the Academy.

Luke stood near one of the windows, scrolling through his phone. As I approached him I was struck by how tall he was, since I'd only ever encountered him seated in the library reference room.

"Hey," I said, coming up beside him.

"Hey. You hungry?" he asked, pocketing his phone.

"I am."

Luke had a car on campus and he took me to a bistro type restaurant in town. It was a trendy place, with creaky wood floors and intriguing art hanging on the walls. The menu was quite extensive, if a little difficult to navigate, and the place was packed with people. We were seated in a corner at a small table for two.

"I have no idea what to get," I laughed.

"Here," Luke said, taking my menu. He pointed out some of his favorite selections and I managed to decide on an artisan burger of some kind.

After we placed our order, Luke said, "So tell me why you became a dream researcher." He placed his arms crossed on the table and leaned forward so he could hear me talk.

It was hard not to smile. "Well, I've always remembered my dreams. I started a dream journal in middle school and used to draw pictures and write stories based on the things I had dreams about. Then in high school, we had a unit in science on cognition and neuroscience. It was the first time I ever learned what really goes on when we dream. I studied psychology and cognition at college in New York, but one of my professors told me about this place and wrote a letter of recommendation for me. Here I am."

Luke kept his eyes on my face as I spoke. He replied, "It's no surprise you were recommended. You seem very dedicated."

"Maybe 'obsessed' is a better word," I countered, laughing.

"What are your plans then after you complete your studies at the Academy?"

I shrugged. "Research. I don't know if I'll continue it here. I'll probably end up back in New York at my old university."

Luke nodded. He was a good listener and kept the conversation going, so it was easy to relax with him.

By the time I returned to my room on campus that evening, I felt genuinely content. However, although I enjoyed my time with Luke, I still said nothing of my recurring nightmares. It did strike me as an odd contrast that the person I felt least comfortable with on campus, Vincent, did know about my situation, while I was hesitant to even mention it to Luke.

I spent the evening with Evan, Alex, and Sophie in the lounge. I hadn't yet spoken to Sophie about my agreement with Vincent, but I planned to before the evening was over. We had reserved the lounge TV for a couple of hours and were enjoying a newly released fighting video game Sophie had picked up earlier that day. The game required a moderately high level of skill in terms of reflex and strategy, but of the four of us, Sophie and Evan were the most competitive. Alex and I went back and forth teasing the two of them, until I thought Evan was ready to throw his controller at the TV. At that moment, Vincent walked in and approached me.

"Can you come to my room for a minute?" he asked rather abruptly, addressing me only and ignoring my friends.

Alex and Evan exchanged a look. Sophie was watching me to see what my response would be. I put my controller down and followed him out of the lounge. He silently led the way until we had entered his room and closed the door.

"I need to run you through the program again to check something," he told me. "I was looking over the data earlier..." He stopped talking suddenly. "What?"

"Huh?"

"What's wrong?"

I tried to think of how to word what I wanted to say. "If you show up and drag me to your room in front of my friends, they're going to wonder what's going on."

Vincent's eyes were unreadable. "I tried getting in touch with you today. You don't check your email," he said.

*Shoot.*

"Then let me give you my number so you can send me a message if you need me," I replied. I took out my phone and we exchanged numbers.

"You can meet me in the lab at 11:30," he informed me.

I left his room and returned to the lounge. Sophie and the guys were still playing the game, but they paused it as soon as I came in. I braced myself.

Alex grinned at me. "The tech guy, huh?"

I rolled my eyes. "He just had a question."

"Yeah, I always invite girls to my room to ask them 'questions,'" Evan said.

Sophie was giggling.

"He was asking for help on an assignment," I said. "We *are* paired in lab you know."

"So, he just had to make you go to his room on Saturday evening? Elena, I've never seen that guy talk to anyone," Alex commented. "He's got a thing for you."

I looked at Sophie, trying to convey a message of distress, but she either didn't notice or chose not to, because she was laughing even harder.

*I'm in high school again.*

"Are we still playing the game?" I asked, trying to change the subject.

Thankfully, that did it. We played for another hour or so, but it was starting to get late and I needed to meet Vincent soon. The guys wanted to go to a movie and Sophie seemed to want to go with them. I excused myself, saying I was a little tired, which made Alex chuckle. Then I practically ran to my room and shut myself in. It was 11:30 by then, but I wanted to give them a chance to go out so they wouldn't see me and get suspicious. I heard them down the hall.

*Oh no.*

I peeked out of my room. They were standing in Sophie's doorway, deciding what movie to see. I couldn't get to the lab without passing them and it was already ten minutes past the time I should have met Vincent. I took out my phone to message Sophie and saw a text from Vincent that read: *"I'm in the lab."*

I responded: *"Something came up. I will be late."*

Then I sent Sophie a message: *"You need to get the guys out of the hall. I have to meet Vincent in the lab."*

I watched her pull out her phone and read the message. Next thing I knew, she had ushered the guys down the hall, leaving me the opportunity to race to the lab, unnoticed. When I got there, Vincent met me at the door to let me in.

"Sorry I'm late," I said.

"Just sit over there." He motioned to a lab chair.

I wasn't sure if he was offended or just wanted to go back to his room, so I quickly sat down in the chair he had pointed to. He didn't sit next to me.

"You're not going to observe?" I asked.

"I need to watch the monitor while you dream," he answered.

"What are you looking for?"

He was engaged in typing something on the main computer terminal. "Not sure yet," he murmured distractedly.

I didn't ask any more questions.

Vincent came over to me and checked on the dream specifications to make sure everything was set properly.

"You can put the mask on now," he said.

I did so, and ten minutes later, woke gasping. My rapidly pounding heart was pumping ice through my veins and I felt shaky with fear.

Vincent came over to me. "Let's talk in my room."

I followed him out of the lab and down the hall, feeling mildly dazed and depressed. I sat in the desk chair in his room, shivering and suppressing a strong sense of weariness.

Vincent was busy on his laptop, so he didn't talk to me for several minutes. Then he finally looked up. "Are you cold?"

I nodded. He went to his closet and pulled out a hoodie, handing it to me. It was black with a green logo I didn't recognize. Vincent wasn't very tall, but the hoodie was still long on me. It smelled clean.

"Tell me about the dream," he said matter-of-factly.

I was tempted to ask him why he needed to hear it again, when he had witnessed it several times already, but I refrained, and instead relayed everything to him, as clearly as possible. While I spoke, he sat cross-legged on his bed, typing on his laptop.

"So, what did you learn?" I asked wearily.

"Hmm?" He was quiet for a few seconds. Then he said, "I want to compare the dream to your cognitive response, so I'll let you know soon. Can you tell me at what point in the dream you felt afraid?"

That question was unexpected. When I thought about it, I realized I was not afraid at the beginning of my dreams. Most of the time I just felt frustrated or worried that I would get caught by the shadow figures. The real fear I experienced was always in the basement, near the stairwell where the small being beckoned to me. I explained all of this to him as he typed.

After a few moments of silence and Vincent typing, my fatigued mind traveled back to the afternoon I'd spent with Luke. Naturally, I didn't want to appear too available, yet I hoped another opportunity to spend time with him would present itself soon.

"You can go back to your room," Vincent said suddenly. "I'll talk to you tomorrow."

Whatever he was doing had him completely absorbed. I marveled at this irritating talent of his for a moment, then I got up and left.

I reached my room just after 12:30 am. Sophie had sent me a message expressing her need to hear the latest update. Exhausted as I was, I responded, inviting her to come to my room so I could tell her in person. I'd already thrown on a pair of pajama pants, but I didn't remove Vincent's hoodie. It was comfortable.

Sophie knocked quietly and gently opened the door. I had stretched myself out on the bed and was scrolling through apps on my phone, not really paying attention to anything in particular. Sophie sat next to me and leaned against the headboard.

"So that was fun earlier, huh?" she laughed, referring to my embarrassment over Vincent dragging me to his room. "Are you guys a 'thing' now?"

I sighed and dramatically dropped my head on my arms, cringing at the inevitable teasing I could expect from Alex over the next week. "You know it was about the dreams," I corrected her, as I lifted my head.

"*I* know that, but the guys don't. Poor Evan looked a little shocked when he watched you leave with Vincent."

I'd been trying to ignore Evan's crush on me for some time, so I didn't respond to that last comment.

"Vincent's going to help me hack into the dreamscape program," I told her, pushing myself up into a sitting position. "I met him last night so he could watch my dream, and something he saw convinced him to help me. He has a condition though," I continued, "he wants to be able to interact when we hack in."

"What, like talk to you while you're dreaming?" Sophie frowned.

I shook my head. "No, he wants to be *in* the dream, but part of it as well."

Although I could have told her about the small figure in my dream, and how it had somehow seen Vincent, something held me back from doing so. I began to think that perhaps it would be best to keep such details to myself, until things became clearer.

Sophie's eyebrows now lifted, replacing her frown with an expression of disbelief. "That's sort of weird, don't you think?"

I shrugged. "Those were his terms. I do want his help, and this is the only way I'm going to get it."

Sophie was quiet. I saw her glance down at my hoodie. "*That's* not yours." Her eyes moved back to my face.

"It's Vincent's. He lent it to me after I logged into the program. I was cold."

Sophie nodded, but I suspected she restrained herself from saying what was really on her mind. "You're not worried you guys will get caught sneaking into the lab and messing with the program?" she asked.

"I know there's a possibility that will happen, but what can we do? We need to have access to the program and lab equipment. Vincent seems to know what he's doing, so I guess I'm not really too worried."

"I hope you're right. I'd hate to see you get kicked out of the Academy because this guy screws something up," she said.

I decided it might be time to change the subject. "You know, I did have an actual date today. I meant to tell you about it."

Sophie sat up attentively. "With who?"

"Luke Phillips," I said, smiling at the expression she rewarded me with after hearing his name.

"That guy is *hot*. I didn't know you two knew each other."

The remainder of our conversation revolved around my day with Luke. I had already decided, just based on Sophie's reaction, that it might be wise to keep my future encounters with Vincent as secret as possible. In fact, I almost regretted that I'd told Sophie anything about my agreement with him. I couldn't put my apprehension into words really. I certainly could not have predicted then that what Vincent and I would find once we hacked into my dreamscape would uncover a troubling secret connected to the Dreamscape Program.

# CHAPTER 5

"We should try to get into that locked room in the west wing," Sophie said to me at lunch on Sunday. She stirred her half iced-tea, half juice beverage as she spoke. "I'm dying to know what's in there."

"I don't know if I want to go back in that place. Remember what I told you?" I said, referring to the room in my dream.

"There's gotta be an explanation. Maybe once you go in that locked room, you'll stop having those dreams and..." she lowered her voice, "you can quit your crazy plan with the tech nerd."

I laughed. "I see."

I almost resisted further when I realized this might be an opportunity to behave as though going into the mansion were the answer to the dreams. If I went with her and told her the dreams had stopped afterward, I wouldn't have to give her any more information about my plans with Vincent. There was a part of me that felt guilt at even having thought of this, but it was too convenient a circumstance to pass up.

"Ok, I'll go with you," I said.

Sophie seemed pleased. "How about tonight? Come on, the sooner we make it happen, the better," she pleaded.

I shrugged. "I guess tonight is fine."

I saw Sophie's eyes glance over my shoulder. "Looks like you have a visitor."

As tempted as I was to turn around, I kept eating my lunch and endeavored to remain casual.

"Hi," I heard Luke say as he came up beside me. "Mind if I join you?" he asked, politely.

"Sure," Sophie responded for both of us.

I smiled at Luke as he sat down next to me.

"Luke Phillips." He extended a hand to Sophie.

"Sophie Leon," she returned, shaking hands with him.

The three of us traded the usual "getting-to-know-each-other" discourse. Sometime during our exchange, I received a message on my phone. I had a feeling it was from Vincent, but not wanting to appear rude, I excused myself to use the restroom. Sure enough, the message read: *"I need to see you. Come to my room."*

*He sure is bossy.*

I replied: *"I'll be there in a little while."*

Although I realized how ungrateful my attitude was, Vincent's interruption into my day meant less time I could be spending with Luke. Admittedly, I did feel a little annoyed at that moment.

When I returned to the table where Sophie and Luke sat, they were rather engrossed in conversation.

"You should come with us," I heard Sophie say as I sat down. She looked at me. "Luke wants to learn more about this mansion too," she explained. "Tell her what you told me," she prompted him.

"This mansion was originally owned by a wealthy French scientist by the name of Abel Dumont. I read a couple of his research articles, and let's just say he had some wild ideas about dream research," Luke began.

Sophie's tone was full of meaning as she added, "Dumont wanted to find a way to treat nightmare patients with some kind of technology."

"You mean like the Dreamscape Program?" I inquired.

"Not exactly," Luke replied. "It's unclear how he planned to do it, but he refers to 'treatments' using 'new equipment' in his articles. There are only a few articles available in the library though, and they're all written in French. I think perhaps his research was incomplete. He went bankrupt eventually and moved back to France. The mansion fell into disrepair until it was donated to the Sleep Research Foundation eight years ago."

While Luke spoke, Sophie's attention was fixed on me.

"Is Abel Dumont still alive?" I asked.

"I don't know. Probably not," Luke said.

As interested as I was in learning more, I was conscious that Vincent was waiting to talk to me.

"So, we'll meet later then?" Sophie suggested. "Luke thinks he can help us get into that locked room."

"Oh, good. Yeah, just text me later," I said, getting to my feet. "Sorry, I have to go."

Sophie gave me a curious look. Luke waved. I left the cafeteria in haste.

I knocked once on Vincent's door and heard him say, "Come in." He was sitting hunched at a computer screen eating ramen noodles with wooden chopsticks and watching Japanese anime. I sat on his bed as he paused the show.

"Have you slept at all?" I asked. Vincent was in the habit of wearing dark pants and trendy, yet unusual t-shirts. I noted that he still wore the same clothing I saw him in the previous night.

"I've been busy," was the reply.

"What did you find?"

He looked thoughtful. "I noticed something was off when I checked your results from that first time you logged in. I don't think your brain calibrates very well to the Dreamscape Program. It triggers your amygdala, which is why you feel fearful."

"Wait, I have these dreams when I'm not logged into the program too though," I countered.

"Yeah, that's what I don't quite understand. It's almost as if...your brain is on repeat when you enter REM." He shifted in his chair a little and ran a hand through his hair. "I'll be honest, I think the sooner we 'reset' your dreams, the better. It's probably not mentally healthy for you to continue to dream something and never reach a solution."

I knew what he was getting at. Dreams function as a means to process emotions and problems from our waking lives. In general, a repetitive cycle such as the one I experienced was often associated with mental illness. Although the thought had already occurred to me, it was one I had attempted to ignore.

I sighed and leaned forward. "So how much time do you need?"

"We're going to have to run a few tests before we try it for real. I'll probably need you to come to the lab again later. It's hard to say exactly how long it will take — a couple of weeks maybe?"

"Ok, but I do have something planned this evening," I said. "Actually...I learned something interesting that may be connected to my nightmares." Vincent's expression remained unchanged as he waited for me to continue. "I heard the man who originally owned this place was involved in some kind of research to eliminate nightmares. Can you tell me anything else about the Dreamscape Program? Who came up with the original plans?"

Vincent leaned back in his chair. "I don't really know. A team had been working on it for a long time before I was contracted to work on it. Most of the program code had already been written."

"What part of it did you work on?"

"Debugging and troubleshooting mostly. They were having difficulty with the program freezing up for a while, so I had to modify some of the code," he explained.

I was somewhat impressed by this information. I suspected Vincent was more than merely a "tech nerd." It sounded as though he'd been contracted as a specialist.

"Well, a friend of mine is working on a nightmare research project. They've been using the program to *induce* nightmares," I told him.

"Yeah, I heard they were doing that. That's what I thought had happened when I first viewed your dreamscape. I thought you'd put in the wrong data somehow and it triggered the nightmare sequence," Vincent said. "Last night when you logged in, I actually intentionally changed the parameters to induce the nightmare sequence. It didn't seem to change anything though," he reflected. "That's how I figured out your brain wasn't calibrating well to the program"–

I held up a hand. "Can we just back up a second? You *changed* the parameters? Were you going to tell *me* this?" I made little effort to hide the annoyance in my voice.

Vincent expressed mild confusion. "I thought you wanted my help with this?"

I sighed. "Yeah, I do. Just tell me when you do things like that."

He nodded slightly. A lapse in conversation ensued and I could sense Vincent's attitude had changed.

I got up. "I'll text you later. I've got some things to take care of today."

Vincent barely acknowledged me. He swiveled his chair back around and resumed his anime show as I left the room.

I was frustrated. Though I had full faith in Vincent's acumen with technology, I certainly lacked confidence in his social abilities. It would have made little difference if it weren't for the fact that he was messing with my brain without my knowledge.

At length, evening arrived. I felt particularly drained and marginally discouraged that day. My sleep each night had been reduced to roughly five hours on average, resulting in perpetual lethargy and even minor dizziness if I stood up too quickly. I'd spent the entirety of the afternoon in bed, binge-watching TV shows on my laptop. I guess I was feeling sorry for myself.

My phone beeped, interrupting my pity party. Sophie's text read: *"Are you ready? I'm coming over."*

I didn't move right away. But eventually, I pulled myself off the bed and found something black to wear. Sophie knocked just as I was putting on my shoes.

"Come in," I said.

"Hey, Luke's waiting for us near the west wing," she told me, as she opened my door.

"Ok. I'm ready."

"You feeling ok? You look sort of pale," she pointed out.

"I've been in bed all day, actually. I'm fine though. Let's go."

"What happened earlier today? Did you go see Vincent?" she asked as we walked.

"Yeah. He just had some questions," I replied. I didn't tell her what Vincent had discovered about my brain not calibrating well to the program, or that he had run the nightmare sequence without my knowledge. It would only add to her argument that I should discontinue my plan with him.

It didn't take long to reach the west wing. Luke greeted us as we arrived.

"You didn't wear black?" Sophie said.

I shook my head and laughed.

"What? Was I supposed to?" he asked, confused.

"No," I said. "She thinks we're ninja-thieves or something. Don't listen to her weirdo ideas."

Sophie elbowed me gently. "We need to be inconspicuous, that's all."

"It's fine," I said to Luke. "So how do you plan to get us in that room?"

"With this," he said, revealing a small device that resembled a screwdriver.

"Nice. Let's get this over with then," I said.

I brushed by Luke to push the door open, and led the way through the mansion hall to the locked room at the end. Everything was just as we'd seen it the last time, so I moved rather quickly. Luke wandered at a slower pace, poking his head into rooms as we passed them. Sophie kept up with my pace.

"Why are you rushing?" she whispered to me.

"I don't want to be here," I informed her. That was only part of it. I was conscious that Vincent would be waiting to hear from me. I was supposed to meet him in the lab again later.

Sophie must have seen through me. "You're meeting Vincent later, aren't you?"

I didn't reply and she didn't bring it up again.

We waited at the locked door for Luke, who had been inspecting every room he passed. I glanced into the room across from where we stood and imagined I was in my dreamscape. It wasn't half so frightening as the last time, but I realized that due to my current state of exhaustion, I was likely a bit numb to my emotions.

"Luke?" Sophie called quietly. He'd disappeared into one of the rooms.

"I'll be right there," we heard him say.

He came toward us and pulled out the lock-picking device he'd brought with him. It wasn't long before we heard a significant "click." Luke pushed the door inward and we entered the room.

What met our vision was rather surprising: a well-maintained library. The room stood in stark contrast to the rest of what we'd come across in that part of the house. Certainly, the wood and furniture appeared old and somewhat worn, but it was evident that the room had been dusted and even polished. At the center of the room in front of the floor to ceiling windows was a massive mahogany desk. It was clearly decades old, yet in superb condition, as if it had been covered for some time to protect it from decay. Behind the desk was an antique leather chair. An oriental carpet had been laid in the middle of the floor, and long, lavish green curtains decorated the immense windows.

"This is unexpected," Luke murmured.

We immediately set out to explore the room, which was filled with books and manuscripts along the built-in bookshelves. I found it truly strange that while the rest of this wing had been left to deteriorate, this room alone had been preserved.

"I think they're going to extend the faculty offices," Luke stated. "They must have started with this room."

"It looks like original furniture though, doesn't it?" Sophie observed. She was trying out an overstuffed wingback chair, positioned near a vast fireplace.

I came toward her and glanced above the fireplace mantel at a vintage oil painting, depicting a handsome, if aloof-looking man with impeccable hair and pale eyes. There was a small plaque at the base of the bronze frame that read simply: *"Abel Dumont 1942."* I was rather fascinated by this portrait. I guessed the subject to be around thirty years old. He had clearly acquired his fortune at a young age, for he was very well dressed in a three-piece suit and wore a bejeweled ring on his left pinky finger. I gazed at the portrait for some time.

Sophie had gotten up at this point and was perusing the mahogany desk. Luke shuffled through books and papers somewhere behind me. I got lost in thought, wondering what sort of person Abel Dumont had been.

"Elena, come over here," Sophie said, interrupting my meditation.

She had been endeavoring to open drawers — most of which were locked — and had found some very old photographs of the mansion grounds.

"It was much smaller then," she commented.

Indeed, most of the Academy we currently knew was missing from the photos. The library facilities and research lab had been built only recently in the last decade or so.

"He was pretty loaded," Sophie remarked, nodding toward Abel Dumont's portrait. "I'll bet Dr. Belle is renovating this room for herself."

Dr. Belle was one of the Academy chairmen. She was a brilliant scientist, but many people found her to be intimidating. We didn't see her often around campus.

Luke wandered toward us, carrying a large, loosely bound manuscript. He set it down on the desk.

"What did you find?" I asked.

"I'm not sure exactly. It's all written in French, so it's taking me a while to read," he said.

"You *read* French?" Sophie lifted an eyebrow and shot me a meaningful glance.

"Not very well," Luke argued, still leafing through the manuscript.

I moved closer so I could have a look. "May I see it?"

Luke nodded. The manuscript was yellowed and had been both type and handwritten. It contained many intricate drawings labeled in French. The drawings appeared to be a machine of some kind. I flipped the manuscript over and read the front cover:

"*Les Cent Ans de L'Enfant – Ésaïe 65:20*"

Abel Dumont's name was initialed beneath the title.

Luke leaned over to have a closer look. "The Child of a Hundred Years," he translated. "The other part is a scripture reference from the Bible – Isaiah 65:20."

Sophie got up and went toward the bookshelves. She came back carrying a large King James Bible. We were relieved to find that it was an English translation.

She handed the Bible to Luke and he leafed through it until he came to the book of Isaiah. He read aloud for us, "*There shall be no more an infant of days, nor an old man that hath not filled his days: for the child shall die an hundred years old; but the sinner being an hundred years old shall be accursed.*"

We were quiet for a moment. Luke continued to read from the Bible.

"What is that supposed to mean? I didn't do well in religion class," Sophie admitted.

Luke was still reading, but paused to say, "It's a reference to the new Heaven and Earth foretold by the Biblical prophets. I'm not getting the connection to the manuscript though," he said, frowning.

"Take it with you," I suggested. "The manuscript I mean. Maybe you can figure it out if you read through it."

Luke gave me a look of uncertainty.

"You should take it," Sophie agreed, glancing at me as she spoke.

Luke considered for a moment. "You two are a bad influence," he conceded.

We spent some time putting things back the way we'd found them – except for the manuscript – then Luke carefully shut and locked the door, erasing any evidence of our heist. It was sort of thrilling to have successfully achieved what we set out to do. The three of us parted ways that evening, convinced we had found a clue that would reveal something about the nature of Abel Dumont's cryptic research project.

I made a stop at my room to regroup and sent Vincent a message on my phone, informing him I could meet him in the lab. Exhausted, I lay on my bed, waiting for a response. None came. I must have fallen asleep after that, because the next thing I knew I was running from shadows and pursuing the terror of the dark basement stairwell.

# CHAPTER 6

I didn't hear from Vincent until the following day, before meeting him in lab for our paired dream session. He had emailed me to say something came up, which is why he couldn't meet me in the lab the night before. I wondered why he didn't simply text me instead.

I had to drag myself to breakfast. I should have probably stayed in bed, but I didn't want to miss the lab session, and I was a little worried Vincent might change his mind about helping me if I didn't talk to him soon.

After I'd eaten, I went straight to his room and knocked on the door. When he opened it, I could see the room was dark and he looked much the way he had the first time I came to his room to tell him about the dreams.

"You look awful," I said.

"Nice to see you too," he returned. He promptly fell back onto his bed and faced the wall.

I hesitated, unsure if I were welcome, but since he neither invited me in nor asked me to leave, I shut the door and pulled up his desk chair so I was sitting nearer to where he lay.

"Migraine?" I asked quietly.

He moved his head in assent.

"Will you be at lab today?" It was insensitive to even ask perhaps.

"Maybe," he mumbled.

I sort of assumed the reason he didn't meet me the night before was due to the headache, although I couldn't be sure. I decided not to ask.

"I'm sorry for getting angry yesterday," I said. "I really appreciate what you're doing for me. I know no one else here could, or would for that matter." I paused and sighed. "If there's anything I can do to help with the process I will. Just tell me. I need to get rid of these nightmares. I need to be able to sleep again." I allowed some desperation to be heard in my voice. It was no exaggeration that I'd been suffering from sleep deprivation and mental weariness.

Vincent was silent. I determined it might be better to leave and give him time to think instead of press him any further.

"I hope you feel better soon," I said, as I got up and pushed his desk chair back where it belonged. Then I left his room.

I wanted to believe that the reason I went to see Vincent that morning was purely by way of apology. However, the truth was that I was assuaging my own concerns about his willingness to assist me in my plan. I tried not to think on it any further that morning.

By the time lab came, I had no expectation that Vincent would show up. I brought my laptop, just in case, so I could get work done in Vincent's absence. To my surprise, he did appear just before the session began.

"You made it," I said, as he took a seat next to me.

He didn't look at me. "Wouldn't want to deprive you of the chance to make some observations," he answered.

Despite my attempt to smooth things over between us, Vincent was giving off a rather arctic vibe.

*The revenge of Iceman.*

I ignored it and readied myself to view his dreamscape.

Our instructor signaled it was time to begin. I was thrown into the unusual state of semi-consciousness the Dreamscape Program induced in the observer. I traveled through darkness and watched images form as if they were in the back of my mind's eye, merely a shadow of a thought and not yet a true idea.

As I fell into Vincent's dreamscape, I was oddly aware of his resistance to me being there. I moved as though against a current of thought, abstract, yet still cognizable. Also, his dreamscape hinted at incompletion, as if he were trying *not* to dream. Or perhaps he could not fully enter REM in his current mental state. I wondered if his migraine persisted and blocked the program's dreaming function.

Then suddenly the dream slammed into clarity. I stood in an open field, the grass an unrealistic green, and the sky silver-gray, filled with perilous clouds preluding a storm. I turned to see Vincent standing atop a grassy knoll, dressed as though he were part of a quest. The wind angrily whipped his long, black coat and two long, curved swords were strapped to his back. He stood motionless, surveying the area, his attention fixed at a cave at the bottom of the hill. With the wind, he was off down the hill, moving faster than anyone possibly could. He practically flew as he ran headlong toward the cave. I was close behind, tied to him as it were, by an invisible string. Then, as if someone had clicked "skip" on a remote, we were inside the cave, creeping slowly, avoiding the creature presiding over that dark place. It knew we had entered. Vincent's body tensed and he reached for his weapons.

It was strange – I actually *felt* Vincent's apprehension. More accurately, I shared it with him. The link we had forged within the program truly joined me to his consciousness, so that although he was unaware of me, I was fully aware of what he felt at that moment. I lingered on that feeling, realizing that I had never felt so fully connected to any human being.

The walls of the cave moved aside, rearranging the scene and revealing the monster, which resembled a dragon, now that we could see it for what it was. Vincent braced himself and attacked the creature while I reflected on how much his dreamscape mirrored a video game.

Then, just as dreams often change unexpectedly, we emerged from the dragon's cave, with no evidence we'd ever entered it at all. Vincent had resumed his usual attire and he was seated in his room, working on his computer. His door opened and I watched myself enter the room and sit on his bed. I looked almost doll-like, with porcelain skin and shimmering hair, yet my shoulders sagged in dismay. The Elena I watched in Vincent's dreamscape very obviously didn't want to be there. I sat beside myself on the bed, intrigued and a bit ashamed at how Vincent perceived me.

I was abruptly pushed from Vincent's dreamscape, as if by physical force. We had run out of time. The disconnection left me feeling empty and alone, and for a moment, I was overcome by a wave of panic at the realization I would not experience someone else's emotions until I next logged in with Vincent. Confusion followed at this curious response to my involvement in Vincent's dreamscape. I determined it might be best to examine it from a scientific perspective, as part of my research.

Vincent awoke, pale and still. The hair across his forehead was slightly damp with sweat and his breathing was shallow. He moved as if in pain, but sat up and wasted no time preparing to leave the lab.

"Wait," I said, grabbing hold of his arm.

He visibly winced and squeezed his eyes shut for a moment.

"Let me help you," I offered.

"I'm fine," he replied. "I'm just going back to my room."

"Can I come by later?" I asked.

He nodded. Then left without giving me time to say anything else.

I sat back in the lab chair and breathed an impatient sigh.

That afternoon I had a mentor meeting scheduled with one of my professors. We met in his office on a bi-weekly basis to discuss my research projects and dissertation plans. I liked Dr. Hammond. He could appear unassuming at times, yet he was straightforward if he thought I was straying off track in my research. He clearly respected his students and had high expectations for our work.

Dr. Hammond's office, though small, was clean and organized. He offered me tea or coffee as I took a seat by the window in one of the lounge chairs.

"I'm fine thanks," I said.

He sat across from me. "So how are things lately?" he asked conversationally. He leaned his elbow on the arm of the chair and rested his chin on his hand.

"Fine I suppose. I've been buried in work, of course," I said, rolling my eyes good-naturedly.

Dr. Hammond smiled and nodded. "How's the paired research with Vincent Miller going?"

I shrugged. "Fine."

Dr. Hammond was quiet for a moment, like he was waiting for me to continue. "Did something happen?" he asked me.

I was confused. "What do you mean?"

Dr. Hammond swiped a hand across his beard. "Vincent requested a lab partner change this morning."

I had to force my mouth to stay shut as he told me this.

"Do you know why he would make such a request?" he asked.

I shook my head, unable to think of a good reason.

As Dr. Hammond pondered this, I ran through all the possible explanations for Vincent's request for a new lab partner. I'd apologized to him that very morning for my behavior the previous day. When it came down to it, I didn't think I'd behaved unreasonably to begin with. I was thoroughly frustrated with Vincent's lack of communication and apparent disinterest in our agreement.

"Well, don't let it bother you. This sort of thing happens sometimes. Maybe he just felt like he wasn't getting anywhere in his research," Dr. Hammond suggested. We moved our conversation forward, but my thoughts stayed fixed on what he had just relayed to me, so much so that I was in a state of agitation for most of the day.

I think Evan and Alex could sense my dark mood at dinner, because they sat on either side of me and forced me to watch what they believed were "comedic" videos on their phone. I found the videos distasteful and difficult to watch, which encouraged the guys even more. They seemed amused at my disgust. As it turned out, they did succeed in lightening my attitude. I was silently grateful to them for making the effort.

I'd put off seeing Vincent that day, concerned my hands might accidentally end up around his neck. But eventually, I could no longer forestall the inevitable and at close to 8:00 pm, found myself gingerly knocking on Vincent's door.

"Come in," I heard him say.

I swung the door inward as Vincent paused whatever game he was playing on his computer. I sat on the bed.

"Feeling better?" I asked.

"Yeah. Thanks," he replied.

The first thing I noticed was that he still avoided eye contact with me. It was obvious he was uncomfortable.

"So, I spoke to Dr. Hammond today," I began.

Vincent nodded.

"Why don't you want to be my research partner anymore? What did I do wrong?" I didn't hide my exasperation. "I tried to apologize this morning..."

Vincent finally looked at me. "No, it's not that." He fidgeted slightly then sighed. "I just don't want you in my dreamscape anymore," he said.

The vague panic I'd felt earlier that day momentarily surfaced. I pushed it aside. "Why not? I thought it was going well," I argued.

He sighed again. "I'm still going to help you, ok? We can go to the lab tonight and work on things. Just don't worry about it."

He gave no further explanation and it was clear that no prodding on my part would induce him to disclose the reason he didn't want me in his dreamscape. As much as I tried not to let it offend me, I was unsuccessful. A wall had grown then that seemed impenetrable, but I surmised that what really bothered me was that he would be free to view my dreamscape while I was forbidden to experience his.

"Well, I can tell you've got video games on your mind," I commented, aiming to break some of the ice between us. "Your dream was pretty cool."

A small smile played on Vincent's lips. "That's a recurring dream I sometimes have. The cave is from one of the first games I ever played. I always get excited when I find it in my dream."

I smiled too. "It's too bad we couldn't go into my dreamscape armed like that. We could attack those shadows if they tried to come at us."

A thoughtful expression took the place of Vincent's smile. "You mean like a mod," he speculated. He swung around and punched a password into the keyboard.

"A mod?"

Vincent typed for a moment. "A modification. You use it to alter a computer game. So, if you wanted to make game play harder, or play with a character you wouldn't normally be able to play with, you could create a modification allowing you to do so."

"And we could do that with my dreamscape?"

"Well…in a sense, that's what we're doing anyway." He frowned and tapped on his keyboard. "I should have thought of adding weapons though."

I smiled to myself, inwardly pleased that I'd been able to contribute to the hack plan. Truthfully, I was aware of how useless I was to him, aside from my dreamscape. He didn't even want me for a lab partner anymore.

"Let's go to the lab," he said suddenly.

Once we arrived in the lab, Vincent had me sit in a chair while he got things ready. He maintained a fixed expression of determination while he worked. It was as though a switch had been flipped in his brain and he needed to accomplish whatever task he had set out to do. I said nothing as he worked, deciding I would give him the chance to tell me, as I'd requested earlier that day.

He came over to me. "I want to run you through the dream sequence with a trial mod. I'm using one I had saved from a while ago. I think it will work with the program."

I nodded. "Ok. What kind of mod is it?"

"It's just a weapons mod. We can change it later, after we see whether it will work or not," he explained.

"Are you going to observe?" I asked him.

"I should stay on the monitor this time," he said.

With that, I logged into the program to test the new mod. The dream proceeded as usual, except that at some point I was aware of a foreign object in my hand. Upon closer examination, I found it to be a red-handled katana. Even dreaming, I was puzzled. I think I tried to put the sword down, but to no avail. It stayed in my hand as if glued there by some unseen force. I must have accepted this new commodity as part of the dream, because I eventually began using it on the shadows. I was pleased to find that the katana swept the shadows away from me and gave me fresh endurance in the face of fear.

My ability to fight the shadows triggered an awareness that I was dreaming. As a result, the dream was out of sequence and somewhat disjointed due to my lucid involvement. At one point the dream changed entirely and I was neither in the mansion nor fighting shadows. I was home. The flood of images I experienced then seemed an attempt to make up for all the dreams I hadn't had in the last several weeks. It was too much for me.

I'm not sure what happened exactly, but the next thing I knew, I was gasping for air as Vincent gently shook me awake.

"Elena," he said, as he tried to get me to respond.

"I'm ok," I replied. I sat up carefully and took several slow, deep breaths. "What happened?"

Vincent leaned against one of the lab chairs, and looked at the ceiling. Then he blew out a breath, slowly. "Everything was fine, but you suddenly went into some kind of respiratory shock. I have no idea what happened."

It came back to me as he spoke. "It worked," I told him. "I had a katana with a red handle, but once I started using it on the shadows, I became lucid. That's when the dream changed. It was overwhelming. Like all the dreams I haven't been able to dream in the last several weeks rushed in at once." I sighed and closed my eyes. "But the mod worked."

We both said nothing for a moment. I felt rather physically and mentally spent by that point, and began to wonder if what had just taken place had been enough to reset my dreamscape. Oddly, I didn't experience any relief at the thought. It worried me. I didn't want the nightmares to cease until I'd uncovered the mystery behind their recurrence, and I was still convinced that I needed to descend the stairwell to do so.

"Let's go," Vincent said to me.

I got up automatically and followed him back to his room.

Vincent immediately sat at his desk and logged into his computer. I sat on his bed and leaned back against the headboard.

"What if I do the same thing when we log in together?" I asked, worried.

"Hmm?" Vincent continued to type.

"I mean dream about other things? This might not work at all if I can't keep us in the mansion."

"One thing at a time," Vincent replied. "We'll tackle that problem later. You probably just need some practice keeping yourself in one place."

More time lapsed in silence as he worked and I tried not to fall asleep. I think he forgot I was there.

"I'm going to my room," I told him, as I got to my feet.

"Mm hmm."

He didn't so much as turn around.

Back in my room, I fell onto my bed, too exhausted to think further on the day's events. As I wavered on the point of falling asleep, I could feel the shape of the sword hilt in my hand. It wasn't long before I was again trapped in my nightmare, fleeing from shadows and terror. Only now I carried a red-handled katana.

## CHAPTER 7

I had breakfast with Sophie the following day. Since our mansion exploration with Luke, we hadn't had the chance to discuss my dreams or the curious manuscript found in the library. Truthfully, I wasn't in any hurry to talk to her about it because I knew I would end up admitting that Vincent and I still intended to hack into my dreamscape.

"So, Luke is an impressive guy, huh?" she commented, as we found a table near the window in the cafeteria. It was unusually dark that morning due to rain clouds.

I stirred my coffee and nodded. "He's certainly seen his share of the world."

"And he's hot too," Sophie continued.

I smiled. "You interested?"

Sophie shrugged. "You found him first. I'm just giving my approval, as your friend." She took a bite of her bagel.

I didn't reply.

"What do you make of that manuscript we found?" she asked.

"It's puzzling. To be honest, I haven't put much thought into it yet. We probably won't hear from Luke until the weekend though. He told me he was working at the hospital this week."

"I think Abel Dumont was experimenting on people," Sophie stated. "He probably put them in that machine from the manuscript

drawings. I'll bet there are corpses buried in the walls of this place."
She burst out laughing, amused at her own wild scenario.

I smiled, but felt the expression freeze on my face as I was
suddenly hit with an image of dead faces on the walls of the mansion in
my dreamscape. It had been some time since I'd decided my dreams
were linked to something else entirely. I started to wonder if the
connection was something that had happened many years ago. Perhaps
my dreams had less to do with the Dreamscape Program itself, and
more to do with the mansion.

"How are things with the tech nerd these days?" Sophie asked.

"Actually, he requested a lab partner change," I told her.

Sophie's mouth fell open. "Are you kidding? The nerve of that guy!
What the hell is wrong with him? Why doesn't he want you as a
partner?"

I shrugged. "He didn't tell me."

"So, no more hack plan, huh? Wow. What a jerk." Sophie shook
her head in disbelief.

I shrugged indifferently.

I could have corrected her then and explained that Vincent was still
going to help me with my dreamscape, but merely didn't want me
viewing his dreams any longer. I didn't. This was an opportunity to
pretend there was no further link between me and Vincent. It was too
good to pass up.

As if in response to my decision to keep all contact with Vincent
secret going forward, my phone beeped with a message. I knew before
checking it was Vincent. Fortunately, Sophie had her phone out and
was scrolling through her social media.

The message read: *"Come to my room before class."*

I finished eating before excusing myself and leaving the cafeteria.

At my knock, Vincent invited me in.

"What's up?" I asked, closing the door behind me.

Vincent didn't turn around. "I think I found a way to keep you
dreaming longer. We're going to test it out later."

I perched on the edge of the bed. "Yeah, ok."

He turned around to look at me. "Now that we know the mod
worked, what kind of weapon do you want to use in your dreamscape?
We might as well work on that while we're at it."

"Actually, I think I'd like to keep that katana you designed. Believe it or not, I dreamt I had it last night," I told him.

Vincent nodded. "Fine."

"By the way…when you offered to help me last week, I told one of my friends about it. She didn't like the idea though and to be honest, I regretted telling her. Well, she thinks that you don't want to help me with this anymore, and I'd like her to keep thinking that for now."

Vincent looked at me for a moment. "Ok. I don't think anyone should know about it anyway," he agreed.

"Yeah. So, you probably shouldn't talk to me in front of other people, is what I'm trying to say." I suddenly felt very guilty.

Vincent's expression remained unchanged. "I *don't* talk to you," he pointed out.

I was disconcerted by his tone. Heat crept up my neck and threatened to spread across my features, but attempting to act as though his words had no effect, I merely smiled and shrugged. "I know. I just wanted to make sure we were on the same page." Even as the words left my mouth, I thought they sounded pretentious. If Vincent read too far into what I was implying, he would conclude I didn't want to have anything to do with him apart from working on the hack plan. I hoped that wasn't the case, but Vincent's demeanor was so aloof and removed that it didn't seem to matter whether I tried to explain further or not.

"I should get to class. When do you want to run through the program?" I asked politely.

"Not till this evening." He had already resumed typing on his computer. "I'll just text you."

I left without another word.

I went through the day feeling anxious. Logically, it shouldn't have mattered whether Vincent and I were on friendly terms or not, yet I was bothered that our interaction had taken several steps backward. I admitted to myself that what truly troubled me was his unwillingness to allow me into his dreamscape. I was offended. When I considered the situation, I realized that I thought I could somehow help Vincent emerge from his anti-social cocoon. His dreamscape had provided an unfettered glimpse into his soul, thereby connecting us in an unusual manner. That connection had been all but severed.

I spent the afternoon in the library, under the pretense of research and study. Instead, I perused the archives, searching for evidence of Abel Dumont's legacy. I found nothing and left more frustrated than ever.

At last, evening arrived. Vincent had messaged me to come to the lab around 9:00 pm. For the first time, I was genuinely nervous about seeing him. After him requesting a lab partner change, and my suggestion that we not speak to each other in public, I felt our plan was at risk. The thin thread that had loosely tied us together seemed almost completely displaced.

Vincent waited for me near the entrance hall to the research wing. My palms were sweaty and my stomach clenched. Vincent stood motionless, fists crammed into his pockets.

"Hi," I said, coming up beside him.

He gave me a curt nod and led the way to the lab.

As eager as I was to question him about our next step, I remained silent.

The research wing lights had been dimmed, casting eerie shadows and creating a gloomy atmosphere. It wasn't hard to imagine myself already within my dreamscape, running from the black creatures that haunted it. My dreams were more real then than I'd ever known them to be. A sudden cold sensation crept down from the back of my neck into my shoulders and spine. I sped up, trying to match my pace with Vincent's.

All that was heard as we entered the lab was a faint hum of equipment, but I felt safe somehow, encased in the glass lab doors. Even being next to Vincent was comforting, cold as he was.

It wasn't my imagination; he was absolutely ice.

He neither looked at me, nor behaved as though I were in the room. I could feel my stomach clench even tighter as I fought the unbearable sinking feeling that my partnership with him was slipping away. It was so intense I could barely breathe. Simultaneously, I questioned my irrational feelings. Why should it bother me so much whether we were on friendly terms? I couldn't answer myself and was left feeling vacant.

"Elena?"

Vincent was saying something to me but I hadn't been listening.

I shook myself slightly. "Sorry, what?"

"I need you to sit in the lab chair. I'm going to start the session."

I did so without a word.

After a few seconds, I realized Vincent was watching me.

"What's wrong?" I asked him.

He shook his head. "You don't seem...normal," he said.

"Sorry. I don't know why, but I'm really nervous," I confessed.

"We're just running some tests. I'm going to put you in a generated empty space, to see if you can practice staying in your dreamscape," he told me. "You'll be able to hear me speak."

"How?"

"Well...it's hard to explain. We started to write this feature into the program, but never finished, so in a sense, you'll be in a debug room, I guess," he explained.

"Like in a PC game," I suggested.

He nodded. "I'm going to have to give you some directions. We'll see how this goes."

"Ok," I said.

I slipped away more gradually this time and found myself in a curious empty space, not quite black or white. After several moments of adjustment, I felt the handle of the katana in my hand and remembered what was happening.

*"Elena? Can you hear me?"*

"Yes. This is so weird. How can we talk?"

*"You're not fully unconscious,"* was the reply. *"Did the weapon mod work?"*

"Yes. I have the katana in my hand," I told him. I did a few practice swings.

*"Good. Can you move around?"*

I took a few paces forward and felt myself grow slightly dizzy. Then I noticed there wasn't any floor. I started to panic.

"I think I'm going to fall. There's no floor," I told him.

*"Just stay calm. You have to make a floor. Try thinking about the floor in the Academy,"* he suggested.

I stayed very still and pictured the carpeted halls beneath my feet. I thought of a hard surface under that and the steadiness of walking on level ground. As I imagined, the Academy floor appeared, and as if a chain reaction had been triggered, walls and doors appeared and the floor stretched itself into a hallway that turned a corner at the end.

"This is so bizarre," I mumbled.

*"Did it work?"*

"Yeah. I'm in the Academy."

*"Ok. Try taking a few steps forward again."*

As I did so, I consciously accepted where I was and walking grew easier.

"This is incredible," I said aloud.

*"You can create your own dreamscape. Try moving around to different places."*

I moved through an empty Academy, void of shadows or anyone for that matter. I started running and swinging my katana as I went. It felt good to have complete control of my environment. On a whim, I ran up the wall and found that I could easily run along the sides of the walls if I chose. Meanwhile, I turned corners with alarming speed. As I ran I was filled with a rush of adrenaline. I could have sworn I was really moving.

*"How's it going?"* Vincent asked.

"Great. I can move around so easily here."

*"That's good. Ok, now I need you to try something. I want you to go down to the basement and find the stairwell."*

I hesitated. "I don't know where to find it."

*"Just think about it. Change your surroundings."*

I was worried I wouldn't be able to recreate the basement, but after a moment found that it came so easily, I had put in almost no effort at all. I held up my katana, just to reassure myself it was still in my hand, and then stepped forward until I was several paces from the stairwell.

"I made it to the stairwell," I said. "Now what?"

*"Go down."*

My heart thumped hard in objection to that request.

I took a step forward and the dizziness returned.

"I don't think I can," I said.

Vincent didn't reply.

I moved forward again, more slowly this time. As I put one foot in front of the other, I noticed the stairwell didn't get any closer. In fact, it seemed to be moving farther away.

"I can't get to it."

*"Just picture it right in front of you."*

I stopped moving and did as he said. The stairwell moved toward me, looming black and dismal as it approached until I was right on the edge of the top step. Looking down I could see nothing.

"There's nothing down there," I said.

*"There are stairs. Walk down the stairs."*

I breathed slowly and put one foot out. Once I felt assured I wouldn't fall, I continued, one footstep at a time, descending into darkness. I walked for a while before Vincent spoke again.

*"Did you make it down?"*

"I'm still going. There's nothing though. The stairs are endless."

"Keep walking. Let's see what happens."

I continued, obediently. As the minutes slipped by, my thoughts wandered. I imagined what it would be like to hack in with Vincent — what we would find at the bottom. In answer to my meandering thoughts, I reached the end of the stairs and suddenly Vincent appeared before me. I almost called out his name, but remembered the real Vincent could hear me.

We were in a dimly lit, featureless room. I didn't pay any attention to my surroundings, because I was too fixated on seeing Vincent in this contrived manner. He looked as he ever did, hair slightly mussed and a little too long. His face was almost luminous, and his eyes, grey as a storm cloud, intensely fixed on my face. He gazed at me, expressionless. I wanted to speak, but kept silent.

*"Elena? Are you at the bottom?"*

"Yes," I breathed, too fascinated by the fake Vincent before me to look elsewhere.

*"What's down there?"*

"It's"—

Before I could describe anything further, the false Vincent changed suddenly, as though a mask had been ripped from his face. His entire figure shrunk nearly to the size of a child, but wiry and humped in an abnormal way. At this transfiguration, I found myself paralyzed in fear. I could neither move nor speak as the creature gazed upon me with glowing eyes filled with hatred. Its mouth hung open and it reached a tremulous hand forward. Then it sprang toward me.

I don't remember the exact moment of waking; only that I heard screaming far away and the next thing I knew, Vincent was shaking me hard and saying my name over and over. I heard a voice sobbing his name in reply and remember clinging to him in desperation.

"It was there," I cried. "How was it there? Oh, God."

I'm fairly certain I fell to pieces then and allowed the sobbing to wrack my body almost to exhaustion. I didn't let go of Vincent. I don't remember how he soothed me, but somehow, I made it back to his room with him. He gave me a bottle of water and let me lie down on his bed.

I clutched the water bottle and sniffed, turning on my side and staring at the wall. I felt helpless and pathetic. My nightmares had finally gotten the better of me.

"It shouldn't have been there," I murmured. "I didn't want it to be there."

Vincent didn't say anything for a while. He worked on his computer while I managed to gradually regain my composure. Once the emotion had passed, I began to think more rationally. I sat up and took a sip of water. Vincent turned and watched me drink.

I glanced back at him, a bit ashamed of myself for so completely losing control.

"I'm sorry," I said, embarrassed.

Vincent ignored my apology. "You saw the creature. Tell me what happened when you went down the stairs."

I sighed, realizing I would have to tell him I had imagined him there as well. "The stairs went on for a long time. I thought they wouldn't end. I guess I was thinking about hacking in with you and what we would find. The stairs finally ended and then you were there at the bottom. We were in a room, I think. I don't remember what it looked like really." I stopped for a moment, frowning at the memory. "Wait, can't we re-watch it?"

Vincent shook his head. "Nothing recorded. What happened after that?"

"Well, then you spoke to me, so I was about to look around so I could describe the room to you. That's when you changed and turned into the small figure from my dreamscape." I rubbed my forehead and sighed again. "That was the first time I ever really saw it though. It was hideous and old. It's eyes...that thing is evil somehow. I don't know. It reached out for me, then it just jumped, like it wanted to kill me."

Vincent nodded. "It tried to attack me too."

"But how was it *there*? The shadows weren't even in the dream. I didn't think about the figure at all."

Vincent shrugged. "It wasn't a dream. It was your thoughts. You had to of thought of that thing."

"No," I insisted. "I didn't think of it. It came to *me*."

I couldn't explain why I felt so strongly that the small figure had found me, despite my not even fully dreaming.

"It's in the program," I heard myself say. "There's something wrong with the program. In fact, there's something wrong with this whole place."

Vincent was quiet. I'm not sure he knew what to say, but I'm certain the words tumbling from my mouth sounded at least mildly paranoid.

"Listen, I found something in the west wing of the mansion. It's a manuscript of some kind, written by the original owner of this place."

I filled Vincent in on the history of the Academy and gave him what little knowledge I possessed of Abel Dumont. He listened, patiently while I spoke. With effort, I managed to keep my voice steady.

When I finished speaking, I waited for Vincent to reply. "So, you think it's all connected? You're saying Abel Dumont pioneered this program?" he ventured.

"I don't know. Luke has the manuscript, but he's been away all week. I'm waiting to hear from him."

Vincent's gaze fell for a moment. Then he looked at me again. "Despite everything, I think the trial run through was successful. You managed to manipulate your surroundings and stayed in the dreamscape to descend the stairwell. You just have to keep dreaming. We'll probably need to practice a little more before we hack in together."

"Ok. I can't guarantee I'll get it right away, but I'll try," I agreed.

A moment of silence ensued. Vincent's gaze had once again fallen to the floor and I guessed he was lost in thought.

"Vincent," I said.

He looked up at me.

"I want to be your lab partner. Please don't switch."

To my surprise, Vincent's ears turned red as I spoke. He swallowed and looked away. "I'll think about it," he said.

# CHAPTER 8

I had several more sessions with Vincent in the lab at night that week. He continued to coach me through the debug room, until I became rather adept at manipulating my surroundings. I also developed my skill with the katana. At times, I would create shadows in the program and practice fighting them. Other times when I felt brave enough, I conjured the small figure and tried not to flee in terror. I half expected the creature to invade the practice space again, but thankfully it did not.

As the week progressed, I managed to stay in the program for longer periods of time. I knew I wasn't really dreaming, but I was conditioning myself to face the unknown mystery that awaited me in my dreamscape. Oddly enough, my new skills transferred to my dreams at night so that I became much more confident with the katana, which never left my hand. Vincent and I wondered if I would end up descending the stairwell naturally as I practiced more, but it didn't happen. We concluded it was because I wasn't always lucid in my dreams.

Vincent said nothing of remaining lab partners with me and I didn't push it. Instead I tried to establish myself as a serious student in his eyes, and redeem myself from the total meltdown he'd witnessed me have earlier that week.

I didn't tell Sophie about my nightly rendezvous with Vincent, and he and I didn't speak in public if it could be helped. On the surface, we seemed successful in our preparations for the dream hack. I grew more anxious to speak with Luke as the days passed, however, because I wanted more information on the manuscript we'd found. Luke had let me know he would be back on campus Saturday and he intended to spend time with me, if I were available.

That Friday, Sophie had convinced me to go out with her and Alex and Evan to a concert in Los Angeles. She came to my room early that evening to fix me up for the outing.

"Hey. I haven't seen you much this week," she commented as she set down her makeup and hair tools on my desk.

"Lots of research this week," I said. "My goodness, is this a date or something?" I asked, nodding to the beauty stash she'd brought with her.

Sophie grinned. "Well, Evan will be there." She gave me a sly look and lifted an eyebrow.

I rolled my eyes. "Come on. You know I'm not interested."

She shrugged and pointed to the chair. I sat compliantly and she began to sponge my face with foundation.

"Are you still having the dreams?" she asked.

I hesitated. We hadn't talked about it recently and I'd hoped she had thought the dreams had naturally disappeared. I couldn't bring myself to lie about it.

"Yes," I replied.

She nodded. "I thought so. Then Vincent is probably still working on your hack plan."

*Of course. She's too intuitive not to have guessed.*

I didn't answer her, but I didn't need to.

"I had a feeling something was going on. You've been so elusive lately."

"I didn't want you to worry," I said.

"It's not that I'm worried about you guys getting caught really," she responded. "I just think you're putting too much trust in Vincent's ability. What if he screws something up and you end up brain fried?"

"That's not likely to happen."

"No, but it could," she insisted.

I didn't argue.

Sophie changed the subject as she brushed through my hair. "Have you spoken to Luke recently?"

"Yeah. He wants to see me tomorrow," I told her.

"Good. I've been thinking about that manuscript all week. I'm dying to know what it's all about."

"Me too," I agreed.

"So maybe your plan to hack the dreamscape program with Vincent will intersect with what's in that manuscript," she suggested. "I think it's all connected."

"So do I."

Sophie sprayed my hair with hairspray and gave me a last look before saying, "All done."

I glanced in the mirror and was impressed with the result. She had kept my make up more on the neutral side, but appropriate for a night out, and my hair was quite silky.

"Nice job," I said. "Maybe you should have been a beautician instead of a dream researcher."

Sophie laughed. "Yeah, I think you're right. I'm going to get myself ready now, so I'll see you in a bit."

I got myself dressed and glanced at the clock. There was still some time before we had to meet the guys in the lobby. I had spoken to Vincent earlier that week about an issue with my laptop and he'd said he would take a look for me. I decided to drop it off before the new week began.

I knocked on Vincent's door and heard him call *"come in."*

As usual, he didn't turn around when I entered. He was playing a video game on his computer and he had the volume turned up rather loud.

"What's up?" he said, still engrossed in the game. It was quite a graphic, gory game. I watched him blast some gruesome looking creature, which exploded, spewing guts everywhere.

"I brought my laptop." I placed it on an empty space on the desk.

Vincent paused the game and turned. His eyes did a once over when he finally looked at me. "What's wrong with it?"

"It's just really slow and some of the programs keep crashing," I explained. I had brought it to him shut off so he could witness it for himself. I powered it on.

Vincent put his game controller down and watched the startup screen defrag. His eyes flicked sideways at me again. "Going somewhere?"

"Yeah. Sophie got tickets to a show in Los Angeles."

Vincent swung the laptop toward him and typed something into the terminal. "What band are you seeing?"

I leaned against the desk. "Some weird name. I don't remember."

"Tellurian?" he guessed.

"Yeah, actually."

"I heard they were coming through." He kept typing. "I'll need to hang on to this tonight."

"Yeah, that's fine." I pushed off the desk. "Thanks for doing this. See you around." I left his room and made my way to the lobby.

Evan and Alex were already waiting when I arrived. They had taken the opportunity to spend a little more time than usual getting ready as well, or so the smell of cologne suggested.

Evan drove that evening as we headed out to the concert venue. Honestly, although I did my best to enjoy my time away, I kept thinking of Luke and the manuscript. I felt certain there was an important clue within its pages that would bring some of Abel Dumont's obscurity to light. Repeatedly I thought of the passage of scripture from the book of Isaiah and the phrase "child of a hundred years." I wondered if it was meant as a description of the small creature from my dreamscape. That seemed the most sensible explanation, but it did nothing to clarify the true nature or significance of that terrifying figure from my nightmares.

In sleep, I still fled from the clutches of shadows and haunting faces on the walls of the mansion. My hand was ever wrapped around the handle of the red katana Vincent had created for me, and I often made it very close to the edge of the stairwell before the small being appeared, its eyes now gleaming with greed at my desire to descend. But I woke every time, or was cast from the dream into darkness and spent the night restlessly turning on my bed, hoping to at least achieve a state of semi-sleep.

After very little sleep from the night out, I woke Saturday morning, famished and impatient. I threw on some sweat pants and a hoodie and went to the cafeteria, which was open all morning on

Saturdays and Sundays for brunch. I piled food onto my plate and found a seat in the corner where I could read. My phone beeped halfway through my meal with a message from Vincent that read: *"Come by. Your laptop is ready."*

I replied: *"I am devouring a mountain of food in the cafeteria. Care to join me?"*

Since Sophie had figured out that Vincent and I were still working on the hack plan, I figured it didn't matter whether we were seen together. That, and he still hadn't officially changed lab partners.

Vincent didn't respond to my message, but five minutes later I saw him enter the cafeteria with my laptop under his arm. He briefly scanned the room and headed in my direction. I kept my eyes on my book as he sat across from me and put the laptop on the table.

"Is there a delivery charge?" I asked.

Vincent raised an eyebrow and the faintest hint of a smile appeared on his face. "I'll waive my usual fee."

"What was wrong with it," I asked, sipping my coffee.

"I just reinstalled the operating system and cleaned it up a bit. Should work fine."

"Great. Thanks."

"Sure," he said.

I continued to eat as Vincent sat with me. He eyed my food and watched me eat for a moment.

"How was the show last night?" he inquired.

"It was good. By the way, Sophie knows we're working together. She sort of guessed and I didn't want to lie. She knew about it before anyway, so it doesn't really matter I suppose. I just wanted you to know," I explained.

He nodded. "That's why I can talk to you in public again," he stated, a bit sardonically.

"Well...it wasn't that you *couldn't* before. I just didn't want you to come up to me in front of people I knew if there wasn't any reason for us to speak..." I stopped, hoping he would understand what I was implying.

There was no opportunity to hear Vincent's reply. Luke walked over to us and sat next to me.

"Hey," he said.

I smiled at him. "Hey."

Vincent got up without a word.

"Thanks for your help," I said to him.

He gave me a nod and left.

"Who was that?" Luke asked.

"Vincent Miller," I answered. "He's my lab partner. He just fixed my laptop for me." I quickly changed the subject. "So how was your week?"

Luke laughed. "Busy. Very busy." He leaned an elbow on the table and turned so we were facing each other. I noted that his hair was slightly damp from showering. He smelled really good.

I tried to push aside any thoughts of Vincent then and endeavored to give Luke my full attention. He was certainly very interested in hearing about my week. His eyes watched my face as I spoke and his expression changed in response to what I said. Inevitably, despite my efforts, I did find myself comparing Vincent and Luke. I'd spent so much time with Vincent that week, in the confines of the lab, that it was refreshing to speak to someone who responded to me as person.

"So you're free today, right?" Luke asked.

"Yeah," I said.

"Good. I have plans for us, and I've been looking forward to seeing you all week," he admitted.

I tried to keep my grin under control.

"Oh, another thing," he said, leaning forward. "I read through some of that book we found in the library. I want to talk to you about it."

"I was hoping you did. I've been dying to hear about it, honestly."

"Well then let's start with that. The book is in my room," he said.

I had finished my meal, so we left the cafeteria and went straight to Luke's room. Upon entering, I learned much more about him than I'd previously known. Books were piled on his desk — some open, some with numerous tabs sticking out of the pages; a quick glance told me most were medical texts. He had added his own touches to the room: several plants rested on the window sill and eclectic posters decorated the walls. There was a guitar on a stand in the corner near a small amplifier.

Luke motioned to a wingback chair. "Have a seat," he offered.

I slipped off my shoes and curled up in the chair. Luke found the manuscript and brought it to me, pulling the desk chair over as he did so. He sat down.

"Don't get your hopes too high," he began. "It's an old-fashioned French dialect, so it's a bit tedious to translate. The first part of the book explains Abel Dumont's theory of dream function. It's stuff we already know, or have ruled out in dream research. Then he goes into some kind of strange idea about dreaming connected to lifespan." Luke flipped the pages and read a portion in French, following with an English translation: "'The controlled dreamer possesses the ability to prolong life, but this is hard to achieve.'"

"'Prolong life?'" I repeated.

"It gets weirder," he said. "Dumont explains that a device is needed to help control an individual's dreams. That's what the second half of the book is — all those drawings and notes are the machine he built to control dreams. There's also something about nightmares, but I haven't gotten very far with that part yet. There's still quite a bit to translate," he concluded.

I pondered the implications of the report I'd just been given and felt more certain than ever that my recurring dream was linked to the strange history of the mansion.

"If we could only find more information on Dumont's research," I said aloud.

"That would shed some light on things," Luke agreed. "You could always ask some of the faculty here if they know anything," he suggested. "There may not be a need for all the secrecy — aside from the whole sneaking into the west wing and taking things that don't belong to us." He laughed.

"Yeah, you're right." I laughed too.

"So let's get out of here," Luke said. He closed the manuscript and returned it to the desk.

"Where are we headed?" I asked him, sliding my feet back into my shoes.

"There's a local art show in town this weekend. That doesn't sound too boring, does it?" he asked.

I smiled. "Not at all."

It's funny how something like timing is taken for granted. Even more ironic that despite Vincent's tendency to stay secluded in his room, he did in fact need to leave it now and then, if only to use the bathroom. Just as Luke and I emerged from his room, Vincent passed us in the hall. Luke, unaware of my situation with Vincent, didn't even notice him pass as he locked up his room, but in that split second, Vincent's eyes connected with mine. Then I watched his gaze flick to Luke and harden. Vincent didn't even pause as this took place. He walked briskly by.

*Oh boy.*

I felt like a kid who had just been caught sneaking out of my room at night. This was going to complicate things.

Despite the tightness in my chest, I managed to pretend as if everything were fine. It was a beautiful day and Luke was very attentive and pleasant to spend time with. Although he and I hadn't yet made any kind of physical contact, I was conscious of the chemistry between us. We spent most of the day together and even stayed out for dinner. I didn't get back to campus until early evening.

That was two Saturdays in a row I'd spent with Luke. Again: timing is everything. A few weeks earlier, and perhaps I would have allowed things to progress as they naturally did when dating someone new. As it was, I was hesitant to even label my outings with Luke as "dating." I was careful to stay at least a little unavailable so Luke wouldn't spend too much time trying to get my attention. Of course, that's not how these things work. The less available I made myself, the more Luke pursued. It wasn't long before he was texting me regularly. I got used to juggling texts between Vincent and Luke; careful not to let on to each one who was texting me at any given time.

Vincent didn't reach out to me that evening. I guess I figured a night off from lab duty wasn't such a bad thing. I'd hardly had a break since the night before, so I put on my pajamas and crawled into bed with my laptop. It's not often I fall asleep while watching shows on my computer, but I was exhausted after so much activity.

My dream proceeded as usual, but with one exception: I was lucid from the beginning. It was as though I had been slowly immersed into the dream, and that slow immersion had prompted the comprehensible sensation that I was dreaming. I checked to be sure I held my katana, and made a steady path through the mansion, slaughtering shadows as I went. The awareness that I was dreaming filled me with remarkable courage. I was outraged and angry that I couldn't get out of the dreamscape.

I went on an absolute rampage.

Sooner than usual, I was in the basement, standing atop the stairwell. I waited for a moment for the small figure to appear. Nothing happened. A thought occurred to me then. Since I had the power to make decisions, and knew that descending the stairwell would end the dream, I turned around and went the other way. As I moved around the basement, I found another passage leading somewhere unknown. I followed the passage as it twisted several times, but found myself at a dead end. Feeling along the wall was to no avail. Then, turning to go back, I nearly jumped in alarm. The stairwell was behind me and I saw the creature waiting for me.

"What are you?" I said. I gripped the handle of my sword.

The creature's mouth moved. It waved to me, bidding I follow it down.

"I can't go down there. I'll wake up."

The small figure crept forward and opened its mouth, which enlarged to an impossible size. In its maw, I saw the faces from the mansion wall. They were no longer dead and lifeless, but twisted in agony. Their groans filled me with hopelessness and horror. The creature came closer to me, and I knew it meant to pull me inside as well.

My eyes shot open in fear. I was panting and sweating as I propped myself up in bed and took an unsteady drink of water from my nightstand. A quick glance at the clock told me it was after 1:00 am. The bedside lamp was still on and my laptop was open next to me. I gently closed it and sat up in bed, smoothing my hair as I did so.

When I had composed myself, I grabbed my phone. Vincent hadn't texted me all evening, yet I had a suspicion he would still be up.

*"Are you awake?"* I typed.

A pause.

*"Yes,"* was the reply.

*"I need to talk to you. Can I come over?"*

*"Sure."*

I was up in an instant.

That trek down the hall to Vincent's room was the longest I'd ever taken. I kept seeing the image of the creature in my mind, its mouth hanging open as it tried to suck me in. I moved faster, and when I reached Vincent's room, I didn't even knock. I flung the door open and closed it quickly behind me.

Vincent was stretched out on his bed, with laptop and earbuds. He wore gym shorts and a t-shirt.

"Bad dream?" he asked, without looking up. He tugged an earbud from his ear.

I smiled, in spite of myself. "You could say that."

"Tell me about." He continued to type and scroll on his laptop.

I sat on the end of the bed and pulled my knees up to my chest. "I was lucid," I told him. "I don't know how, but from the beginning, I knew I was dreaming. I fought the shadows and went down into the basement. But, because I knew I was dreaming, I went a different way."

Vincent looked at me.

"There was a hallway that kept turning, but it was a dead end. I turned to go back the way I'd come. The stairwell was right behind me and so was the creature. It tried to get me to come down." I sighed. "I spoke to it. I asked it what it was, but I couldn't hear what it said, so I told it I couldn't go down the stairwell. Vincent...it came toward me and opened its mouth." I leaned forward as I spoke. "I could see those faces in its mouth, the ones on the wall in the mansion, only they weren't dead, they were screaming. I think the creature wanted to suck me in. It was awful." I stopped talking.

Vincent sat very still. His eyes were fixed on me, but I couldn't tell what he was thinking.

"I made that part up, right? I was lucid, and I wasn't in the program. I must have made it up," I insisted.

"Possibly," he said.

"The dream keeps getting weirder. I'm worried that when we hack in together, we won't make it down that stairwell. What if that thing gets us?" I heard panic rise in my voice as I spoke.

"It won't get us. We'll be armed and you'll be lucid. You'll slice it in half if you want to."

"But I was lucid this time and I didn't kill it. What if it can't be killed?"

Vincent was quiet.

"I just don't know if this is going to work. I'm going to be stuck having nightmares forever and that thing will eventually eat me." I was intentionally petulant, weary of pretending I had it together. By that point, it didn't matter much. Vincent had already seen me fall to pieces once before and I had come to terms with him switching lab partners.

Another minute of silence passed.

"Do you want to watch a movie?" he asked me.

I nodded.

Vincent opened his laptop and placed it in the middle of the bed. I moved up next to him and leaned against the pillows. We selected an indie film that I'd heard was pretty funny, but it actually turned out to be more of a romantic drama with some odd humor strung throughout.

I had nearly forgotten about Vincent's subtle response to seeing me with Luke earlier that day. He didn't bring it up and behaved as though it never happened. Naively, I thought that meant it hadn't really bothered him after all.

Later on, I marveled at how Vincent's presence alone was enough to comfort me. Despite his sometimes aloof and unfeeling disposition, he possessed a steadiness I found reassuring.

At that moment, Vincent's room was the safest place in the world.

# CHAPTER 9

My recent nightmare filled me with more eagerness than ever to get to the bottom of my dreamscape mystery. In fact, I found it nearly impossible to think of anything in the days that followed. Each time I closed my eyes, I saw the gaping mouth of the small monster from my dreams, and the faces it had consumed, scream to me in anguish. I felt sorrowful when I thought of the future, as though mine had already been determined, and I began to see the dreams as more of an omen, and less a scientific phenomena. I found myself relying heavily on Vincent for the answer I sought.

We didn't go to the lab at all that weekend. Vincent spent it primarily writing code, so I spent Sunday catching up on my work for the coming week. Luke texted me quite a bit throughout the day, but I didn't see him again that weekend.

To my relief, the nightmares resumed their normalcy Sunday evening, so that I did at least manage to rest without as much terror as the previous night.

Then Monday's lab session came.

I had prepared myself for a new lab partner assignment all week, and although I hadn't yet received an email confirming the change, I didn't want to get my hopes up.

I arrived in the lab a little earlier than most of the other students. I sat in the chair and watched the technicians work at the computers. My thoughts traveled to Abel Dumont's manuscript and Luke's suggestion that I simply talk to one of the faculty about it. I had to admit, there was a chance I'd created a mystery out of nothing. Perhaps it would be helpful to try to get an outside perspective on things. I decided I would try speaking with Dr. Hammond later that day.

After several minutes, I found that I really wasn't all that surprised when Vincent walked through the door and came up beside me. He placed his backpack on the floor and sat in the adjacent chair, setting the parameters as he did so.

He looked at me.

"You know, you look a lot like my other lab partner," I said to him. I squinted as though I were eyeing him up.

"That's because I'm wearing the other guy's face," he replied.

I burst out laughing. "That's disgusting."

Vincent grinned. "How was the dream last night?"

"It was more normal than Saturday. No guarantees for today's nightmare experience," I said, lightly.

"Being lab partners with you is like watching the same bad horror flick on repeat," Vincent muttered. "Here's hoping that little freak tries something crazy this time."

"I'm ok with that *not* happening," I contradicted. "At least not until you can actually help me fight the thing. Speaking of which, I think I'm going to be way better than you at fighting." I shot him a good-natured look as if to challenge him.

As he opened his mouth to reply, our instructor gave the signal to begin the lab session. For the first time ever, I actually looked forward to having a nightmare. It amazed me how relieved I was that Vincent wasn't going to switch lab partners. It wasn't just that I wanted to be able to view his dreamscape. I still didn't want anyone else to see mine. It had been close to two months since the nightmares started and as disturbing as it was to experience the same dream every time I closed my eyes, I wanted nothing more than to unlock the mystery beyond the basement stairwell.

I started dreaming. Since the mod wasn't running, I was unarmed that time in my dreamscape and everything happened in slow motion. There was something different aside from that, however. Something felt off. Though I wasn't lucid, I was compelled to get out of the mansion at all costs, so I didn't make the same decisions as in previous dreams.

I pushed myself hard, yanking doors and windows in an effort to free myself from the prison of the mansion. I think I started screaming as I tore through the place, fleeing from shadows. There were more of them than before. Their numbers had increased so dramatically that it was difficult to turn a corner without bumping into them. They reached for me with sinewy, black arms, trying to pull me into the walls and make me one the dead faces. Somehow I *knew* that's what they were trying to do.

Then at last, I turned a corner and was met with a dead end. Out of the wall, the small creature appeared, grinning with malice. It waved to me, and the wall behind it transformed into the black stairwell. I was in the basement. The creature opened its mouth, then suddenly stopped. It was then that I remembered that although I couldn't see him, Vincent was with me.

The small figure reached a decrepit hand forward and tried to grab the air. It was reaching for Vincent. I wanted so desperately to be able to see him there, and in a that moment of despair, I charged forward and slammed my body into the ancient monster. We tumbled down the stairwell together.

I woke, calmer than I would have expected after such a dramatic dream. But when I opened my eyes, I had tunnel vision and tried not to move much until it passed. I heard Vincent sit up next to me. He leaned over and whispered my name.

"I'm awake," I said. "I can't see very well."

"Can you sit up?"

"Yeah." I pushed myself up and slowly stood next to the chair. "It's hard to see. My peripheral vision isn't so good," I explained.

Vincent took my hand and led me out of the lab. He didn't let go until we had reached his room. I sat down on his bed and stared at the floor. Vincent stood in front of me, arms crossed.

"How's your vision?" he inquired.

"It seems ok now," I replied. "I have another class to get to though"—

"Forget it," he interrupted. "That thing in your dream, it *saw* me again." Vincent ran his hands through his hair and paced back and forth.

"What the hell *is* that thing? And why did you attack it — unarmed no less?"

He was getting worked up. I'd never seen him like that before.

"We gotta get in there soon and annihilate that thing," he continued, still pacing. "I think it wants *you* Elena. It doesn't like me being there."

"I've been telling you that, haven't I? That's why I came up with the whole hacking in idea. We need to get down that stairwell." I kept my voice steady.

"But this shouldn't be *happening*. This could be really dangerous. Why haven't you told anyone else about it yet?" He stopped pacing and glared at me.

I stood up. "What do you think they'll do? Run tests. They'll use the program and run tests on me to see why I'm having the dreams. Or they'll force me to drop out of the program and I'll have to go through treatment. That's *not* going to happen. You said you'd help me. When can we do this? I want it resolved." I glared back at him, determined to make him understand.

He sat down in his desk chair and breathed out a sigh, rubbing his face with his hands. "Yeah. Ok," he said. He swung the chair around and began to type on his keyboard. "We're going to do it this week. I'm thinking Friday night, but there are a few more things we need to try."

I came up beside him.

"We have to practice logging in to the debug room together. I want to test the dream-joining feature," he said.

"That's the part you designed?"

He nodded. "It's still never been tested though. The thing is, the Academy knows I've been working on it." He stopped typing and glanced at me. "It's kind of funny that you approached me with this whole dream hack thing. I had been wanting to try logging in with someone, but I'm not supposed to do it without prior approval. We're technically not going to launch this for another few months. They think it's still incomplete."

"You finished it on your own?" I guessed.

"Yeah, something like that. Anyway, we're going to test it before the real thing. I'm not sure this feature will function properly when merged with your dreamscape. I think it kind of depends on you."

"How so?"

"Well, that's why we've been running you through the dreamscape design feature, to see how well you control a lucid dream. You seem to do better in there than your own dreamscape. Which makes me wonder..." he paused.

"What?" I pressed.

"I wonder if you're in someone else's dreamscape?" he finished.

I shook my head. "You're going to need to explain."

He turned so that he was facing me, and gave me an apologetic look. "Sorry I freaked out earlier," he said.

"It's fine. We're even now." I smiled to show him I didn't hold it against him.

His eyes fell and he looked back at the computer screen. "It's possible your dreamscape overlapped with someone else. Maybe that's why certain parts of it feel like they're...forced."

*So he felt that too.*

"I also think that creature from your dreams is using the paired dream function somehow. I don't know. That part still doesn't make sense," he said.

"None of it makes sense. How can I still be having that dream, even when I'm not in the program? It just repeats over and over. It's getting worse now." I leaned against his desk. "Vincent, please don't bail on me. And don't tell anyone." I looked at him seriously.

He nodded ever so slightly. "We'll pull it off." His demeanor changed suddenly. "By the way, that thing you said about being a better fighter than me – I wouldn't get my hopes up if I were you." He smiled to himself.

I lifted an eyebrow. "Really? I'm looking forward to it then."

He laughed. "You're so competitive. But really, I can't wait to get in there and rip that little monster to shreds."

I had a sudden thought. "Do you think there's a basement in the Academy?" I wondered aloud.

"Possibly. This place is a lot bigger than you would expect."

"What if there really is a stairwell that leads to some kind of secret? Want to do some exploring?" I asked.

"I thought you had your own exploration team already assembled," he responded, with slight derision. "Don't you keep these things separate? You know, 'tech nerd for hacking into scary dreams' and 'pretty friends for mansion explorations?'" He looked up at me and grinned.

I smacked his arm. "You're a piece of work, you know that?"

"So is that Luke character you pal around with," he murmured, as he punched something into the keyboard.

I could have easily shot back with a sarcastic remark, but I held my tongue. I couldn't overlook what I knew to be true: Vincent was jealous. I understood how he felt. The last time I'd logged into the program with him, I felt the same possessiveness that he seemed to be exhibiting now. We were connected through the program and we needed to feel secure in that connection. I realized that my fears of Vincent switching partners or bailing on me were unfounded. He was in fact the *only* person I could rely on.

"So, is that a 'yes?'" I asked, ignoring his comment about Luke.

"Maybe," he replied. "Let's focus on the program first. I want to get you out of that nightmare."

"Yeah. I'm good with that."

I left his room shortly thereafter, and headed to Dr. Hammond's office. I didn't have an appointment, but I knew Dr. Hammond would be in his office during that time of day anyway. I still wanted to ask him about Abel Dumont.

"Elena," he greeted me, as I knocked on his door frame. "Come in." He got up and motioned to a lounge chair. "So Vincent withdrew his request for a lab partner change. I'm glad things worked out."

"Me too."

"How can I help you today?" he asked, taking a seat near me.

"I just had a few questions for you, actually," I began. "I heard a rumor recently about the original owner of the Academy. Um, I believe his name was Abel Dumont? Can you tell me anything about him?"

"What sort of rumors have you heard?"

"Oh, just something about him coming up with the idea for the Dreamscape Program. There was also a rumor that he was still alive somewhere in France," I said.

Dr. Hammond looked thoughtful. "I wonder where you heard that?" He gave me a searching look that made me feel a little nervous. Then he smiled at me. "You're quite inquisitive. Unfortunately, I can't give you very much information. I've only been part of the faculty for about four years now, and I'm not so familiar with the history of this place. Dr. Belle is the one you want to speak with. She's been part of our work from the beginning. I believe she has office hours on Tuesdays and Thursdays if you'd like to see her," he suggested.

I nodded. "That sounds fine. I'll talk to her," I said.

He continued to look at me. "You feeling alright? You look pale."

"I'm fine." I forced a smile. "I'm just getting over something," I lied.

"Well don't push yourself too hard," he advised.

I thanked him and left rather hastily. It was only Monday, so I would have to wait to speak to Dr. Belle.

Alex and Evan descended on me at dinner that evening.

"There she is," Alex said, sitting beside me.

Evan took the other seat next to me.

"Why are you weirdos surrounding me?" I said. I had been enjoying my meal alone. The truth was, I was trying to eat fast and leave so I could get some studying done before meeting Vincent in the lab later that evening.

"You're always rushing around," Alex observed. "We just want to spend time with you." He patted my arm patronizingly. I yanked it away with pretend disgust.

"There's a video game tournament in the longue tonight," Evan told me. "Want to come by?"

"I'd love to, but I have loads to do," I said. "Why is it happening on a Monday night anyway? I thought you guys only did those things on the weekend."

Alex shrugged. "We didn't set it up. We're going to crash it though. Show those tech nerds some real gaming." He leaned back in his chair and let out a laugh.

I rolled my eyes. "Pass. My sensitive nature can't handle seeing you two get yourselves wrecked."

"You're so feisty," Alex commented. "That's why I like you Gray. You know how to make a man feel good about himself."

I nudged him, but smiled at the remark.

"You two sound like a bitter old married couple," Evan mumbled.

"Jealous man? It's ok. I haven't made my mind up about this one yet anyway"– Alex started to say.

Evan reached around me and smacked Alex in the back of the head. Alex had begun to dodge the blow, but was still hit. He burst out laughing.

"Would you two please behave?" I said, with mock exasperation.

The two of them went back and forth for a moment, calling each other some rather childish, inappropriate names. I just shook my head and laughed.

After they'd settled down, Evan asked, "How are your paired lab sessions going?"

"Fine." I shrugged as though there wasn't much to say.

"What's that Vincent guy like?" Evan asked.

"He's kind of quiet I guess. Sort of anti-social." I was really just repeating what I'd heard about him. After spending more time with Vincent over the past couple of weeks, I knew better, but I wasn't about to tell the guys that.

"Let us know if he tries any funny business," Alex said.

I smiled at the thought of Vincent trying "funny business" with me. Although I'd gotten the sense Vincent was attracted to me, he seemed too diffident to do anything about it.

Evening slipped into night and I made my way to the lab. As usual, Vincent waited for me by the entrance to the research wing. He used his keycard to let me in to the lab.

"I talked to Dr. Hammond this afternoon," I told him. "I asked him about Abel Dumont. He said I should speak to Dr. Belle."

Vincent was making preparations on the computer. "Are you going to?"

"I think so. I'm just really curious to learn about the history of this place."

"Yeah, that's what you'll *tell* her," he stated.

I sat in the lab chair and waited for him to finish.

"It's ready," he said. He took the seat next to me. "I don't know what this is going to be like," he told me. "There's a chance we'll both feel a bit...disoriented. I don't know. Oh, and I made some adjustments to the mod."

"Like what?"

"You'll see. Ready?"

I nodded.

"One more thing: I'm controlling this dream space," he explained. "You'll get a turn tomorrow."

We logged in.

I was alone in a dark room. Completely dark. I couldn't even see the outline of my hand, though I could feel the handle of my katana.

*"Elena,"* I heard Vincent call.

"I can't see anything," I said. "Where are you?"

*"Just hold on a sec."*

Then the black literally rolled away and was replaced by an orange sky at sunset. I felt a breeze on my face and looked out at a massive, empty city. I was atop a skyscraper.

Vincent came up beside me. He wore a long black coat and two swords strapped to his back, just like the last time I'd logged into his dreamscape.

"Is this really you, or am I dreaming it?" I asked.

"You're not dreaming it. It's *my* dream, remember?"

"So we're both lucid...and we're in the same dream. It worked."

Vincent nodded. "Yeah."

"What modifications did you make?"

"Your gear, mostly," he said, nodding at my attire.

I looked down at myself and saw I too was outfitted like a video game character. I wore a black leather bomber jacket and knee high boots. Around my waist was a utility belt with a flashlight and other small tools.

"This is wild," I exclaimed.

"You haven't even seen the place yet. I made it especially for you," he said, with irony.

"Then let's not waste time."

I followed Vincent to the other edge of the skyscraper until we found the stairwell leading down to the next floor.

"Stairwells, huh? I get it," I said.

He laughed. "That's not all. You're going to want to use that." He motioned to my katana.

The stairwell we descended wasn't like the one from my dreamscape. It looked just as you'd expect a staircase to look in a massive, multi-level skyscraper. At least, it did at first. The deeper we went, the darker it became. Before we were left in pitch black, however, Vincent stopped at the door leading onto the actual floor of the building.

"What floor is this?" I asked.

He shrugged. "I don't know how many this place has. I don't think there's an exact number. I just thought we should get some practice in before going down any more flights."

He opened the door and unsheathed his weapons, slowly. I did the same. We wandered through a dimly lit hall, passing offices and other rooms that looked as though they hadn't been touched in a very long time. The more rooms we passed, the more disheveled they appeared, until there was furniture upended and papers strewn everywhere. I thought I saw what looked like blood smeared across the wall. Something about the place felt familiar.

It didn't take long before I heard a strange, feral noise in the distant. The more we crept along, the louder it became, but now it sounded like low growls and other guttural sounds. Again, I was struck with the familiarity of the place.

We turned a corner.

Vincent stopped as we looked out at a large, open office space, dotted with cubicles and more decrepit than anything we'd seen so far. Then out of the shadows they appeared.

Zombies.

# CHAPTER 10

"You're not on my favorites list right now Miller," I breathed quietly.

"You don't know what you'll find down that stairwell in your dreamscape," he replied. "Just thinking worst case scenarios."

"You can say that again," I complained. "Can we just go back the way we came?"

"It will be fine. It's a dream, remember? Now's a good time to practice."

He was done talking. I could see he was already itching to slice up some zombies.

*This is what I get for recruiting a gamer nut.*

Vincent strode confidently forward, swinging his two swords in a synchronized manner, as though he were some kind of expert. A moment later, I saw evidence of his expertise. If I had blinked, I would have missed him, he moved so quickly. Before I knew it, two zombies had fallen.

"You coming?" he called over his shoulder.

"Right behind you," I said.

A zombie dragged itself toward me from the corner of the room. I met it halfway, bringing my sword up in a diagonal arc. I was pleased to find my weapon easily moved through its flesh, neatly cutting it in half. It fell to the ground and I moved forward to catch up with

Vincent, who was already felling zombies like trees in his wake. I followed suit, though I didn't move with nearly equal speed.

We cut our way through the large open space until we reached the other side. Vincent wiped the blood off his weapons and put them back in the sheathes. I stood still, trying to discern if we had indeed eliminated the threat in that room.

It was quiet.

"This isn't your first time doing that," I surmised.

Vincent laughed. "You're not the only one who's been practicing."

"Tell me it doesn't get any worse than that?" I pleaded.

"That was just a warm up. Now we go further down."

He didn't wait for my protest. I could tell he was enjoying himself. Though I felt nervous about what lay ahead, I began to enjoy myself as well.

"We're going to try something here," Vincent said, once we were inside the stairwell again. There was a gleam in his eye. "Remember: you don't have to follow the rules, so try not to limit yourself."

With that, he jumped over the edge of the rail and flew down into the darkness below. I hesitated, still lacking confidence in my ability to land in one piece. Then I jumped as well.

I fell headlong, trying to catch up to Vincent. The more I fell, the darker everything became. I switched on the light attached to my belt and could make out Vincent's outline, still falling.

"Vincent!" I called to him.

He looked back at me over his shoulder. "Get ready to slow down."

I found that although I had no control over the dream's surroundings, I had plenty of control over my own actions. I made myself fall more slowly, just by thinking about it. Vincent was doing the same thing, and allowed me to catch up to him.

"I think we're almost at the bottom," he told me.

The next moment, we landed, more gracefully than I would have expected.

"You ok?" he asked.

"Yeah. How much longer do we have?"

"We'll probably wake up soon. Let's keep going and see how far we get," he said.

Without our flashlights, we would have been in pitch darkness. It was difficult to see ahead as we made our way to the basement door. Vincent tried the handle and I heard him make a frustrated noise.

"It's locked," he said.

"Is there another door?"

"No. This door shouldn't be locked. I'm controlling this space," he explained. Although he whispered, I could hear annoyance in his voice.

Suddenly the air around us shifted. It grew colder and the darkness felt denser.

"Vincent," I whispered. "I think something's here."

We moved away from the door.

From the shadows crept a recognizable shape, ghastly and small. It shuffled toward us, with glowing eyes and a grinning face.

We both drew our weapons, but it didn't matter. The floor disappeared and we fell even further into the abyss below.

Waking was tedious and felt like climbing upward through a sludge-filled hole. My limbs were heavy and my head pounded unbearably. At last, I opened my eyes and stared at the lab ceiling for a few minutes, still unable to think clearly. When I looked at Vincent, he seemed to be having even more trouble waking.

"Vincent."

"I'm awake," he said. "Someone put a spike in my head though."

We managed to get up, rather groggily, and with effort, Vincent took care of erasing evidence of our having used the program. I helped him back to his room.

"Let's talk about it all tomorrow," he requested. "I just need to sleep."

I could see he was in tremendous pain, so I left him and returned to my room.

Naturally, my mind replayed the adventure several times over. I felt a mixture of excitement and fear at the fact that the dream joining had worked. I don't remember getting much sleep that night, but when morning arrived, it brought with it anticipation for the next phase of our process. We were getting closer to the moment of truth…or so I believed at the time.

Vincent spent most of the day in his room with a migraine. I tried not to bother him until he'd recovered.

I stopped by Dr. Belle's office that afternoon, but she wasn't in, so I met Luke in the library. I was conscious that I took advantage of Vincent's disability that day to see Luke, and I ignored my better judgment which told me to steer clear of him — at least until Vincent and I had achieved our goal.

"How's the nightmare research?" I asked Luke, as I slid into the chair next to him. We were fortunate enough to be alone in the usual small reference room toward the back of the library.

"Slow going," was his reply. "To be honest, I'm thinking of leaving the project and switching to coma research. It's more along the lines of my undergraduate thesis anyway. How was your lab session yesterday? I haven't tried dream pairing yet."

"You really should. Experiencing someone else's dream is fascinating," I told him.

Our conversation varied from research to fragments of our own lives. Luke pulled out his phone at one point to show me pictures from his summer trip to Europe. He moved closer to me so that I could see, brushing his arm against mine as he scrolled through the pictures. Anyone watching would have concluded we were both quite attracted to each other — and they would have been right. Throughout our time together, however, I felt a disproportionate loyalty to Vincent that hindered me from getting too carried away. I didn't move my arm away, but I didn't make any other movement to give Luke the impression I wanted anything else to happen. It took some willpower.

My phone beeped and I knew without looking it was Vincent.

"Sorry," I said. "It's my lab partner."

Luke pulled his phone away and busied himself while I checked my message. *"Come over. Let's talk,"* it read.

*"Ok. I'll be there in 10 minutes,"* I wrote back.

"Luke, I have to meet him to discuss our lab session," I said.

Luke nodded. "I'll text you later."

I left him and made a quick stop at my room to drop off my things and use the bathroom. When I got to Vincent's room, he was sitting on his bed with his laptop. I sat at the edge of the bed.

"How's the head?" I asked.

"Attached," he replied, without looking up.

"So it worked," I said, referring to the dream joining.

He nodded. "Yeah. You're up next, but first we try it in the debug room." He closed his laptop. "Let's talk about that thing that kicked us out."

"What? You mean the small creature? I thought you brought that there to make it feel more like my dreamscape."

"No. I wanted to get in that room in the basement, but I couldn't. That shouldn't have happened. And that *thing* from your dreamscape appeared...that's what kicked us out of the program." He looked annoyed.

"Maybe I'm not understanding. You *didn't* dream it? How did it get there?" I asked, incredulous.

"I don't know. Whatever it is, it's messing with our plans. I'm concerned it won't let us down that stairwell," he explained.

"But it wants me to go down. It keeps beckoning to me," I argued.

Vincent sighed. "I think it wants you to come to it, but not go down the stairwell. I don't know."

"Listen, let's take a break from the lab tonight," I suggested. "I want to see if this place has a basement, and we might be able to find more evidence of Abel Dumont's research." I thought it might be a good idea to spare Vincent another migraine, and I was growing more curious as to the true nature of Abel Dumont's original research. I felt certain we would find something important if we searched the place.

"Yeah. Ok," Vincent said. He was staring at me with a rather smug expression.

"What?"

"Just thinking about what you said...something about being a better fighter." He smirked.

I crossed my arms.

"It's ok. You can admit that's really why you don't want to log in tonight. I would be embarrassed too if I fought the way you do," he said, lifting an eyebrow.

"You just wait until you log into *my* dreamscape," I shot back at him. I wasn't bothered by his arrogance. I could tell he was putting it on to mess with me. I sort of figured it was his way of flirting.

I spent the rest of the day getting work done. I even took a brief nap so I wouldn't be too exhausted later. Sophie popped in on me after dinner and I shared with her Luke's translation of the manuscript so far, but I didn't tell her I was planning to explore the Academy that night — or that Vincent and I had successfully logged into the same dream together.

We waited until 10:00 pm to venture out, and began our search in the research wing, only because we knew there were lower levels to explore. I reasoned that files and equipment would likely be stored in that part of the campus.

Sneaking through the Academy at night was sort of exhilarating. In fact, I was so excited, I didn't even feel nervous. Or perhaps I'd been exposed to so much fear in my nightmares that I was becoming immune to it. Either way, this exploration was much less frightening than sneaking into the west wing. There was something else, however: Vincent. Throughout our search, he kept making random, sarcastic comments that made it challenging not to laugh and make noise.

"You're too loud," he whispered to me, as I tried to suppress a bout of giggles.

"Stop making me laugh!" I protested.

We had found a stairwell leading down several floors in the research wing. Vincent had programmed a master keycard to get us into various off-limits places.

"This place doesn't end," he commented, as we descended another flight of stairs.

"I think the medical students work down here," I said.

At last, we came to a metal door that seemed to lead to basement storage. Vincent swiped his keycard and opened the door. We shone our lights on another stairwell, leading down into darkness. I began to feel a little nervous.

"You ready?" he asked.

I nodded.

We walked down the stairwell, which turned out not to be very long after all. In fact, we found ourselves in a sort of sub-basement, filled with boxes, crates, and other sheet covered items. We peered beneath several sheets to find expensive-looking furniture and elaborate décor.

"I think this stuff is from the original mansion," I said.

The sub-basement went on and on. In the far corner of the room there was a large, awkwardly shaped object covered in a sheet. I stopped.

Vincent came up beside me. "Shall we?"

We each took a corner of the sheet and lifted. Then we pulled it off and used our lights to illuminate the area.

We stood gaping for a moment at what we found beneath it.

"What is *that?*" Vincent murmured.

The thing before us was an ancient-looking machine. It was made of bronze, or another metal of some kind, and had arms and levers sticking out everywhere. In the center of the machine was what looked like a reclining chair with several thin tubes hanging off the arms, and a helmet attached to the top. The whole thing was rather grotesque.

"I've seen this thing before," I said slowly. "The manuscript we found had sketches that looked like this. It was Abel Dumont's machine."

Vincent circled the machine, examining it more closely with his phone light. Then he began snapping photos of it from different angles. "I wonder if it still works," he mused. He crouched down in search of a power cord. "This plug looks weird," he said to himself. He continued to fiddle with the contraption.

I skimmed through some boxes nearby, lifting lids and absently checking the contents, until I became aware of what I was finding inside of those boxes. There were dozens of yellowed files, containing transcripts and research data. Several of the files had x-ray images of brain scans.

*Bingo.*

I dragged one of the file boxes over to a crate so I could sit while I read through the research. The transcripts were filled with names, numbers, and statistics, but there were portions of dialogue as well. They looked something like this:

*Date: 11/10/1951*
*Subject: Helen Locke*
*Age: 35*

*Description of sleep complication: Subject has suffered from sleep terrors since childhood (age 5). Sleep is frequently interrupted at night and subject is showing signs of physical, emotional, and mental deterioration. Subject will often awake with an accelerated heart rate, convinced she is in danger. Psychiatrist prescribed sleep medication, but nightmares persist.*

*Recommended treatment: Shock treatment*

There were many similar cases, and each one had undergone severe treatment to rid them of their nightmares. Some of the patients suffered permanent brain injury, while a couple even passed away. There was some description about the nature of the nightmares as well. Many patients were chased and hunted. Some of the dreams were much darker and more disturbing than others, eerily resembling my own nightmares.

I stumbled across another discovery in the files. The machine was referred to as "Somnium Medicus," which in Latin translated to "Dream Healer." There were many experiments in which a patient who had suffered from nightmares for a prolonged period of time, was given treatment using the Somnium Medicus. These were the files I found most fascinating. It looked as if in some cases, it had worked.

Helen Locke was one of the more successful cases. She had been treated weekly using the machine for six months, and the results were significant. Not only did the machine eradicate the nightmares, it improved her sleep so well that there were reports of her appearing younger and healthier than ever. One of the last documents in her file was a transcript of a recorded interview with her.

*Date: 05/21/1954*
*Subject: Helen Locke*
*Age: 38*

*Interviewer: Tell us about how your sleep has improved. Have you had any nightmares? What about wakefulness and insomnia?*
*Subject: I've never felt better. I sleep so soundly and I feel amazing everyday. My family has noticed (laughs). But really, I feel wonderful.*
*Interviewer: You came in because you had some concerns though. Tell us about them.*
*Subject: Well, I'm thrilled with the way I feel. The only thing that's bothered me is that (pause) I actually don't dream anymore, and I mean never. Um, it's just black every night. (laughs) I guess it's not a bad tradeoff, considering how horrible my dreams used to be. But I guess (pause) I don't know. I miss having dreams. I feel like a sense of mine was taken away, you know? Like I've become*

*blind or something like that. The dreams I used to have reassured me somehow. I'm not making sense. (laughs) I just wondered if there was a way to get them back?*

The transcript ended and there seemed to be no further research data on Helen Locke.

Vincent kicked something and swore.

"What's wrong?" I went over to where he stood. He was holding one hand in the other.

"I cut myself on this stupid machine," he said, irritated. I trained my light on his hand to find that it was practically dripping with blood. The cut, though not very deep, spread diagonal across his palm and bled profusely.

"Let's get this cleaned up in one of those sinks upstairs," I suggested.

We went back up the stairwell and found a maintenance room with a sink and an emergency first aid kit. As I washed and bandaged his hand, I told him about the box of research data I found.

"Somnium Medicus?" he repeated, when I told him about the machine's true nature. "That thing looks more like it creates nightmares than heals them," he muttered.

"I won't argue with you there," I said. "Do you think it still works?"

"The power cord looks different. It's probably European or something. Anyway, I sure as hell wouldn't try it, even if it did work," replied Vincent. "We should go back down and cover it up again."

We returned to the sub-basement to put things back the way we'd found them. I selected several files to take with me so I could read through them more when I had time. Then we left the basement and made our way back to the dorm wing.

Despite our intentions to spend time in the lab each night during that week, we only made it there once more, on Thursday night. Vincent was very busy working on some project for his research track. Turns out he had fallen behind in his effort to assist me with my hack plan. As a result, I didn't see much of him until we met to run another dream joining test later that week.

Busy as I was with my own workload, I managed to read through some of the files I'd taken with me from the sub-basement. It was rather dry reading – lots of data and forms documenting tests that had been run on patients. What interested me most was reading through the description of various case studies, relating to the nightmare research. There were many more than I would have originally guessed. Something that intrigued me from the data was that many of the patients reported similar results as Helen Locke: the treatment with the Somnius Medicum had successfully abolished the patient's nightmares, but with it, all other dreams as well. Patients expressed initial relief at the outcome, however, some of the later files also recorded complaints and a desire to reverse the process.

I tried to find evidence of Abel Dumont's theory of prolonging life through controlled dreaming, with no success. That particular aspect of the machine was not even mentioned in the files. I wondered if Abel Dumont had abandoned his original idea. Perhaps it was unachievable to begin with. It was certainly unlikely.

Thursday afternoon, I managed to find Dr. Belle in her office. Naturally, I had no intention of telling her of my adventures in the basement of the research wing – or my recurring nightmares for that matter. I merely wanted to see if she could give me any information about Abel Dumont himself.

I knocked on her doorframe. She was seated at her desk, working on her computer.

"Excuse me Dr. Belle, do you have a moment?" I asked.

"Come in," she said, without looking up.

I took a seat across from her. Her office was impeccable. The carpet looked as though it had just been vacuumed and the smell of lemon-scented furniture polish faintly hung in the air. She liked expensive furniture.

Dr. Belle looked up as I took a seat and gave me a polite smile. "How can I help you?" she asked. I guessed her to be in her mid-forties. Her brunette hair framed her almost pretty face and she wore glasses that looked a little too big for her. Otherwise, she was very neat, if a bit plain looking.

"Well, I'm Elena Gray," I began. "I'm in the dream psychology program."

"A pleasure, Elena. How is your research going so far?"

We spent a few minutes discussing my past studies and my plans for my dissertation. She wasn't much for small talk, so it wasn't long before our discussion turned to the reason I had stopped in.

"I've heard some rumors about the original owner of this place, Abel Dumont. Dr. Hammond suggested I ask you about him," I told her.

She gazed at me for a moment, a thoughtful look on her face. "What have you heard about Monsieur Dumont?" she asked.

I repeated what I'd said to Dr. Hammond. "I heard he pioneered the Dreamscape Program. Is he still alive today?"

"No," she replied. "He died before the facility was passed on to the Sleep Research Foundation. It was left to us in his will," she explained. "As for your other statement, he didn't exactly 'pioneer' the program. He conducted dream research in his own time, but that was long before anything like the dreamscape program existed."

Her response left me a bit perplexed. Clearly, she had to know of the manuscript and machine M. Dumont had designed. Yet she offered none of this information to me then, leading me to conclude that what - I'd recently uncovered wasn't common knowledge. I wondered why.

I didn't want to impose on her time any longer. I thanked her and left shortly after.

At dinner that evening, Vincent made a rare appearance in the cafeteria. He didn't try to sit with me though. Instead, he lived up to his anti-social reputation and sat alone. I noticed he'd brought his laptop with him and stayed busy on it while he ate. I glanced over at him once or twice during the course of my meal, and wondered if I should go over to him, but decided against it.

It wasn't long before he got up and seemed ready to leave the cafeteria. He had nearly left the room, when Rachel stopped him at the exit. It may have been my imagination, but I thought it looked like she was waiting for him. She talked to him for a couple of minutes, giggling and touching his shoulder; clearly flirting with him.

Vincent finally managed to detach himself from her. At least, I guessed that was what he might be trying to do, but maybe he liked the attention. I wasn't really sure.

Later that evening, I received a message on my phone from Vincent. The cryptic nature of the message intrigued me, because it was still too early to go to the lab. I made my way to Vincent's room, but stopped short when I turned the corner. There was Rachel, standing at Vincent's door, giggling about something again. Vincent was standing just inside the doorframe so he didn't see me. I walked slowly down the hall, and thought that maybe I'd just keep walking, pretending I had somewhere to be. As I passed them, Vincent called my name. I smiled and Rachel smiled back, but she looked like she wanted to get back to flirting or whatever.

"Are you coming in?" Vincent asked meaningfully.

Rachel's smile kind of faded into a look of confusion. Vincent stepped out of the doorway, took my arm, and pulled me into his room.

"Good night Rachel," he said, shutting the door in her face.

He sat wearily on the bed, leaned back on his arms, and stared at the ceiling for a moment. Then he sighed.

"Must be rough," I teased.

Vincent shut his eyes and laughed ruefully. "I thought she got the hint before, but she's persistent."

I shrugged. "Some girls like a challenge."

"That so?" he said, disinterestedly.

I nodded. "Yeah, so pulling me in here may not have been the best move. You just added fuel to the fire." I was really just trying to have a little fun with the whole scenario. These things generally amuse me.

Vincent's eyes expressed mild horror. "I'm never leaving my room again," he mumbled.

I smiled and chuckled a little. "No interest then, huh?"

Vincent gave me an *"Are you kidding me?"* look and rolled his eyes.

"Poor Rachel," I said with exaggerated sympathy.

"I'm ready to change the subject," he responded, getting up.

He sat at his desk and looked at me expectantly, so I sat next to him. Then he pulled out two game controllers and hooked them into the computer. While he loaded the game, I removed my shoes and sat cross-legged in the chair. Vincent very briefly eyed my cat patterned socks and then turned his attention to the monitor as he clicked through the game menu.

It was a multiplayer role-playing game. We selected our characters and a mission level, and began to play. Ironically, we choose a mission that took place in a very old, dilapidated mansion. Distorted, monstrous figures kept coming at us seemingly from out of nowhere. Vincent took most of them down in a single shot. I had a hard time hitting anything at first, but improved after a little while. I freaked out a few times when something jumped out at us, my reaction creating entertainment for Vincent. Overall, it was a very intense and challenging game.

After a while, Vincent paused the game so we could take a break.

"Did you get caught up on things?" I asked him.

"Sort of. They've got me working on some pretty boring stuff right now. I'd rather do your thing," he admitted.

"Are we still going to the lab tonight?"

"We have to. I don't want to hack into your dreamscape without prepping you first."

"I read through those files I took," I told him. "That machine really erased people's ability to dream, but there was no mention of it prolonging life."

"Because that's impossible. By the way, how have *your* dreams been?"

"A little different. I may be imagining it, but they don't seem as distinct as they were. I've been worried they'll disappear before tomorrow night," I confessed. "That would be awful."

"Well, your goal all along has been to get rid of them, right?"

"Sort of. You *know* there's more to it. We need to go down the stairwell, and find out about that thing living in my dreamscape," I said.

"I think 'invading' is a better term for it," he responded.

I was quiet for a moment. "I spoke to Dr. Belle this afternoon. She didn't say anything about the original machine or Abel Dumont's research. Why wouldn't she tell me something like that? What are they hiding?"

"Why are you so sure they're hiding something? Maybe it's just not important," he offered.

I frowned. "You don't really think that, do you?"

He shrugged. "There's always the chance we're getting worked up over nothing."

"You wouldn't have said that the other night, after that thing appeared in your dreamscape," I objected.

"But why are you so certain it's connected? Your nightmares and the machine we found..." he shook his head. "We just don't know yet."

It was useless to argue. We were counting on the hack to provide the answers we sought anyway.

Vincent put his controller down. "Shall we?" he said.

I nodded.

We left his room and made our way to the lab. It was my turn to host the dream joining, but not in my dreamscape. Vincent wanted to try joining in the debug room first. The real hack would take place tomorrow night.

"Make it as crazy as you want," he said. "We could use the practice."

We started the dream joining feature and logged into the debug room. It was dark, as we were used to when entering the dream design space. I wasted no time creating the mansion and could see that I was still equipped with the upgraded mod.

"Vincent?" I called.

"I'm here," he said. "Nicely done."

"We did it. This will work with my dreamscape?"

Vincent shrugged. "Let's hope. What you'll need to focus on most is your resistance to waking. For now, let's just practice fighting."

We spent the rest of that session attacking the shadows I created. I tried to make them larger and faster than usual, but whatever their shape or speed, they were no match for me or Vincent. I found it easier to fight in my own dream space, as I knew what to expect. Vincent did as well as he had with the zombies. He was clearly channeling his video game skills successfully in the dreams. It was impressive.

To our relief, waking was less dramatic than the last time. It wasn't long before we were back in Vincent's room. He worked on his computer and let me borrow his laptop so I could do some reading. I stretched out on his bed and scrolled through several research articles. I was tired from our lab session. I ended up falling asleep on my arms, while in the middle of reading. It was a wakeful sleep; I didn't dream and I could still hear the sound of Vincent typing. Eventually, soft music began to play and I must have dropped off completely.

I opened my eyes and tapped the laptop's mousepad to check the time. I'd been sleeping for close to two hours. Vincent still sat at his desk.

I slipped my feet over the side of the bed and smoothed my hair. "Got anything to eat?" I asked.

Vincent held out a bag of chips he'd been working on.

I got up and took it from him. "Thanks," I said. "I'm thirsty too."

Vincent gave me an intentional look, as though I were causing him great inconvenience.

"If it's not too much trouble, of course," I added, with falsified concern. I smirked.

He pushed himself up from the desk and went over to his mini-fridge. I expected it to be full of those energy drinks guys like to guzzle, but it contained a variety of Japanese beverages instead. He pulled out a green iced tea and handed it to me, saying ironically as he did, "Anything else?"

"Yeah," I said, leaning on his desk. "Your laptop is better than mine. Wanna trade?"

I stared at him and threw a chip in my mouth, deliberately chewing much louder than necessary.

"You gotta give me back my hoodie first," he replied, playing along.

I shook my head. "Nah. I'm keeping that."

"Suit yourself. It looks better on me though," he said smugly, resuming his seat at the computer.

I took a small, wadded piece of paper from my pocket and casually placed in on the edge of the desk. Then I flicked it, hitting Vincent in the side of the head with it.

He stopped typing and lifted an eyebrow. "Oh, so you want to play *that* game?"

He flicked a pen cap my way without so much as aiming. I put my hands up to block as it sailed toward me. As he continued to fling several small objects at me, I had a hard time finding anything else to use as ammunition. Laughing, I practically tripped over my own feet trying to get to the bed so I could grab a pillow to smack him.

When I turned, he was right behind me. He caught my arm before I could attack, picked me up, and threw me onto the bed. I recovered quickly – although I was laughing so hard I was practically breathless –

and we resumed our battle with pillows. Vincent leveled glinting, grey eyes at me as we attacked each other and I found that it secretly thrilled me to see him that way.

After a few minutes, I threw my hands up in surrender. "Ok! You win," I said.

He grinned and dropped the pillow, catching his breath. At first, he looked quite pleased with himself for being victorious, but then I watched as his expression changed and his ears reddened. He avoided eye contact with me and hastily returned to his computer.

I sat still for a moment, processing what had just occurred and decided it would be best to simply leave without trying to say anything. Vincent appeared to be engrossed in his program anyway, although his shoulders still heaved very slightly.

"See you tomorrow," I said as I left the room.

As soon as I'd closed the door, I allowed a giant smile to spread across my face. I had to cover my mouth with my hand to muffle more giggles as I rushed down the hall to my room. Then I collapsed onto my bed, laughing so hard I was afraid I would be heard. I buried my face in the pillow until I could regain my composure.

*Maybe Alex was right.*

# CHAPTER 11

Hack day had finally come.

I went through the day, counting down the hours until that fateful moment arrived. It was agonizing. Pretending everything was normal was the worst part. The only person beside Vincent who knew what would happen that night was Sophie. I ended up telling her, just in case something went wrong. I asked her to check in with me after the lab session, to which she agreed, albeit reluctantly. She wasn't so pleased with my plan to begin with.

My nightmares hadn't disappeared, as I had worried they might, but they seemed to have taken a back seat in my thoughts. I started to wonder what would happen *after* the nightmares were resolved. At the root of those thoughts was my partnership with Vincent. Without the thread of the dreams tying us together, no doubt the time we spent in each other's company would lessen. I still couldn't quite determine whether that would bother me. On the one I hand, I would be free to spend more time with Luke. However, the friendship I'd developed with Vincent was something I didn't want to lose. It was a complicated situation.

As if to further complicate the issue, Luke asked me to go out with him that night. I had to turn him down, naturally, making up some excuse about a skype call home. I hoped he didn't think I was just trying to avoid him, but I was too preoccupied to worry about it then.

As night fell on the campus, I imagined the shadows were waiting for us to fall into sleep. The mythology of my dreamscape seemed so intertwined with the mansion, that I'd almost come to accept it as part of the Academy; we were merely visitors. The shadows roamed about and the small creature ruled, snatching souls unaware. Such were my thoughts as I readied myself for the true adventure that awaited.

Smiling, I took Vincent's hoodie from my closet and slipped it on. The clean smell still clung to it, unexpectedly calming my nerves. Whatever horrors we met in my dreamscape, I felt certain we would come out the other side. I was immensely relieved that Vincent was hacking in with me.

I met Vincent in the usual place, right outside the research wing. His eyes immediately traveled to the hoodie I wore.

"I told you I was keeping it," I said.

"I *gave* it to you," he corrected. "You're not touching my laptop again though," he mumbled, turning to lead the way to the lab.

We had waited until well after 11:00 pm before entering the lab that night. Vincent planned on giving us around ninety minutes in the dreamscape. Somehow, along with all the other details of the plan, he had created a save feature so that we could re-access the dream and pick up where we left off. He told me he tested it on his own dream and it worked fine. There was a chance we would crash the program with all the features he had integrated, so he made some additional adjustments to the computer. It took a little longer than usual.

I leaned back in a lab chair and placed a halo on my head.

Vincent stood next to me.

"Well, I guess we're ready," he said. "You'll be lucid, so let's not waste any time getting to the basement. Try to keep us in the mansion though, and we should probably stay together. I don't know what will happen if we separate."

"What about the creature?"

"Let's see if we can get around it for now. The priority is the stairwell. We can worry about that stupid thing later," he said.

"Ok."

Nerves kicked in again and my heart pounded hard in response. I took a few breaths to steady myself.

"Alright. Here we go," Vincent said quietly.

We placed the masks on our faces and fell into darkness.

At some point, I tried to jerk myself awake, but was already too heavily asleep. For a moment, I thought I would just continue to fall. Then suddenly I was standing in the hall leading to the research lab. Vincent was already there, waiting for me. I was confused at first, wondering why he looked like he was about to attend a cosplay convention.

"Why are you looking at me like that?" he asked.

I shook myself. "We have to hack in tonight. Why are you wearing that?"

"We're already in your dreamscape," he told me.

Though I was lucid, I felt disoriented and skeptical that the Vincent before me was the real one. I'd dreamed of him before.

"How do I know it's really you?" I said.

"Good question. You could take my word for it," he suggested.

"I just don't feel so clearheaded," I explained.

Vincent stepped closer to me. "Let's go. We don't want to waste time."

I started moving forward and gradually my sense of what was happening returned. Vincent walked briskly beside me, allowing me to set the pace and direction. Without speaking, we drew our weapons and turned a corner. The shadows waited, arms open as if they had been waiting forever, longing to cling to us.

Vincent grinned. "Here goes," he said.

He sped toward them, swiftly clearing a path for us to pass through. I wasn't far behind, having finally recognized the situation we were in. It took effort at first to disencumber myself from the weight I carried as the dreamer. It was heavy, almost as though being lucid were a burden to carry.

Once we took care of the shadows in that proximity, Vincent stopped at the end of the hall, panting. "Elena, make it lighter. I can't fight like this," he said. He leaned an arm against the wall, his shoulders rising and falling as he tried to catch his breath.

"I don't know how to," I moaned. "I'm *too* conscious this is a dream."

"You're doing fine. Try to focus on the task at hand. One thing at a time," he encouraged.

We continued our journey through the darkened halls.

I centered my thoughts on merely walking through the mansion; putting one foot in front of the other. It wasn't long before moving became easier. It struck me that the heaviness only occurred when I endeavored to control the dreamscape, which meant that I actually had very little control, even lucidly dreaming. I remembered what Vincent had said about my dreamscape belonging to someone else. Perhaps his theory was correct after all.

Moving through the mansion was slow-going, and it was almost as though the shadows knew what we were trying to do. They came at us, relentlessly.

"What are these things anyway?" Vincent muttered as he sliced one in half.

I shrugged. "I have no idea. They've always been part of the dream."

"They certainly don't want us getting through. What happens if one gets you?"

"I don't know."

Vincent was quiet for a moment before saying, "Then let's not give them the opportunity."

We worked our way through a hall dripping with what appeared to be black vines, woven into the fabric of the building. It wasn't difficult to slice through them, but consumed a good deal of time. Once we passed through, we had made it to the west wing.

"We're going to the room with the faces," I said calmly.

There were less shadows here, but the stillness created its own suspense. I noticed more details, passing through that part of the mansion. It wasn't falling apart like the west wing we knew in the Academy. It was younger looking, as if it were lived in.

When we reached the end of the hall, I wondered if we could enter the library instead of the room with the faces on the wall. Oddly enough, there was no door where the library should have been.

"This is strange. There should be a door here," I mused, running my hand along the wall.

Vincent had already turned into the other room.

"Elena," he called.

"What is it?"

"Look." He motioned to the wall. "This is a little too cliché, don't you think?"

I stared at our own faces, sticking out of the wall, pale and deathlike.

"Yeah. It is cliché," I agreed, quietly.

"I don't know. It just feels like a bunch of horror movies mashed up into one bad dream," he continued.

I said nothing as I watched the faces writhe in pain. There were more of them than I remembered dreaming about previously. Faces of people I'd never seen before.

"We should keep going," Vincent said.

As he spoke, the whole scene shifted and we were in the basement. It was difficult to know for certain how it happened. I wasn't controlling the dream, it just moved on its own, as though it were part of a pre-recorded background.

"Nice," Vincent said.

"That wasn't me," I told him.

Vincent moved toward the elevator shaft. "What if we went down this way?"

"You're kidding."

"Have you ever tried it before? We know you might wake up when you go down the stairwell. Or that thing will try to get us. Maybe we can get around it." He looked at me expectantly.

As much as I hated to admit it, Vincent had a point.

"Ok. It's just that…I can't control anything here. I don't know what happens next." Even as I spoke, panic crept its way into my voice.

"We can control our own actions though. Just stay close to me and slow down when I tell you to," he advised. He gave me a look of confidence. "We'll be fine. This is it: you're going to find out what's down there."

I nodded, wishing for some of his fortitude. The fact was, the fear had begun to grip me, gradually. Even knowing it was just a dream wasn't enough to dispel the overwhelming sense that I was going to die. I felt hopeless.

As if in response to my fear, the dreamscape blurred around us until the sky opened up into a glorious blue. A gentle breeze swept across my face and I smelled the ocean. We were on the most beautiful beach I had ever seen, with perfect clear blue-green water, and sand soft and white. There was no danger here.

"Elena, we shouldn't be here right now!" Vincent's voice was urgent. "We'll run out of time. We need to go back."

My heart was racing. I shut my eyes tight and tried to think of the basement and the elevator shaft, but it was no use. I couldn't take us back. I was too terrified of what we would find down there.

On that glorious beach, it was difficult to even think of it anymore.

I took several steps closer to the ocean and crouched down, tracing my fingers through the sand.

"Let's just stay here for a moment." I looked up at Vincent. "Please."

He sat down next to me, resting his arms on his knees.

We didn't speak for a while.

"This is the place *I* try to find," I told him. "I don't know why I rarely do. I think of it almost every night." I leaned back and stretched my legs out in front of me. Then I looked at Vincent. "Maybe the dream is over. Maybe there isn't anything left."

He didn't answer at first. Then he asked quietly, "What do you want to do?"

Without a word, I lay down in the sand and he lay down next to me. I shut my eyes and breathed the clean air, listening to the soothing sound of the ocean waves. Then I felt Vincent take my hand. The warmth and firmness of his hand in mine brought with it peace. As my heart rate slowed, the beach gradually disappeared.

When I opened my eyes, the basement had returned and we stood at the edge of the elevator shaft. Vincent didn't release my hand.

"Let's go," he said.

I allowed him to pull me with him into the elevator shaft. As we fell, I wrapped my arms around his waist and squeezed my eyes shut. I was a coward. If not for Vincent, I doubt I would have ever jumped.

The further down we went, the colder the air became, and instead of slowing, we fell even faster. I felt as though there was nothing left. Perhaps the dream had emptied into infinity and we would find ourselves floating in space somewhere, lost to the world. Maybe this was death itself: not a light at the end of a tunnel, but a never-ending fall into darkness.

"Vincent." I said his name, just to be certain we were still alive.

"It's almost over. Get ready to slow down."

I don't remember whether I actually tried to slow down, but somehow we decelerated until at last we floated gently to the bottom. I didn't release Vincent at first, wanting to be certain I stood on level ground. I opened my eyes. There was nothing to see but blackness. The only light came from our own flashlights, which threw a dim circle around us so we could vaguely make out each other's features.

"We should keep going," Vincent whispered.

I still had my arms around him. I was afraid to move.

"I feel your fear," he murmured in my ear. "It's been a part of your dreams for so long, you don't even know what you're afraid of anymore. But I'm here. I'll stay with you."

Gently, he freed himself from my embrace. He took my hand and led me on into the darkness. There was nothing. No sound, so scent. Not even the cold. Everything had disappeared. We wandered through emptiness for ages.

Vincent stopped. "What are you thinking about?" he asked.

"I don't know...death I suppose."

"Stop thinking. What you said about having no control..." he shook his head. "I don't think that's entirely true. I think you're blocking us from moving forward. Just try not to think."

I paused to clear my thoughts. Not trying to think was more challenging than finding the courage to press on. I channeled my energy into that one idea: courage. We had to keep moving.

Very slowly, the darkness lifted, as though a blanket had been removed, or someone was gradually undimming the lights. We could see boxes and crates and nondescript shapes covered with sheets.

We were in the sub-basement in the research wing.

"This doesn't make sense," I said slowly.

"Are you sure this isn't you?" Vincent asked.

I sighed. "I don't know. Maybe it is after all."

I tried to think of somewhere else — my dorm room or the Academy lab, but nothing changed around us. We were still in the sub-basement.

"It's not me," I said.

"Let's look around then," Vincent proposed.

We moved around the room, lifting sheets and lids as we did so. The room was eerily identical to the sub-basement, with two exceptions: everything was covered in a heavy layer of dust...and the Somnium Medicus machine was missing.

I grew uneasy.

"Let's go up," Vincent said, pointing to the stairwell.

I was struck by the irony of climbing stairs in my dreamscape, instead of descending them. At the top of those stairs, we found ourselves in the medical research wing of the Academy.

"This is weird. We're just back in the Academy." I shook my head. "Maybe we should have gone down the stairwell instead of the elevator shaft?"

Vincent didn't reply at first. We kept walking, making our way back to the main floor of the research wing.

"No. This is different," he said quietly. "It looks very old."

I could see what he meant. Dust covered everything – even the floor. When we walked, we left distinct footprints, marking our path. It was strange, however, that despite the dust and natural decay, everything was exactly as it had been the other night when we explored the place – until we reached the lab.

We stopped at the entrance to the lab and peered inside.

"I don't like the look of this," Vincent said.

The lab was completely void of lab chairs and computers. The only thing we saw inside was the Somnium Medicus machine. It looked new and gave off a slight glow as it hummed in the empty space.

We moved toward the glass doors to the lab. They opened on their own, as if we were welcome.

"Ok, this is the real creepy part," Vincent noted.

I said nothing as we cautiously approached the machine. It was alluring somehow. I felt it almost call to me.

"Elena?" Vincent grabbed my arm. "What are you doing?"

"I want to try it," I said.

Vincent's hold on my arm grew tight. "No. Let's get out of here."

He pulled me with him until we exited the lab. I could still see the machine through the glass windows, waiting for me.

Vincent made me keep moving, away from the lab and the machine. I followed him automatically through the empty halls of the Academy. He was heading to the dorm wing. We stopped outside his room.

He looked at me and shrugged. "I was just curious," he said.

We opened the door to his room to find it undisturbed. The computers were as Vincent had them set up in the real world, along with the rest of the furniture. Aside from the dust, there was one other difference: another Vincent was there, but he lay on the bed, unmoving with arms crossed over his chest. We could immediately see he was lifeless.

Vincent lifted an eyebrow and looked at me. "Well, now we know the future: The Academy gets overrun by crazy shadows and we're all put into comas in our dorm rooms. Looks pretty bleak." I knew he said it to make light of the situation. I wished I shared his nonchalant attitude.

As we exited the room, I could *feel* its presence before I saw it. It waited for us at the very end of the hall, the familiar form of the small creature, calling to me.

"Look who's come to play," Vincent said grimly.

"I don't want to fight it yet. What if the dream disappears when we kill it? We need to keep looking," I whispered.

"Yeah. Then let's go the other way."

We hastened down the hall in the other direction. I couldn't bring myself to look back.

"It's not following us," Vincent informed me.

"That's because it knows how to find us," I said.

"Just stay away from the research wing," Vincent warned. "I have a feeling that thing wants to put one of us in the machine."

Even as he spoke, I had to fight the desire to go back to the lab. I could still feel the machine pulling me toward it, longing for me. The feeling grew stronger, even as we moved further from the lab. I tried not to speak of it, and even began to wonder if I could get away from Vincent and find a way back to the machine.

We ended up in the Academy lobby. I stopped moving.

"What's wrong?" Vincent asked me.

"This just seems pointless," I said. "We're not getting anywhere."

Vincent looked at me knowingly. "We're not going back to the lab."

"But that's the only place left to go," I argued.

He shook his head.

We stood there for a moment, each contemplating our next move. I was frustrated. This hadn't turned out the way I'd expected, though I wasn't even certain what my expectation had been. I guess I thought something would click. I thought the answer would become clear to us right away; the mystery would be solved.

The ground tremored. I looked at Vincent uneasily.

"Let's go," Vincent said.

We made a hasty retreat and heard a loud crash behind us. The roar grew until it was deafening.

"It's the shadows," I yelled.

They had broken through the walls, swarming like angry, dark insects, too numerous to count. As we ran, they came at us from different parts of the mansion, so that our escape route led in only one direction: the research wing.

Suddenly, a shadow landed on Vincent's back and took him down.

"Run, Elena! Keep going!" he shouted.

The next moment, he was engulfed in black.

Chapter 12

I had no choice but to push forward. I practically flew through the mansion until I finally reached the lab. Then, safely inside the glass doors, I turned to see the shadows filling the hall outside. For some reason, they didn't try to get in.

*They wanted me to come here.*

I knew it was the only explanation. The small creature didn't need to chase us — that's what the shadows were for.

The Somnium Medicus hummed soothingly behind me. I wanted to go to it more than ever.

"Vincent, wake me up," I pleaded aloud. "Please. I can't stay here anymore."

I had already begun to approach the machine. It's gold color gleamed, appealingly. I put my hand out to touch it.

*"Wake up Elena!"*

I felt dizzy.

*"Wake up!"*

I fell backward and saw light behind my eyelids. I still heard the faint hum of the machine.

"Get up Elena," Vincent said.

Obediently, I opened my eyes and sat forward. My head pounded in protest.

"Vincent," I whispered.

"We're awake now. How do you feel?" he asked.

"I don't know. Are you sure I'm not still dreaming?"

"You're awake," he reassured me. "Let's get you back to your room."

"Wait. What happened to you? The shadows got you..."

"I woke up as soon as they covered me," he explained. "I guessed they were trying to get you back to the lab with the machine. I could sense that's where you wanted to go anyway. I tried to wake you up before you could sit in the machine."

"I was about to," I confessed. "But it's the creature that wants me to get into the machine. Why does it want that? What's going to happen?" I sighed. "This was pointless. We didn't learn anything."

"It wasn't pointless. We got to explore the dreamscape, like you wanted. Why don't we talk about it more tomorrow? You'll think more clearly after you've had a chance to rest," Vincent said.

We didn't speak again until Vincent had brought me to my room.

"You sure you're ok?" he asked. He lingered at the door, as though he didn't want to leave me alone.

"I'm fine. I'm a little nervous about what will happen when I fall asleep though."

"Call me if you need to," he offered.

I thanked him and closed the door as he left.

Sophie texted me soon after to make sure I was ok. I let her know everything was fine, but that I needed to sleep.

I don't remember dreaming that night, which made it impossible to know whether the plan had successfully erased the nightmares. In fact, I found myself hoping it hadn't. Our first attempt at hacking into my dreamscape hadn't yielded any evidence as to why I was having the dreams to begin with, and I had begun to care more about finding the connection between my dreams and the Academy than returning my dreams to normal.

I slept long and heavy until mid-morning. My head ached when I finally woke and the hopelessness I had experienced in my dreamscape lingered, making it difficult to find the desire to do anything other than lie still doing absolutely *nothing*. I wasn't hungry, but made myself get something to eat in the cafeteria, just so I would get out of bed.

The background noise in the cafeteria was oddly soothing and somehow dispelled the gloom that had settled on me from my dreamscape.

Luke came up next to me as I grabbed a tray. "Good morning Elena."

"Good morning," I returned.

"I was hoping to see you today."

I smiled in reply.

"You feeling alright?"

"Yeah. Just didn't sleep well."

"Can I sit with you?"

I nodded and we found a seat by the window.

"How was your skype call?" he asked.

"Huh? Oh, fine."

I took a bite of my bagel. Luke watched me for a moment.

"You sure you're ok? You seem out of it. May I?" He reached a hand across the table and felt my forehead. He frowned. "You don't have a fever. You just look a bit off."

"I'm fine, really," I said.

Luke studied me for another moment, then he said, "By the way, I read more of the manuscript."

I stopped eating. "What did it say?"

He smiled. "You're really interested in that thing, huh. Alright, here's the deal: I'll tell you what it says if you go out with me tonight."

I tried to suppress a smile of my own. "Looks like you finally pinned me down."

He lifted an eyebrow. "So that what's it takes to get your attention – midnight mansion explorations and vintage French manuscripts. You're a rare one."

I finally allowed myself a grin.

"So 7:00 tonight?" he confirmed.

"Yeah. I could use a night out."

My phone buzzed next to me. It was Vincent.

"I'll see you later then," I said to him. I got up rather hastily, checking the message as I left:

*"You awake?"*

*"On my way,"* I wrote back.

I didn't even knock when I opened Vincent's door.

"How were the dreams?" he asked.

I sat on the bed. "I didn't have any."

"I thought that might happen. It's fine. There's more to do in the dreamscape yet, anyway." He turned his chair so he could see me and gave me a puzzled look. "You look sick."

"I'm fine. Just tired."

He shook his head. "I don't think you're fine. Your pupils are enormous and your face looks...shiny."

I sighed. "I'm just not wearing makeup."

"Oh." He looked uncomfortable.

I changed the subject quickly. "Vincent, when we're in the dreamscape, can you feel what I'm feeling?"

Vincent nodded.

"So you know how afraid I was?"

"I told you I could feel your fear," he reminded me.

I suddenly remembered clinging to him as we fell down the elevator shaft – and how I refused to let go of him when we landed. In fact, Vincent had seen me more vulnerable than anyone I'd ever known, aside from my family. But even they didn't really understand my feelings like he did.

"I've been thinking about it. Maybe it was wrong to go down the elevator shaft. All along you've wanted to see what was down the stairwell. We need to try again," Vincent said.

I nodded in agreement.

"I wonder why the machine was in the lab?" Vincent said thoughtfully. "It's obviously important in your dreamscape somehow. I wish we knew why. That would probably help."

"I may be able to help with that part. Luke told me he discovered more from the manuscript. He's going to share it with me later," I paused and laughed uneasily. "He wants me to go out with him first though."

Vincent smirked. "Trading information for dates?" He swung his chair back around and added, mostly to himself, "I should have thought of that."

"Why don't you bring Rachel? We can make it a double date," I said, a bit more flippantly than I intended.

"Pass," he said flatly. "What time are you going out?"

"At seven. I'll let you know as soon as I learn something."

"Don't rush on my account," Vincent replied. His attention was already fixed on his computer. The atmosphere had suddenly grown tense.

*There's that icy wall again.*

Silence followed, until the lull in conversation grew awkward. There was plenty more to say, about the dreamscape and our plans for the next hack in, but it was clear we were finished for the time being.

"Well, I have some things to do. I'll see you later." I got up and left.

When evening arrived, I felt more tired than I had earlier that day, and even after taking a nap, the weariness remained.

I still didn't dream.

Sophie came by to help me with my makeup and catch up on things. I managed to give her just enough information to satisfy her curiosity about the hack in, yet held back certain details. She was more interested in my relationship status anyway.

"Does Vincent know about this date?" she asked, as she brushed my hair.

"Yeah," I said. "Why do you ask?"

"Well, doesn't it complicate things a little? I sort of thought Vincent had a thing for you."

I laughed wryly. "What gave you *that* idea?"

Sophie gave me a look in the mirror. "Come on Elena. He rejected Rachel, but he wants to spend time with you. Alex thinks you guys are secretly dating."

I rolled my eyes. "Alex thinks a lot of things. Anyway, *you* know why we spend so much time together."

"Yeah. It just doesn't seem fair to Vincent, I guess." She stopped talking and ran the hot iron through my hair.

I attempted to get Sophie's mind off my relationship status for a moment. "Sophie, do you feel Meghan's emotions in the program? I mean when she dreams?"

Sophie nodded. "I feel very connected to her now. That's why I think you should be careful with Vincent. I'm sure you guys feel it too."

"I wonder why they didn't warn us about that when we were paired up?"

She shrugged. "It's still an experimental technology. Maybe they didn't know."

I laughed again. "There's a lot they don't know."

Sophie's expression changed. "What?"

"Never mind."

"They'll probably just switch the lab partners after a while. You know, to keep the research fresh," she said.

I was quiet. More than anything now, I didn't want to lose Vincent as a lab partner. It made me anxious to think of not working with him anymore, and that anxiety produced an agitation of its own. I didn't like how attached I was becoming to him. I kept trying not to admit to myself how dependent on Vincent I'd become, especially in my dreamscape. I'm sure I wouldn't have made it half as far without him. In fact, the whole plan would have failed but for him.

That evening, Luke took me to a cozy restaurant with live music. The musicians performed on a little stage and the restaurant was dimly lit, creating an off-Broadway feel. We sat at a rather undersized table in a dark corner of the room, far enough away from the band so we could hear each other talk. Luke had styled his hair differently and was wearing just the right amount of cologne. I was impressed at how good he was at finding date spots.

Throughout the evening, I fought the temptation to ask Luke about the manuscript. It was all I could think about and I'm afraid I didn't enjoy myself as much as I might have under other circumstances. I began to realize how obsessed I was with uncovering the mansion's secrets — and understanding its correlation to my dreamscape.

After dinner, Luke took me back to the Academy and invited me to his dorm room to look at the manuscript. He made some tea for us as I pulled off my shoes and sat on his bed.

"Here," he said, handing me a steaming mug.

He brought over the manuscript and sat with me on the bed. I saw he had put tabs in some of the pages. It looked as though he'd read through it rather thoroughly.

"It's sort of dry reading, after the initial dream theory and all, but there's something in here you might be interested in," he began, opening the manuscript to one of the tabs. "Here it is." He pointed a finger on the page and read from a separate page of notes he'd made while translating the text.

*"'Harnessing dream energy dates back to the 8th century BC. This technique is often disregarded as superstition, and strong dreamers are dismissed as mere abnormalities. Yet I have seen the power of strong dreamers, especially those who have nightmares. Their nightmares can be stored in the Somnium Medicus for a limitless supply of dream energy. With enough dreamers, the machine will grant one longer life.*

*I have designed the Somnium Medicus to heal the subject's dreams by scanning their brain waves during REM and tracking their dream patterns. The machine recalibrates the subject's brain pattern and "resets" their dreamscape.*

*I am not sure how many dreamers are required to achieve enough dream power to prolong life, and the procedure will likely take years to test. Test subjects will be acquired from the local asylum.'"*

Luke paused reading and flipped the pages until he was near the end of the manuscript. "There's a note here. I think it was written later:

*'The machine comes with a cost I had not anticipated. It takes nightmares and leaves the recipient with nothing. In fact, it steals dreams. Something else very strange has happened to the machine, as though it has a life of its own. It worries me. I am afraid to use it again.'"*

Luke stopped reading and glanced at me. "What do you think?" he asked.

I tried to hide my excitement at what I'd just heard. "It's interesting, but must be fiction. It sounds too much like a sci-fi novel," I laughed.

Luke looked thoughtful. "No, I think some of it is true. He's too specific with his theories and research. I've been wondering what happened to the machine he built? I'll bet finding it would provide some answers."

"Maybe it was destroyed," I offered. I was beginning to worry Luke would go on a search of his own to find what Vincent and I had in the sub-basement.

"Perhaps. There must be some other evidence of what took place though, if someone went through the trouble of saving this manuscript."

He had a point.

"Is there any other explanation about the 'Child of a Hundred Years?'" I inquired.

"It's vague. The prophet Isaiah lived during the 8th century BC, so I believe Abel Dumont traced this dream energy technique to that time in history. I've yet to explore it further. I wonder if Abel Dumont left a journal behind? The manuscript is more research based than personal. Want to go back into the west wing and see if we find anything else in the library?"

I hesitated, conscious of Vincent waiting for me to contact him so we could continue our hack plan that night. "I'm a little tired tonight," I admitted. "I think I'm coming down with something." It was partially true.

Luke nodded, understandingly. "Another time then."

We discussed the manuscript a little more that evening before I returned to my room. If Luke had expected anything further to happen between us, he didn't push it.

I waited a little while before making the trip to Vincent's room. I didn't want Luke to see me in the hall and wonder.

My phone buzzed. Vincent had texted: *"Are you coming over?"*

*"In a few minutes,"* I replied.

*"Tell him you have a headache,"* he wrote back.

I smiled. Clearly Vincent thought I was still with Luke.

Instead of replying, I finally left my room and made my way over to Vincent's.

"How was it?" he asked as I entered.

"Informative. I have to tell you what I learned about the machine," I began.

"I'm listening," he said, still working at his computer.

"It has to do with those files we found. The machine was indeed designed to 'fix' dreams. But it also stores the dreamer's energy and it can be used to prolong an individual's lifespan. Somehow, it's based on an ancient technique," I told him.

"Sounds farfetched."

122

"I know. It gets weirder: there's an addendum at the very end of the manuscript. Dumont explains that the machine steals people's dreams."

"We knew that already," Vincent cut in.

"Yeah, but he also says the machine developed 'a life of its own.' He was afraid to use it again. Luke wants to go back to the library to find more of Abel Dumont's writings. I told him I wasn't feeling well though," I explained.

Vincent had turned to look at me as I spoke. "There might be more in the basement as well," he said.

I nodded. "We need to keep looking. It's all linked, somehow."

We let some time pass in silence.

"Do you want to go back into the program tonight?" he asked me. His eyes carried an astute expression that I wasn't used to seeing in him. As though he understood how much of a burden it was for me to host the dream joining and face the nightmares again.

I sighed. "Yes."

"The stairwell this time?" he asked.

"The stairwell."

Vincent utilized the save feature on the program for this next hack in. Instead of starting from a new dream altogether, we decided to log in as close to the basement stairwell as possible. We weren't sure how well it would work, as there was the chance we would end up making the same decisions as before while using a past dream. However, we reasoned that logging in this way could save us time and give us the opportunity to explore further than we had previously.

Last time, we had tried to merely avoid running into the small creature in the basement. We prepared ourselves by discussing a plan of attack, in case we encountered the creature again and it impeded our desire to descend the stairwell. We agreed that no matter what, we needed to try to stay together – and away from the Somnium Medicus.

Before long, we were in the program again, standing in the room with ghastly faces on the wall, just before the dream shifted and put us in the basement. The save feature had worked, but it took me a little longer to adjust to my surroundings. I felt disoriented. Thankfully, Vincent patiently explained to me what was happening, as we cut down persistent shadows. Then the dream changed and we were in the basement.

Everything felt different than before. The air was stale, as though time had passed and no living thing had been through that place in ages. The atmosphere was heavy with oppression and sorrow. The lights were dimmer than I remembered them.

"Why does this feel so different?" Vincent wondered aloud. "It should be the same dream."

We approached the stairwell and I pulled open the doors, as I always did. We were met with pitch darkness and an overwhelming fear that death would meet us below. It was paralyzing. I looked at Vincent and could read by his expression that he felt just as afraid at that moment as I had, every time I opened the doors. We said nothing, waiting for the small, hideous form to appear on the stairwell, and beckon to us.

It never came.

Vincent finally spoke. "We should go down."

I nodded, but neither of us moved at first.

"Elena," Vincent said.

"We're going to die if we go down," I whispered.

"I've been having the same thought, but it's not going to happen," he said. "This isn't real. We *have* to go down." He reached for my hand and pulled me with him onto the stairwell.

That descent into darkness was worse than the fall down the elevator shaft. Every step brought a new depth of fear. I sensed something waiting for us below, and a foul smell grew ever stronger the further we went. I thought it was the smell of death itself, and wondered how it could be so potent in a dream.

"It smells like death," Vincent observed quietly, echoing my thoughts. "How is the smell so strong in a dream?"

"I was thinking the same thing," I replied.

At last, we reached the bottom of the stairs. Our flashlights cast dim light on a concrete floor, stained with some kind of muddy substance. The walls dripped with it and the smell was worse than ever.

I covered my nose with my arm. "This is disgusting," I complained.

"Elena...I think I can hear your thoughts," Vincent said. "Everything you do and say is exactly what I'm thinking. It's much stronger this time than the last time we logged in. Must be part of the dream joining feature."

"Then you already know what I'm worried about..." I began.

"You think this is your own fear taking shape in the dreamscape," he finished. "Let's move forward and find out."

It was another basement, or tunnel, more decrepit than anything we'd seen up to that point. Our boots almost stuck to the sludge substance on the floor, making our progress slow and cumbersome. The smell was revolting and I grew slightly sick from it.

The further we went, the narrower the passage became, until we walked in single file. The air grew colder and more damp, despite the closeness of the tunnel.

"Where are we?" Vincent asked, half to himself.

Just hearing his voice was reassuring. I was so struck with terror it was hard to breathe.

"Have you noticed how mushy the ground is becoming?" Vincent asked in a whisper. "And this sludge is deeper now."

It was true, my feet nearly sunk into the substance on the floor and I avoided touching the walls because they were covered with more of the muck. Then suddenly the ceiling began to get lower. After several more minutes, we saw it would become necessary to crawl through the rest of the way.

"Maybe we should go back," I said.

"Let's see where it takes us. Just a bit further," Vincent encouraged.

I silently obeyed, afraid that if I said anything else I would burst into tears. I was feeling rather overcome with emotion as we made our way through that filth-ridden passage. More than anything, I sensed the fear of death as never before — as though we willingly climbed into the jaws of doom. I'd never felt fear as I did then.

Then at last, we were through. We pulled ourselves out of the mire and stood up to find that we were in yet another basement. This was unlike any we'd seen thus far, however. It was clearly quite old, with natural stone walls and a dirt floor. Though the revolting stench still lingered, it was overpowered by a musty, aging smell.

Vincent came up next to me and laid a hand on my arm. "Are you ok?" he asked in a low voice.

"I don't know," I whispered back. "I've never been so afraid. What if we never make it out of this place?"

Though there was little light, I could tell Vincent's eyes were fixed on my face as he replied, "We'll make it out. It's just a dream. Nothing can happen to us."

We journeyed through the basement and found that it broke off into several different tunnels.

"I don't know where to go," I told him.

"Maybe it doesn't matter. Just keep moving," Vincent suggested.

I did as he said, following a number of twists and turns until we came to a dead end. On the floor was a giant metal hatch, smeared with the muck we'd just crawled through.

"We have to go down again?" I moaned.

"Come on. We have to be getting closer," Vincent said.

"This is the most optimistic I've ever seen you," I shot back, sullenly. "Why are you enjoying this nightmare so much?"

"I just think we're getting close to finding the answer to all of this. You have to remind yourself that the fear isn't real. The program is stimulating your amygdala, so the emotion is contrived. It's almost deliberate though, how it's all set up," he mused.

"What do you mean by that?"

"I don't know yet," he said slowly. "It's not important right now though. Let's go down that hatch."

I sighed.

It wasn't difficult to get the hatch open, but a wretched smell came up to meet us, bringing with it a stronger sense of the horror below. We didn't speak as we climbed onto the rusted, metal ladder. Vincent went on ahead of me. I started to have racing, panicky thoughts the lower we went. I thought about climbing back up quickly, closing the hatch and running away. I could force myself to wake; anything to get away from the nightmare.

"Elena..." I heard Vincent say. "Stay calm."

I didn't reply. He could hear everything I thought anyway. From then on, I tried to focus on *not* thinking.

The ladder eventually ran out and we were on level ground again, standing in a shallow puddle. There was a groaning sound.

"Something's down here," Vincent whispered.

My heart thumped unbearably.

It was almost impossible to see even a foot ahead of us at that point, but we pressed on, feeling along the walls as we did. They were cool and cut from stone. We were underground. The stench and the groaning increased as we progressed, until it felt as though the ground beneath us shook. I drew my katana, concluding that whatever it was, we were going to have to fight our way through. Vincent followed my lead and readied himself as well.

Then all at once, the tunnel ended, and we were in a cavernous room, which was clearly the source of both the smell and the groaning. Unfortunately, we couldn't see a thing.

"Stay together," Vincent whispered beside me. "Can we cast more light?"

I tried to concentrate on light, and the small circle surrounding us did in fact become more luminescent, casting a faint glow at least a few feet ahead of us. Then the room itself undimmed very slightly and we saw a giant, moving figure in the far corner of the room. It was formless and nondescript, but it writhed and squirmed, groaning as if in pain.

"What is *that?*" I breathed.

"We should turn around..." Vincent started to say.

There was no time. The creature moved like liquid along the walls until it was behind us, blocking the way we'd come. It was quick and noiseless as it slithered and the groaning filled the room so that it was impossible to tell where the giant form would be without looking at it.

Then the black monster rushed toward us and we were forced to defend ourselves from the onslaught of darkness. I was vaguely aware of the fact that it came at us as individual shadows, as if pieces of it broke off to attack.

The terror I'd been subject to up to that point melted into adrenaline and rage. I whipped my sword through each foe, matching their speed and fluidity. I was aware of Vincent somewhere nearby, flashing like lightning as he annihilated shadows. But we made no progress. The shadows persisted until we found ourselves being pushed backward. They were pinning us in.

"We have to get at the big one," Vincent shouted to me.

*I'll cut around left.*

I knew Vincent would be able to hear my thoughts. Sure enough, he sped off to the right so that we could get around the shadows and engage the larger form behind them. The closer we got to it, the stronger and thicker the hoard. We managed to break through them and were suddenly attacking something much larger and more difficult to cut through. The black monster — whatever it was — seemed to be made out of the sludge substance we'd encountered earlier. Yet it moved impossibly fast and consistently avoided our attacks.

I started to notice the more we attacked, the more we were covered in the creature's sediment. It began to impede my movements. Vincent was slowing down as well.

"This isn't working. We should fall back," I heard him say.

Turning, I realized we had forgotten the shadows behind us. They had made their way back toward us and now we were pinned from all sides.

"This isn't good," I said.

I heard Vincent abruptly cry out. His leg was wrapped in a black rope of slime attached to the larger mass, like a tentacle. He made an attempt to stab it, but before he could, it yanked him off his feet and dragged him toward it.

"Vincent!" I shrieked, bolting after him.

I couldn't get to him in time. He was swallowed up in the monster and I was left alone in my nightmare.

# CHAPTER 13

"Vincent," I said aloud. I sat up. The nightmare had vanished, taking with it the shadows and the monster.

Vincent was still beside me in the lab chair, but he hadn't woken up yet.

"Vincent," I repeated. I got up and shook him gently. He remained motionless. He was very pale. "Vincent!" I said, more desperately. "Wake up!"

He didn't move. I put my ear to his mouth to find that he was just barely breathing. I checked the computer monitor. His vital signs were very faint.

"No, no, no. This isn't good," I said aloud shaking my head.

I logged Vincent out of the program and gently removed the halo from his head. His body was completely limp in the chair. In a desperate attempt, I tried to perform CPR. I was so nervous though, I probably did it wrong. It didn't work anyway.

As the minutes slipped by, I fought the growing panic building inside me, and tried to think of what to do.

*Luke.*

"I'll be right back," I said to Vincent. Maybe he could hear me, even if he wasn't awake.

I flew down the hall, back to the dorm wing and straight to Luke's room. Then, as quietly as possible, I knocked several times on the door.

"Elena?" Luke said, as he opened the door. He looked confused. I could tell he had been sleeping. "What's going on?"

"I need you to come with me," I said in a low voice. "Please. It's very important."

Luke blinked. He went back into the room and came out wearing a hoodie and sweatpants.

We didn't speak as I led him through the halls to the research wing. I'd had the sense to grab Vincent's keycard before leaving the lab, so I got us in quickly and brought Luke straight to Vincent.

"He won't wake up," I said. "We were in the program, but for some reason, he got stuck."

Luke stared at me as I spoke. I saw him trying to make sense of the words coming out of my mouth. He didn't ask questions. He immediately began checking Vincent's pulse and vital signs and opened his eyelids.

"He's comatose," he stated. "What happened?"

"It's a long story..." I replied.

Luke glanced at me. "Well, you got me up to help him. You might as well tell me."

Judging by his expression, he was not in any mood to be diverted from the truth.

I sighed. "I've been having these nightmares," I began. "Vincent was helping me get rid of them."

"How?"

"He created a hack program so we could explore my dreamscape together lucidly," I explained. "This is the second time we've gone in together. I didn't know something like this would happen..."

Luke was quiet.

"I think the dreams are connected to that manuscript we found in the library," I told him. "I think there's something wrong with the Dreamscape Program. Vincent and I...we found the machine from the manuscript – the Somnium Medicus. It's in the basement. It was in my dreamscape last night as well."

"So this hack program...it let you be in the dream at the same time?"

I nodded. "We can talk to each other. We're even armed in the dreamscape."

Luke frowned. "Why?"

"There are things in my dreamscape that try to get me. We use a weapons mod to fight them."

Luke considered this then asked, "What happened right before you woke up?"

I described the dream to him quickly. "He was taken by the monster," I said. "It must have trapped him in the dream."

"That's not how it should work though," Luke protested. "It's probably something else to do with the program. A dream can't actually hurt him. It was in your dreamscape."

"I don't think it's my dream," I said. "We don't know how, but we think that maybe my dream overlapped with something else."

"'We?' You and Vincent?"

"Yes. We've been working on this for a few weeks," I confessed.

"I see." Luke's expression was unreadable, but it wasn't difficult to guess what he might be thinking.

"What should we do?" I asked, trying to direct his attention back to the problem at hand.

He sighed. "Ok. I have an idea that might work." He moved toward the computer terminal and started typing. I came around to see what he was doing. There was a window open on the screen with code.

"You know how to write code?" I asked.

He nodded. "Nothing fancy. This particular code isn't something I wrote on my own. It's part of the coma research program the Academy has been working on." He was silent as he proceeded to type and open a couple more windows on the screen. Then he went over to Vincent, repositioned the halo on his head, and put in the required criterion. He returned to the computer. "Here goes..." he said.

I moved toward Vincent and waited for something to happen. "How long will it take?"

Luke didn't answer at first. "It's calibrating. Give it a few minutes."

I couldn't look away from Vincent. He was so still and white, like death itself. I thought of the dead faces on the wall in the mansion.

"Come on," I heard Luke say to himself. He came over and stood next to me to check on Vincent. "The program should stimulate his cerebral cortex and restore wakefulness — if the damage isn't too bad that is," Luke explained.

It seemed to take forever.

Vincent moved.

"Vincent!" I said.

"Hmm," he moaned. His brow furrowed and he brought a hand up to his head. Then he opened his eyes and blinked a few times. He sat up, glancing from me to Luke as he did. "What? Why is *he* here?" he asked, wincing.

I ignored his question. "Are you ok? What happened?"

"Elena, give him a minute," Luke advised.

Vincent rubbed his forehead. "I don't feel so good"— he started to say. Luke moved toward a garbage can, but not fast enough. Vincent had already turned on his side and vomited all over the floor. He coughed.

"I'll take care of it," Luke offered. He left the room to find cleaning supplies.

I put a hand out to touch Vincent's shoulder. His body trembled. "Vincent, what happened?"

"I was in the machine," he said. "I don't know how I got there. I just remember that thing we were fighting pulled me into it, and the next thing I knew, I was hooked into the Somnium Medicus." He coughed again. "It was very dark and I felt something cold in my arm. Someone was there with me, but I couldn't see him."

"'Him?'" I repeated.

I heard Luke returning and dropped my hand. He began to clean up the mess on the floor. Vincent sat up again.

"Why don't you take him to his room?" Luke suggested. "I'll meet you there in a few minutes."

"Ok," I said. I helped Vincent stand to his feet and led him into the hall.

"I don't want that guy in my room," Vincent muttered, once we were out of earshot.

"You seem to be feeling better," I commented. "Listen, you were unconscious. I had to do something."

"I would have woken up eventually."

"Luke said you were comatose. He used the program to stimulate your cerebral cortex."

Vincent didn't respond. We walked in silence until we reached his room. I sat at his desk as he grabbed a bottle of water from the mini fridge and drank half of it in one gulp. "How much does he know?" he asked. He took another swig.

"Pretty much everything. I guess I figured he should know what was happening."

Vincent sighed.

"I thought you were dying..." I said wearily.

He looked at me then. I still wasn't very good at reading his expressions, but I thought there was something like longing in his eyes. Before I could say anything further, there was a quiet knock on the door. Vincent's eyes fell.

"Come in," I called softly.

Luke entered, closing the door gently behind him.

Vincent ran a hand through his hair and sat down heavily on the bed.

"How do you feel?" Luke asked him.

Vincent shrugged apathetically. "My head hurts like a mother."

Luke nodded understandingly. "Well, you did just undergo mild shock treatment. Your head will ache for the next day or two."

"Luke's in the med program," I told Vincent. His mildly antagonistic attitude triggered in me the need to defend Luke's involvement.

Vincent didn't answer. He looked from me to Luke and his gaze settled back on me. I wondered if Luke was aware of the invisible ice crystals forming in the air around us.

Luke shifted and then leaned against the desk. "I want to see the machine in the basement. Elena said you found the real thing."

Vincent continued to stare at me. "Yeah. I'm not going down there tonight though, so you'll have to wait."

"How did you get in?" Luke asked.

"He has a master keycard," I said. "Maybe we can go tomorrow?"

"Yeah, ok," Luke agreed. "I want in to whatever it is you guys are doing."

Vincent and I didn't respond. I wasn't sure what to say. Now that Luke knew, it would be nearly impossible to keep him out of the loop. I reasoned that it would be useful to have a third party involved in uncovering the truth. Perhaps it was for the best.

"You guys are tired, so we can talk about it tomorrow," Luke said.

"Thank you, Luke," I said sincerely.

He gave me a small smile. "Good night Elena." Then he left.

Vincent had already gotten in bed. He was facing the wall so I couldn't see his face. I approached him and sat down on the bed.

"Please don't be angry. I didn't know what to do," I said.

"I'm not angry. My head hurts," was the muffled reply.

On impulse, my hand found Vincent's head and I ran my fingers through his hair, gently brushing the hair from his forehead.

"Mm. That helps a little," he said quietly.

I didn't want to leave him. I stayed for a while, rubbing his head until I could tell his breathing had changed and he was sleeping.

In my own room that night, I got very little sleep. Each time I did try to close my eyes, my brain replayed the most recent dream hack with vivid fervor. I kept seeing Vincent pulled into the black monster, and lying pale in the lab chair. Then I imagined him in the Somnium Medicus. He had said someone was with him. I wondered if it was the small creature or if there was someone else lurking in my dreamscape. It also struck me as unusual that the small creature had been absent in that last dream.

Sometimes hope comes with the dawn of a new day. The next morning, however, left me completely void of that feeling. I stayed in bed much longer than usual, pondering life and just feeling sorry for myself. I couldn't explain why I was so melancholy. It was as though the emotion I'd felt in my dreamscape the night before had clung to me and wouldn't let go.

In a way, though I still wanted to learn the secret behind the nightmares and Abel Dumont's research, I had lost some of my resolve. What happened to Vincent in my dreamscape had scared me more than I realized. I now knew the true terror of the dreams. They were not harmless. A real threat crept behind the use of the Dreamscape Program, and I had somehow found access to its true nature.

I was sluggish most of that morning and stayed in bed thinking. Close to noon, Vincent texted me, wanting me to come to his room. Moving was an unwelcome chore, but I did manage to get up and drag myself to his room. He looked more pallid than usual and didn't seem to be moving as quickly.

"How do you feel today?" I asked.

"I've felt better," he replied. Then he glanced at me. "You seem to be under the weather yourself."

"Yeah." I sat on his bed and leaned back on my arms. "Didn't sleep much."

"Let's take a break from the program tonight," he said. "It may be unnecessary to continue hacking in, if your dreams return to normal."

I frowned. "What do you mean? We still haven't discovered anything that explains why I started having the dreams."

Vincent didn't respond right away. "I thought the point was to get rid of the dreams? Isn't that why you asked for my help to begin with?"

"That's how it started, but you know now there's more going on. We need to figure out how the program is connected to Abel Dumont. Something's not right about the whole thing," I argued.

Vincent's face remained passive. "I don't think I'm so interested in figuring that out anymore."

His eyes possessed a steely look that I hadn't seen in him for some time. I knew it was because of Luke. Without expressing what he was thinking in so many words, he was showing me he didn't want to move forward if Luke were involved.

I decided to respond to his unspoken protest of Luke's involvement. "Listen, it's just one more trip to the basement. Who cares if he's there? We don't have to tell him when we hack in again. We can take a break until he loses interest."

Vincent raised his eyebrows slightly. "Is he *going* to lose interest?" His expression now carried a meaningful look. I knew what he implied.

"I don't know." I sighed and shook my head. "Please don't quit just yet. Let's make the trip to the basement and take a break from the program. Then we can decide what else to do."

We held each other's gaze for a moment. Unspoken words hung heavily in the air as I felt our partnership slipping away.

"Fine. We'll make the trip to the basement," he agreed.

I left his room shortly after and didn't hear from him until that evening.

Luke asked me to come see him later that day. Dancing back and forth between Vincent and Luke's rooms was beginning to feel a bit like human ping pong.

"How's Vincent feeling?" he asked.

"He doesn't look so good, but he says he's ok."

"Did *you* get any sleep last night?"

I shook my head. "Not very much."

"Sounds like you've been through a lot," he observed. He hesitated. "Why didn't you tell me about those dreams you were having?"

I sat down in the wingback chair in his room and looked at the floor. "I didn't tell anyone. Vincent only found out because he saw the dreams during our lab sessions. I guess I thought that if it got around that I was having nightmares, they'd make me stop using the program. After a while, I started to think that maybe I was having the dreams for a reason. That's when I asked Vincent to help me hack into my dreamscape."

Luke listened attentively. Then he rubbed the side of his neck. "That Vincent guy doesn't like me."

I laughed. "What was your first clue? Don't let it bother you. He doesn't seem to like most people."

"He likes *you*."

I could feel my face grow red. I laughed again, and heard the embarrassment in my voice as I replied, "That's stretching things little."

Luke smiled and graciously changed the subject. "I want to see that machine tonight."

"Yeah. I already spoke with Vincent about it and he agreed to go. Oh, I forgot to tell you about the research data I found down there as well. The manuscript translation is consistent with the data. Some patients really were treated with the Somnium Medicus and afterward, they didn't dream. One patient – Helen Locke was her name – tried to get the process reversed. She preferred the nightmares to no dreams at all." I paused briefly, then continued, "When Vincent and I saw the machine in my dreamscape, I had a strong urge to use it, but Vincent stopped me. Luke, he told me last night, after he was taken in the dreamscape, he was put in the machine. He said someone was there with him. I'm worried for him."

"It was just a dream though. You shouldn't worry."

I looked at him earnestly. "It wasn't just a dream."

That night, Vincent, Luke, and I made a trip to the sub-basement in the research center. We said little as we somberly trekked down each flight of stairs. Vincent behaved as though he were being held hostage and forced to act against his will. Though I'm sure Luke was aware of Vincent's mood, he ignored it and paid more attention to me. It was an altogether uncomfortable situation.

Once Vincent opened the door to the sub-basement, he hung back by the entrance. I led Luke directly to the Somium Medicus. We lifted the sheet together and stood in quiet awe for a moment.

"This thing is terrifying," he said.

"Yeah. We thought so too, the first time we saw it."

"Does it work?" He moved around to the back of the machine and found the power cable. "The plug is different. I wish we could turn it on."

Somehow I plucked up enough courage then to sit in the machine. The seat and arms were padded with worn leather, but the machine itself felt cold and uninviting. I reached up and pulled the helmet down carefully, until it covered my face. Then I rested my arms on either side of the machine and imagined it was turned on.

Suddenly, the helmet was lifted from my face.

"What are you doing?" Vincent asked. He had taken the helmet off my head and was standing next to me with a troubled look on his face.

"I was just curious," I replied.

"Get out of the chair," he ordered.

I didn't question him. Luke silently watched the two of us as I stood up.

"There are more boxes to look through," Vincent said, turning as though that's what he had planned to do all along.

I followed him to another corner of the basement. Luke stayed by the machine.

"What's wrong?" I asked him quietly, so Luke couldn't hear.

"Just stay away from that machine. It's dangerous," Vincent answered. He seemed genuinely worried for some reason.

"It doesn't even work."

Vincent didn't try to convince me anymore, so I dropped the subject and instead began to look through boxes and furniture. I hadn't searched this side of the basement last time, but most of it didn't seem so significant. There were old decorative items and even some china sets packed away. I wondered why they hadn't sold any of it. It looked expensive.

"Come look at this," I heard Luke say. Vincent and I abandoned our corner and returned to the Somium Medicus to see what Luke had found.

He shone his phone light on the back of the machine where he had removed a panel. We could see some words engraved in French along with a date.

Luke translated for us:

> *"Here lies the Child of a Hundred Years.*
> *Forever rest in our nightmares.*
> *1950-1958'"*

"Are you sure that's what it says?" Vincent asked, skeptically.

Luke nodded. "I know. It makes no sense."

"It sounds like something you'd read on a gravestone – minus the nightmare part," I added.

"I think the machine was intentionally sabotaged. Wires have been cut here and here"– Luke said, pointing. "I wonder what made it necessary to do that?"

"Remember what the manuscript said? After a while, Abel Dumont was afraid to use it," I reminded him. "He said the machine had taken on a life of its own."

"Did you find any more research data?" Luke asked.

"Not yet. We'll keep looking," I said.

Vincent and I returned to the far corner of the basement and continued searching through the boxes.

"This Dumont guy had a lot of junk," Vincent muttered.

"Expensive junk," I corrected him.

"Who collects weird stuff like this?" Vincent held up an unusual statue carved from black stone. Something about it looked familiar. I came closer and held out a hand to see it. Vincent handed it to me.

"This is from my dreamscape," I said. I traced the statue and turned it around in my hand. It was a crouching, bony figure without a face. "It's that thing that's always finding me," I exclaimed.

Vincent took another look. "Maybe. It might just look like it cause it's all black."

"I wish we could speak to Abel Dumont," I thought aloud. "I want to talk to him about it. He has to know what it is."

"Bingo," Vincent said.

I turned my attention to him as he pulled out a heavy book from the same box. It was written in what looked like Arabic, but was filled with pictures of various statues and symbols. Vincent flipped through it until he came to a picture that resembled the statue I was holding.

"But what is it supposed to be?" I wondered.

"Maybe he can read *Arabic* too," he said, nodding in Luke's direction. It wasn't difficult to detect the not-so-subtle sarcasm in his voice.

After more searching, we didn't find much else of interest. We took the book with us, but the small statue creeped me out, so I had Vincent put it back. Luke seemed to be satisfied with having seen the machine, and we all worked on putting things back the way we'd found them. Then we returned to Vincent's room.

I showed Luke the book and we discovered that he could *not* read Arabic, though he was at least familiar with some of the book's content.

"This is an ancient dream charm," he said, pointing to the picture of the black statue we'd found. "People used it to keep them safe in their homes and to ward off bad dreams." He flipped through more of the book. "I believe most of the artifacts pictured in here are connected to some kind of mysticism or superstition. Were you thinking this might be related to that ancient technique Dumont wrote about in his manuscript?"

I nodded. "The thought had crossed my mind."

"May I borrow it then?" he held out a hand and I gave him the book. "I'll do some research on it."

While Luke and I spoke, Vincent was immersed in something else entirely on his computer. I couldn't help but remember what he said earlier that day, about not being sure he was interested in pursuing the answers behind my dreamscape any longer. I felt myself grow heavy with despair at the thought of Vincent disengaging.

Luke was ready to leave, but he mouthed to me *"Let's talk"* before he said, "Thanks for showing me the machine. I'll let you know what I find out from this." He patted the book. Then left the room.

Despite Luke's absence, Vincent didn't talk to me. I hung around for another minute, scrolling through my phone as if I were doing something important, but the awkwardness in the air refused to dissipate until it became nearly unbearable. I stood up and approached Vincent.

"Are you working on something?"

He shrugged. "Just messing around with stuff." He didn't speak again.

My dignity prohibited me from standing around, waiting for him to talk. "I'll see you in lab tomorrow," I said.

I went to Luke's room from there.

Luke got straight to the point as I sat in his wing back chair. "Are you guys planning to hack in again soon?"

"I don't know," I said with a sigh. "Vincent doesn't seem to want to continue with the plan." It was the truth.

"Because of me?" Luke asked.

"I'm...not sure. I think he's still recovering from what happened last night. We haven't made plans to hack in again yet."

Luke nodded, then said, "You need to let me know when you do. There's no way you guys can go back in there without someone keeping an eye on you. It's too dangerous."

"I did consider that," I agreed. "I don't know if Vincent will go for it though."

"Then he doesn't have to know I'm there," Luke said. "*You* tell me when it happens."

"You don't understand though...Vincent wants to give up on the plan."

"Are you still having the nightmares?"

"I don't know yet. Maybe I'll find out tonight." I sighed.

Luke leaned forward and said with a serious expression, "If he won't help you get rid of them, *I* will."

I gave him a half smile. "Thanks. I'm sure we'll figure something out."

I went back to my room, feeling as though my betrayal of Vincent was complete. It was nonsense really. I'd involved Luke to *help* Vincent. It shouldn't have turned out this way. Logically, Luke was a helpful asset to the team. His discovery of the manuscript and strange writing on the machine had uncovered some interesting clues connected to the Somnium Medicus. In fact, I doubt Vincent or I would have made those discoveries apart from him.

Weary as I was, my mind would not relent from its torrent of thought. I spent some time reading and researching Middle Eastern dream superstition, but quickly grew tired of it and gave up.

As I expected, I didn't sleep well that night.

But I did dream.

It wasn't the same nightmare anymore. I was in the mansion, completely alone now. There were no shadows, no basement, no stairwell, and no creature...but I was afraid. I wandered through the halls, desperately seeking something and never finding it. I opened doors and looked in dark corners, almost hoping shadows would appear, though if I had encountered them, I would face them unarmed, for I no longer held the red-handled katana. I remember trying to find the stairwell, convinced that I had to go down and fight the monster again. Then I realized I was looking for Vincent.

I called his name and ran to his room, flinging the door open to find it vacant. I headed for the lab.

As I approached the glass lab doors, I could already see what I feared I would find. All the chairs and computers had been removed. The Somnium Medicus was the only object in the room, and there, strapped in the machine with the helmet on his head and tubes sticking out of his arms was Vincent. He was still and white.

I pounded on the lab door and called to him. I remember saying they had taken the wrong person – I should be the one in the machine. The doors wouldn't open.

Vincent wasn't alone in the room. Out from behind the machine emerged a tall figure with pale hair and eyes like ice. At the sight of him, my thoughts flashed back to the library in the west wing and a picture hanging above the fireplace mantle.

Abel Dumont.

CHAPTER 14

Monday morning was a return to reality. Though I could hardly wait to speak to Vincent about my dream, I remembered his detachment and apathy the previous day. It was enough to keep me at bay until lab later that morning. Vincent was so late to lab, however, I feared he wouldn't come. When he did finally show up, the session had nearly started already.

"Vincent. Are you sick?" I asked him quietly.

He nodded, but proceeded with preparations to log in.

"We shouldn't do this then...I'll let the instructor know"— I started to say.

He touched my arm to stop me and shook his head. "I want you to see my dreamscape."

I sat back slowly and prepared myself. Then we logged in together.

There was nothing to see but darkness. It felt different than a dark room, however. It felt like empty space and I was very conscious of the absence of a dream. I could sense Vincent's agitation as more time passed and nothing happened. But though I searched for him in the empty dreamscape, he was nowhere to be found.

I thought the agony would never end, yet at last, it did. My head pulsed with questions as we vacated the lab.

"We need to talk," I said to him, once we were in the hall. "Let's go for a walk."

Vincent followed without protest as I led him outside to the courtyard. We found a seat on a bench in a secluded region. He appeared even more sickly in daylight.

"You're not dreaming," I stated.

He nodded. "Yeah. Not since we hacked in that second time."

"Is that why you're sick?"

"I don't know. Maybe. I just feel different."

"Vincent, my nightmare went away." Vincent looked at me, interestedly. "Well, it's been replaced by another dream. I don't know if I'll have it again because I just dreamt it last night...I'm still in the mansion. There aren't any shadows or stairwells. It's just empty. Then I start looking for you. You're not in your room, so I go to the lab and find you in the Somnium Medicus. Abel Dumont was there with you. I couldn't get in though," I finished.

Vincent frowned. "So my dreams have been taken. Didn't you say the patients got better when their dreams were taken though?"

"That's what the data showed, but the patients wanted their dreams back. The transcripts didn't record whether the process was ever reversed."

"Well, it looks like we'll need to keep hacking in after all, but I don't think my dreamscape will be any use. We'll have to keep using yours. I think you're going to need to find me and get me out of the machine," he said.

"Would you consider...letting Luke help us then?"

Vincent sighed and scratched his head. "Yeah. I don't think you should go in alone."

"Wait — you want *Luke* to hack in with me?"

He nodded. "It makes sense. I'll bet if I try to hack in with you, I won't be there. We can try it, but I'm pretty sure that's what will happen. Luke can help you find me and pull me out of the machine. Just make sure you guys don't get caught by the shadows."

"We should do this soon. You don't seem to be holding up too well."

Vincent smiled wryly. "Ironic, isn't it."

After a minute of silence, I said, "What if we can't get your dreams back? We're going to have to say something eventually."

Vincent shrugged. "If it comes to that. Let's not worry about it right now."

We made plans to meet with Luke that evening and explain the situation to him. In the meantime, Sophie had been bugging me to tell her about my date with Luke Saturday night, so I hung out with her for a bit before dinner.

I sat on the floor in her room while she folded laundry on the bed.

"So are you and Luke like an official 'thing' now?" she asked, after I told her about the date.

"I don't think so," I replied.

"Because of Vincent?" she guessed.

"It's gotten a bit complicated," I admitted. "Saturday night, after Luke and I went out, Vincent had a negative response to our hack in and I had Luke come help me wake Vincent."

"Wait a minute — you guys hacked in a *second* time?" Sophie stopped folding and looked at me.

"Yeah. We didn't get as far as we wanted to the first time. And we're going to need to go in again."

"Your nightmares haven't gone away yet?"

"Not exactly...something odd happened during that last hack in though. Vincent isn't dreaming now, so we think we need to fix his dreams by hacking in again."

Sophie was staring at me in disbelief. "Why don't you just tell the faculty what's going on?"

"We can't. It's possible they already know something is...different about the program," I explained.

Sophie shook her head. "So, you guys think there really is some kind of conspiracy happening involving the Dreamscape Program?"

"We think something happened here a long time ago and we want to figure out how it's connected to the program *now*," I corrected her. "If I tell you more, you need to keep it quiet for now."

Sophie nodded. "Ok."

I filled her in on the details of Luke's manuscript interpretation and how it coincided with my nightmares. I even told her about the Somnium Medicus machine in the basement. She didn't touch her laundry as I spoke.

"Sounds like you guys uncovered something quite intriguing," she remarked, once I finished. "Let me know if I can help in any way. To be honest, I feel a little left out."

"*You* were the one who forced me to go searching the west wing to begin with. I wouldn't have made any connection between my dream and the real history mansion of the mansion if not for that little adventure."

Sophie grinned. "That was pretty fun." Then her expression became more serious as she said, "What are you planning to do if Vincent's dreams don't come back?"

"We'll have to tell someone, of course. But I think our plan will work."

We left her room and had dinner in the cafeteria. I wondered why I had told Sophie everything. At first, I'd been so secretive, but now trying to keep the truth from her seemed pointless. Still, for some reason I felt apprehensive about having shared everything with Sophie. I did trust her to keep our conversation quiet, yet perhaps I worried we couldn't keep everything secret for much longer.

Luke met with me and Vincent in Vincent's room later that evening. We told him about Vincent's dream problem and our idea to find Vincent in the dreamscape. He was willing to help.

"Tell me how the dream joining works," he said.

"You'll be in Elena's dreamscape," Vincent explained. "You're both lucid and armed, so you can talk to her and interact. You just can't manipulate the dreamscape."

"How are we armed?" Luke asked.

Vincent pulled up a screen on his computer. "This is the mod I use. It would probably be best if you use the same one tonight, for the sake of time. If we need to change it later we can."

Luke peered over Vincent's shoulder and commented, "This looks like something from a video game."

"It is," Vincent said, a bit impatiently.

"The thing we need to avoid is being trapped by the shadows," I chimed in. "It seems like whoever is in the dreamscape with me is targeted, so be careful."

"I'll pull you out if I see changes in your readings," Vincent said.

"Another thing," I continued. "You'll be able to feel what I'm feeling. We've determined that the program sort of messes with my amygdala, so I'm usually pretty freaked out in the dreams. Vincent has helped me get through certain parts of the dreamscape. It's not easy..."

Vincent didn't comment. He had turned away from us to type on his computer.

"Wait a minute...will it matter if Vincent isn't logged in with us?" Luke asked. "Will we be able to find him I mean."

"My dream consciousness is trapped, so it probably doesn't matter," Vincent answered.

"He does have a point though," I said.

"Let's just try it this way first," Vincent suggested. "If you don't find me in the machine when you're in the dreamscape, I'll log in with you next time. But you would be alone," he said to me.

"So you can only pair two people at a time," Luke stated.

Vincent shrugged. "So far, yes."

It wasn't long before we were gathered in the lab, preparing to hack in once again. Vincent was quiet and moody, but I sensed he was very tired, so perhaps his mood was directly related to fatigue.

"Am I really going to have to fight something in this dreamscape," Luke asked me quietly.

"More than likely," I responded. I smiled at him. "Nervous?"

He laughed. "I'm more nervous about embarrassing myself in front of you."

"It's sort of unfair that you get a dry run. Vincent and I practiced together a few times before the real thing," I told him. "I'm sure you'll do fine. You can move very quickly in the dreamscape. You can even defy gravity and run on the walls. It's pretty cool."

"It's ready," Vincent said.

As Luke and I took our seats, Vincent was watching me. I held his gaze for a moment and nodded to him. His eyes broke away as he turned his attention to the monitor.

"I'm logging you in to Elena's current dreamscape," Vincent said. "Hopefully, it's the same one you had last night."

Luke and I put the masks on our faces and fell into sleep. It wasn't long before I was standing next to him in a deserted Academy.

He took a moment to adjust himself to the weapons mod. He wore the same black coat and two swords Vincent was accustomed to wearing in my dreamscape.

"That's really you, right?" he said to me.

"Yeah. It's bizarre, isn't it?"

He nodded. "So where to?" he asked.

"We need to get to the lab. I didn't run into any shadows in my dream last night, but be ready just in case. Follow my lead."

As we made our way through the vacant halls, Luke commented on the dreamscape. "Everything looks exactly the same as the real Academy, except much older, like no one's been here for a long time."

"We must be in the same place as the first time Vincent and I hacked in," I replied.

After a pause, Luke said, "You're not afraid right now, are you."

"No."

"You're angry…"

I didn't answer. I was too preoccupied with finding Vincent to be bothered.

We turned a corner and were met with what appeared to be a black wall.

"The shadows," I said. "Get ready."

We unsheathed our weapons and began to cut through the darkness. The air was thick with it. I also smelled the familiar scent from the basement and the walls were smeared with sludge.

"It's here," I said. "The thing that took Vincent."

Though Luke held his own next to me, he didn't fight with the same intensity as Vincent had. He moved cautiously and deliberately as we pressed forward. It was probably for the best that he didn't run headlong into the danger. It wouldn't help to lose another person to the monster and the machine.

Our progress was slow, but eventually, we did pass through the darkened hall and leave the shadows behind. Suddenly, the fear kicked in. I smelled the monster ahead and dreaded having to face it again.

"Elena…" Luke said. He quickened his pace so he was beside me as I marched determinedly forward. "It won't take us," he reassured me.

"Just be careful. It's quicker than you think."

We had almost reached the lab by then.

*Vincent.*

I expected to see the black, hulking beast from the basement at any moment. Instead, we arrived at the hall leading to the lab without encountering it, but something else was waiting for us.

"That's the thing that's been haunting my dreams," I said quietly. From where we had stopped in the hall, we could see Vincent in the

Somnium Medicus, and a small, familiar figure standing like a sentinel just outside the doorway to the lab.

"Abel Dumont might be in there too," I said.

"What is that thing?" Luke asked.

"I think it's the same as the one from that book we found. There was a statue of it in the basement, but Vincent and I left it in the box."

"The dream guardian? In ancient times, they were supposed to have protected people from bad dreams, which is why they kept statues of them in their home," Luke said.

"Well here, it's part of the nightmare."

"Are you sure?"

"I'm not sure of anything. I just don't want that thing to catch me." I thought of the creature opening its mouth, revealing dead faces, writing in pain.

"So, what do we do?" Luke asked me.

"One of us can distract it. The other can try to get to Vincent," I suggested. "Luke, try to find a way into the lab. That thing wants *me*."

Luke looked at me doubtingly.

"Just get him out of the machine," I insisted.

We parted ways and I advanced toward the creature by the door. It stood motionless, just like the statue figure. Behind it, just beyond the glass doors, Vincent was prisoner to the Somium Medicus. The desire to get to the machine was stronger than ever, though I couldn't tell if it was because I wanted to sit in it, or I wanted to get at Vincent.

The creature stirred and opened glowing, heinous eyes. It grinned.

"I'm here. I've come back. Please let me through," I pleaded.

It raised its arms toward me and then it opened its mouth. My body froze with terror as I looked down the gaping hole and saw what seemed to be hell inside the small monster. The dead ones moaned and screamed at me in pain. The creature reached for me with longing and caught hold of my arm. I yanked back suddenly and swept my katana through the creature's body. It shut its mouth with alarming quickness and fell back against the glass. Then it hissed at me.

"Get away from me!" I yelled. "I'm taking Vincent!"

I rushed at it then with such savage force, I surprised myself. The creature had recovered from my first attack and was now growing larger by the second. It morphed into something even more misshapen and horrifying than before. The dead faces inside it pushed out until they could be seen on the creature's body. It moved quickly, evading every attempt of mine to cut it down. All the while, I heard my name called again and again, until my head ached with the noise.

I flew up on the wall and crashed down heavily on the monster's back, driving my sword deep into it as I fell. It screamed and reeled back, slamming me into the glass walls of the research lab. They shattered and we fell through. I landed gasping on the floor, mere feet from the machine. The creature was up much more quickly than I. It was on me before I could move. I tried desperately to untangle myself from it, but my katana was pinned down with my arm. The creature sat on me, smiling victoriously as it opened its mouth to consume me.

"Elena!" Luke yelled.

Suddenly, he was in the fray, swinging both swords with unexpected dexterity. The monster released me, and I rolled out of the way so Luke could continue to fend off the creature's attacks. Then I joined in the onslaught and we pushed it out of the lab.

It transformed back into a small being and quickly dashed away down the hall.

"What happened?" he asked.

"Nevermind right now. Let's get Vincent out," I said, rushing over to the Somnium Medicus.

Luke came up beside me as I gently lifted the helmet from Vincent's head and unstrapped his arms.

"Vincent," I said. "Can you hear me?"

Luke worked on unfastening the tubes from Vincent's arms.

"He's cold," Luke observed. "He might not respond. He's not really in the program, remember?"

"What if we were supposed to wake him in here? What if we did this wrong?"

Luke put a hand on my shoulder. "Let's just get him out of here."

We pulled Vincent out of the chair and each took one of his arms around our shoulders. Then we dragged him across the room.

*"Stop. What do you think you're doing?"* a voice said from behind us.

I recognized the voice as the one I'd heard calling my name just moments before. I knew before turning who it was and a look over my shoulder confirmed it to be Abel Dumont. His eyes were like blue fire as he stared at me with contempt. "How did you get in here?" he asked. He started to move forward then, taking slow, purposeful strides.

"Let's go," I said urgently.

"Let me take him," Luke said, hoisting Vincent over his shoulder.

We moved as quickly as was possible, carrying a third person. I felt the mansion physically sway in protest as we hurried away from the lab.

*"Elena."*

Dumont's voice continued to call my name, inviting me back to the lab.

*"Elena, come to the Somnium Medicus. I can heal your dreams."*

His words were smooth and enticing. It was difficult later to describe the conflict I felt in my dreamscape. I wanted to go back to the lab. Luke even began to move faster than I, though he carried Vincent on his shoulder.

Luke called to me, "Elena! Hurry! He's behind you!"

I looked over my shoulder once to see Abel Dumont, still advancing toward us. Somehow, he moved more quickly than I expected. Though I tried to run faster, my legs began to feel rather unsteady beneath me. Then, from behind me I heard a sound like wind rushing up. The shadows had come. They swirled past Abel Dumont and their tendrils encircled my legs, making my progress even more laborious.

"Luke! Take Vincent out of here!" I screamed.

Luke had stopped to see what was happening. The last thing I remember was the look of panic on his face as he called my name. I heard nothing but the thunderous storm of the shadows as they swallowed me whole.

# CHAPTER 15

I opened my eyes and sat up, slowly.

*They took me.*

Beside me, Luke was rousing from sleep as well. "Elena…" he said with concern.

Vincent looked up from the computer. "What happened?"

"We got you out of the machine," I said slowly.

"But the shadows got Elena," Luke finished.

"You're kidding, right?" Vincent came around to where we sat. "You let them take her?" he asked, addressing Luke.

"I was carrying *you*. They rushed up on her quickly," Luke explained calmly.

Vincent's jaw tightened. "You should have dropped me. I mean seriously, you let them *take* her?"

I could sense it was all he could do not to explode on Luke then.

I tried to reason with him. "Vincent, it was Abel Dumont. He came after me. There was nothing Luke could have done. This was his first time in my dreamscape, remember?"

Luke didn't look happy with my attempt to defend him. However, Vincent was too angry to let him reply.

"Let's go back in right now. I'll get you out"– he started to say.

"No," Luke said, standing up. "Elena can't hack in again tonight. You have to let her rest."

"She's not going to *get* any rest. They'll just put her in the machine like they did with me and she won't have any dreams," Vincent argued.

Luke shook his head firmly. "I won't let you try it. You can get her back tomorrow night."

The two of them held each other's gaze for a rather tense moment. Then Vincent swore under his breath and returned to the computer terminal.

"Are you alright?" Luke asked me, once Vincent had moved away.

"Yeah," I assured him. "You did the right thing. Our plan was to get Vincent out. Anyway, who knows? I woke up before they put me in the machine, so it's probably fine."

"I hope so," Luke replied. "What was that thing you were fighting anyway? Where'd it come from?"

"It was the creature by the door. It transformed or something."

Luke shook his head. "I didn't expect any of it to be like that. You've been having dreams like that for weeks you say?"

I shrugged. "More or less."

"Didn't you say something about this not really being your dreamscape?" Luke started to ask.

Vincent brushed by us. "I'll be in my room," he said, looking at me. He walked out without acknowledging Luke.

"I'm sorry," I said. "He should be thanking you for getting him out of the machine."

Luke's expression was thoughtful as he watched Vincent leave. "Not if it means putting you in harm's way."

His observation bothered me. "You were saying something before," I reminded him.

"Right. It's not your dreamscape."

We walked slowly toward the hall.

"I don't think so," I confirmed.

"Which would mean you've linked up with something in the program...so Abel Dumont is actually there? But he's supposed to have died years ago."

"It doesn't make sense," I admitted. "Unless perhaps the person in my dream only *looks* like Abel Dumont. I don't know."

We continued in silence until we came to Vincent's room.

Luke stopped. "I'm not going in. I'll talk to him when he's not so angry with me."

"Ok. Good night Luke. Thanks for your help."

I waited until he'd disappeared down the hall before opening Vincent's door.

Vincent was on his bed with his laptop, typing aggressively. "Did he retreat to his room?" he asked, caustically.

"You were really rude. Luke helped you."

Vincent frowned and stopped typing. "I wouldn't have let them take you," he said candidly. He looked up at me with smoldering, grey eyes.

"Vincent..." I didn't know how to respond to the obvious emotion he exhibited. "Let's just take it one step at a time. We can go back in tomorrow night."

"As long as we don't take 'Mr. Screw-Up' with us," he muttered, returning to his laptop.

I didn't stay much longer. I could see he was irritated with Luke and I was having difficulty coming up with the right words to say to help the situation. I didn't blame Luke. He only did what needed to be done.

As was usual after spending an extended period of time in the program, I didn't dream that night, though I felt as if I were still in my dreamscape. I kept sensing a presence in the room, yet when I looked, I was alone. Abel Dumont's voice called to me softly as well and I kept thinking of the machine in the basement, wondering if it could be fixed. Perhaps I could try it just once.

Life intruded the following day. There wasn't time to think about Vincent's mood or my adventures in the dreamscape. In fact, I spent most of the day in class or working on research. I didn't see or hear from Luke or Vincent until evening.

Luke was the first to contact me with a text that read, *"How were your dreams last night?"*

I replied, *"I didn't have any."*

Then I sent a message to Vincent asking when he wanted me to meet him later that day. He didn't reply until the dinner hour was well past. His message read simply: *"Come to my room."*

"What's up?" I said, as I entered his room shortly after.

As was his custom, Vincent was at his desk, engrossed in working on his computer. "I found something," he told me.

"Did you dream last night?" I asked him.

He shook his head.

"It didn't work?" I didn't even trying to hide the frustration in my voice.

"No, I just didn't sleep," he stated.

"Oh. What did you find?" I came up beside him and glanced over his shoulder.

"Last night, while you were in the program, I did some research. Here"– He pulled up a screen with a graph, showing my dream pattern, then he pulled up a window from another program and explained, "I don't think your dreamscape is just a dream. It's a firewall built into the program." He paused to look at me.

"A firewall?"

He nodded. "I think the fear is built in to keep you away from some other source. The first time you used the program, you bumped into the firewall and got stuck. Since then, you haven't been able to break through it, or return to the actual program itself."

"How do we get past it?"

"My theory? The stairwell. We need to finish that part of the dreamscape."

"You mean the creature in the basement," I said.

"Probably," Vincent agreed. He leaned back and breathed a sigh.

"What's the plan?"

Vincent looked at me, exhaustion clearly written on his face. "I might have overdone it today," he admitted. "And before we log in again, I want to make a few more adjustments to the weapons mod. But maybe tomorrow night we can go back in and try to fight that thing in the basement again."

"Ok," I said. "What about Luke?"

Vincent sat still for a moment. Then gave a slight shrug. "It would help to have someone outside, in case something goes wrong."

"Are you sure?"

Vincent stretched, looking up at me as he did. He put his hands behind his head and locked his fingers together. "You want him involved, don't you?"

"I just think it's a good idea. It really scared me when you didn't wake up." I looked at the floor.

"You sure get scared a lot," he commented facetiously.

I looked back up in time to catch his smug grin, then gave him a playful shove. "Jerk."

He laughed, momentarily erasing the exhaustion from his face and producing a rather pleasing, boyish expression. Once again, I was surprised at how delighted I felt to see him that way. My face grew warm and my stomach did a flip.

Still beaming from his joke, Vincent returned to working on his computer.

"Aren't you going to sleep soon?" I asked.

"Maybe. Just a couple more things to do first." I watched him work for a minute until he looked at me again. "Something on your mind?"

I shook my head. "It's nothing. Guess I was just lost in thought. Have you eaten yet?"

"No, I haven't, come to think of it."

"You're not too keen on taking care of yourself, are you?" I observed.

Vincent got up suddenly. "Let's get some sushi."

"I thought you were tired."

"I'm very tired, but I'm hungry now too, thanks to you."

"I don't have a car," I told him, while he tied his shoes.

"I do," he said.

As I followed him out of the dorm wing and down the stairs to the lobby, I remarked ironically, "You sure you're not allergic to leaving your room?"

Vincent looked over his shoulder at me. "Be nice, or you won't get any sushi."

"I've never even had it, so who cares?" I replied.

Vincent shook his head as we exited the Academy. "I knew there was something wrong with you."

"You mean beside the fact that I have strange nightmares on a consistent basis?"

Vincent stopped in the parking lot next to an expensive, black sports car.

"This is yours?" I asked, raising my eyebrows.

He got in and started the engine. I slid into the passenger seat. The car was pristine, just like his room.

"You impress me Mr. Miller," I said.

He glanced at me, then, seeing my coy expression, rolled his eyes.

"No, really," I insisted.

He responded by peeling out of the parking lot so fast that I flew back against the seat, laughing.

It was already dark. Vincent had the windows rolled down all the way and the music playing a little too loudly for conversation. He also drove a bit fast, but I didn't mind. It felt good to leave the Academy, as though I peeled off a layer of wet clothing and climbed into something soft and warm.

Vincent took me to a small sushi restaurant in town, not quite as trendy as the places Luke had brought me to, but I don't think Vincent really cared about the atmosphere. He claimed their sushi was the best. I didn't know what to get, so I left ordering up to him. It wasn't long before our plates arrived.

Vincent saw me eyeing the sushi skeptically. "Don't worry, it's raw," he said, as he popped a piece in his mouth.

I made a face. "You sure know how to show a girl a good time."

He laughed. "Yeah. They line up for me."

"Now you're just bragging."

I tried to bite a sushi roll in half, and was dismayed to find it fell apart.

"Just put the whole thing in your mouth," Vincent suggested.

I obeyed, and found that I really liked sushi. "This is good."

Vincent smiled and took a sip of water. "I know," he said.

I managed to pry a bit of personal information out of him that evening. His parents had moved to Los Angeles when Vincent was a freshman in high school. He was enrolled in an elite, private school, but left due to some unpleasantness with his peers. Without him saying it outright, he hinted at having been the victim of bullying, and in an attempt to retaliate, got himself kicked out of the school. After that, he refused to attend the nearby public school, so his parents enrolled him in classes online.

The migraines started around that time as well.

"My dad used to yell at me a lot," he admitted. "He was always telling me to get off my computer cause he thought all I did was play games, but I was actually *creating* them. They were pretty simple at first. You know, like those games you can download for free and waste hours playing. So once my dad saw that I was starting to make money from them, he stopped yelling at me."

Vincent's father took advantage of his son's talent with technology and began to find clients for Vincent who needed a computer expert. That was how he ended up working at the Academy. The Academy eventually made an exception for him as a student, because he hadn't yet completed an undergrad program, and allowed him to continue his work in exchange for tuition. I realized then that Vincent was actually a couple of years younger than me.

This brief reprieve from chasing through dreamscapes and running from shadows was enough to momentarily restore the ordinary. It reminded me that Vincent was just a normal guy, and despite our unusual adventures together, life would at some point return to the way it had been before I stumbled into a repetitive nightmare.

There was certainly a part of me that now wished it would never end. It was something I'd been trying to suppress for a while, yet kept creeping to the surface with each new hack in attempt. I was attached to the nightmares. I suppose I was attached to Vincent as well, though at the time, it was difficult to tell whether that connection wasn't something other than our dream pairing experiences. Frequently, I reminded myself that the *program* had drawn us together, and there was no reason to believe anything otherwise.

Back on campus, I dragged Vincent with me to see Luke, who had been texting me throughout the evening, requesting an update on our plans. We entered Luke's room to find him sitting on his bed with his laptop and various papers and textbooks spread out around him. Vincent shuffled into Luke's room behind me and stood rather stiffly near the door. I took a seat in the wingback chair.

Luke removed his glasses for a moment and rubbed his eyes. "So what's up? You guys aren't hacking in tonight?"

I glanced at Vincent. "Vincent has some things to do first. But he thinks he may have discovered something about my dreamscape." I paused again to give Vincent a chance to explain.

"It's possible Elena has bumped into a firewall in the Dreamscape Program. We're going to try to get through it," Vincent said.

"So the shadow things and Abel Dumont are just part of a firewall?" Luke asked, doubtfully.

"Not necessarily. Those elements could be part of what's on the other side of it. The *fear* is the firewall," Vincent explained.

Luke nodded, thoughtfully. "Have you guys considered the Dreamscape Program might have some purpose unknown to the average student at the Academy?"

I looked at Vincent. Then asked Luke, "What were you thinking?"

Luke breathed out a slow sigh. "It's obvious this place has an unusual history — one that isn't common knowledge — but somehow you started dreaming about the past once you logged into the program. I think it's all related."

I nodded. "We came to that conclusion as well."

"Ok. So what if what you're dreaming isn't just a firewall? What if it's the core of the actual program?"

Vincent spoke up. "It's more likely a firewall. The fear is what's preventing Elena from getting through."

"Why do you think it's the core of the program?" I asked Luke.

"The machine," he replied. "I think the machine is the original prototype for the Dreamscape Program."

His theory wasn't completely unexpected. It was something I'd already considered.

"That may be true," Vincent said. "But I still think we need to get through the nightmare part of Elena's dream to see what's on the other side."

Luke nodded in agreement. "Well, you guys have been at this longer, so I'll defer to you."

"Luke, do you think the program does something other than what we were told?" I asked.

Luke shrugged and shook his head. "I don't know. I think it's possible, but whether the faculty even know is the question. Abel Dumont was concerned that the machine took on a life of its own. Maybe that's happened in the program as well."

Vincent frowned. "I'm not sure about that."

"It's possible though," I said, agreeing with Luke.

"So, you'll be alright until tomorrow evening? Your dreams aren't affected?" Luke asked me.

"I'll be fine. I don't know about the dreams, but at this point, it doesn't matter anymore."

Luke's eyes searched my face for confirmation as I spoke. Out of the corner of my eye, I saw Vincent shift impatiently.

"I'll see you tomorrow," I said to Luke.

Luke's eyes moved to Vincent before returning to me as he said, "Yeah. Have a good night."

Vincent had already left and was standing in the hall. "I'm going to sleep," he told me.

He turned and started walking to his room. I was heading in the same direction anyway, on the way to my own room, so I followed him. We moved in silence through the halls until Vincent finally stopped at his door. With his hand on the doorknob, he said to me, "I don't invite girls back to my room on the first date, so you'll have to wait until next time." The corners of his mouth turned up into a rather ironic smile as he enjoyed my shocked expression.

As soon as I caught on to his joke, I replied, "I think you're confused, because I don't go on dates with anti-social tech nerds."

Vincent raised an eyebrow. "You mean you've never had the good fortune until now. It's alright. I get that a lot."

"Someone took their irony pills," I mumbled.

Vincent actually laughed. "The honest truth? I'm just exhausted. You'll have to amuse yourself."

"What gave you the impression I was looking for amusement from *you*?" I asked, with mock indignation.

"You're following me, aren't you?"

"Just on my way to my room, wise guy. Go to sleep already. You're so annoying when you're overtired," I remarked, not without humor.

Vincent's grin was enough to tell me he was enjoying this back and forth. Once again, that endearing, boyish look spread across his face, filling me with the desire to linger so I could enjoy it longer.

Vincent unlocked his door, but stopped to say over his shoulder, "Try not to miss me too much."

With that he disappeared into his room, closing the door behind him.

# CHAPTER 16

I was alone.

The darkened halls filled me with sorrow and longing — sorrow for their emptiness — longing for the company of the shadows. It was unbearably lonely. I wandered until I reached the basement of the mansion, which was much more elaborate than I remembered and the rooms never ended. Just as I thought I was making progress, I would turn a corner and face another corridor filled with empty, dark rooms. I should have been afraid, but I felt nothing. Nothing but the desire to move forward and find whatever was down there. In that basement labyrinth, I felt something calling to me.

At last, I came upon a boiler room of some kind, only inside I found the Somnium Medicus, humming soothingly. I would have sat in the chair if it were not already occupied.

"Elena." Vincent called my name and stepped into the room. "He's not coming out of there. We should let him be."

"Who is it?"

Vincent shook his head. "Listen...I need you with me." He came toward me and grasped my arm, pulling me to him. He pressed me close in an embrace and said softly in my ear, "If you leave me here, I'm going to die."

"I'm not going to leave you," I replied. I wrapped my arms around his waist.

THE CHILD OF 100 YEARS

"That's a relief," he sighed. As he pulled away, I saw it was Abel Dumont who held me.

I pushed away from him. "Where's Vincent?"

Abel Dumont smiled with false cordiality. "You want to sit in the machine."

I stepped back.

"Elena, it is your turn." He held his hand out to me and motioned to the now empty machine. "You must have your turn. Vincent will die if you do not. They will all die," he said, sorrowfully.

My eyes blurred with unwelcome tears. "This is your fault. Why did you make the machine?"

M. Dumont's smile softened. "You do not know. It is much more than merely a machine. You will soon understand, as Vincent does."

"What do you mean by that?"

M. Dumont's expression turned cold as ice. "Why don't you ask him?"

I started awake, audibly saying Vincent's name as I did. My hair was damp with sweat and my heart raced as though I had actually just run through the Academy.

*So I'm not in the machine.*

I was simultaneously relieved and disappointed at this realization. It meant that when we logged into the dreamscape tonight, I would not be a prisoner to the Somnium Medicus. Yet I still longed to try the machine. It worried me that that longing now pervaded my thoughts in the waking world.

*"Why don't you ask him?"*

M. Dumont's words played over and over in my mind until I sat up and got dressed. As an after thought, I glanced at the clock and saw that it was still quite early in the morning. I left my room anyway, but instead of going to Vincent, I went for a walk. It was a mild, somber morning, which filled me with an isolated, hopeless feeling, as though the dream had not ended and I was the only one who remained at the Academy.

I wondered about the dreams: why lately, they were so ridden with loneliness? Why the shadows were sometimes present, but often missing?

*"Why don't you ask him?"*

I walked a bit further before turning around and walking briskly back to campus. As I passed through the halls, I heard the stirring of people getting ready for the day. I went straight to Vincent's room and knocked twice, then put my ear to the door to listen. When I heard nothing, I knocked again.

"Did you need something?" Vincent said, coming up beside me and making me jump. His already dark hair, now wet, looked black as night. A blue towel was slung across his shoulders.

"Uh...I need to talk to you," I told him.

He opened his door and motioned me inside. "It's early. So you really *did* miss me," he said, smiling a bit mischievously.

He hung up his towel on the hook by the door and put his shower stuff away.

Too preoccupied to banter at that moment, I ignored his comment. "I had a dream. You were there...well, it turned out not to be you. It was Abel Dumont. He told me to ask you about the Somnium Medicus. He said you understand what it is..." I stopped when I saw Vincent's expression. He looked angry.

"He's in your head. I knew it was a mistake to let the shadows take you."

"Vincent...is he right? Do you know why the machine was really created?" I pressed.

"How are you even dreaming this stuff? You're not logged in to the program, so how is he talking to you? I don't get it." He paced as he spoke.

"Vincent! Why won't you give me a straight answer?"

Vincent stopped pacing and stared at me. "I don't *know!*" he exclaimed, emphatically. "I don't know why the hell you're having these whacked out dreams and nothing I do seems to fix it!"

We looked at each other in silence for a long moment, as I tried to construct something appropriate to say. Vincent was the first to look away.

"I have to change," he told me. "I have class in a few minutes."

I hesitated, until Vincent ripped his shirt off in front of me and began to get dressed anyway. I hastened to the door and left without a word.

It was unsettling to see Vincent like that, but what bothered me most was that I didn't believe him. In fact, I was convinced he was lying to me; that he did know the true nature of the machine and just refused to tell me. He had merely used an outburst as a means of distracting me from the question at hand. He couldn't be trusted.

*"Why don't you ask him?"*

Abel Dumont's words haunted me that day. I counted the hours until I could log into the program again and find the Somnium Medicus. As time slipped by, it stole my resolve *not* to sit in the machine. I would get away from Vincent. I would find out the secret of the machine for myself.

"Elena? Where are you?" Alex laughed. "You're holding up the line."

"Sorry," I said, moving forward with my lunch tray. I still hadn't put anything on it, so I grabbed a wrapped sandwich and iced tea.

"Let's sit over there," Alex suggested, nodding to a table in the corner.

I followed him, without even thinking. Evan walked next to me glancing at me, concerned.

"What?" I asked. I think my voice sounded rude.

"Nothing. You ok?" Evan ventured.

"Yeah."

We took our seats and I pulled out my phone, placing it on the table beside my tray. Then I unwrapped my sandwich rather mechanically and unscrewed my iced tea.

Alex and Evan sat across from me, watching as I prepared my food for eating, yet didn't touch it. I scrolled through my phone instead.

"Ah, I get it," Alex said, confidently. "You got into a fight with the tech nerd."

"What?" I looked up, confused.

"You're in another world, not eating — at least, not according to your usual standards — and you're waiting for him to text you," Alex concluded.

"Someone should give you the 'observant medal,'" I grumbled, taking a swig of my iced tea.

"Well then, what is it? You're being weird," Alex shot back.

"Wait, are you and that tech guy together?" Evan asked, rather innocently.

Alex rolled his eyes. "Where have *you* been?"

"We're not a '*together*,'" I corrected.

"Even worse. You're pining for him then." Alex laughed.

Evan's face fell. He began to eat his lunch, I guessed to hide his disappointment.

Alex's eyes moved above my head as he watched someone from behind me. "Well, must be your lucky day," he said, lifting an eyebrow.

I didn't even have time to respond. Vincent came up behind me. "Are you going to eat that?" he asked, nodding to my sandwich. He completely ignored Evan and Alex.

"No," I replied.

"Let's go. I want to talk to you." He turned and started walking back out of the cafeteria.

"Trouble in paradise? He's intense, huh?" Alex grinned.

"Shut up Alex." I stood up and left, leaving my lunch tray for the guys to tend to.

Vincent walked a few paces ahead of me. I followed him as he led me down various flights of stairs, into the basement of the research center. Though there were some people around, no one questioned us about where we were going. Vincent stopped just outside the sub-basement.

"Are we going to keep doing this?" he asked.

"What?"

He scratched his head and looked away, uncomfortably. "I can't tell...I mean, I don't know what you're thinking. I only know when we're in the program. But obviously, we can't always be in there."

I shook my head. "I don't know what you're talking about."

Vincent ran a hand through his hair and sighed. "Yeah, ok." He swiped his keycard through the door and opened it, leading me into the basement below. Then He moved to the machine and yanked the cover off.

Unconsciously, I moved toward it.

"Have a seat," Vincent offered.

I gauged his expression, warily.

He shrugged. "It's what you want, right? It's what Abel Dumont is telling you to do. So do it."

I gazed at the machine with newfound awe. My hand moved forward to touch the cold metal.

"Sit in the machine," he said again.

I expected it to be Abel Dumont who spoke, but when I looked again, I saw Vincent watching me intently. His face, darkened by the dim light, was difficult to read.

I sat in the machine. Vincent brought the helmet down until it covered my head, encasing me in darkness.

It was comforting.

Neither of us spoke for a time. To be honest, I thought Vincent had left me there, alone in the basement. I thought perhaps I was still dreaming and the machine would turn on and do…whatever it was it really did: heal dreams, prolong life, unlock the secret to the universe – something.

The minutes ticked by and nothing happened. Then the darkness was taken from me as Vincent removed the helmet.

"Did you get your fill?" he asked. His eyes were sincere as he added, "If you end up in the machine, I'll come find you. It's a nightmare Elena. You think it's going to save everyone and reveal the true nature of the Dreamscape Program, but it doesn't give without taking." He swallowed. "I'm still not dreaming. Yeah, I do get it: I feel…different now. I think the machine does give something, because I haven't had a migraine in a while. Maybe it is longer life, I don't know yet, but I'm not dreaming. I don't know if I'll ever get that back. It scares the hell out of me." He stopped talking then and turned away, so I couldn't see his face.

"Vincent…I have to know. He says everyone will die if I don't have my turn."

Vincent was quiet.

"I have to *know*," I repeated.

"He's using you. I don't know what he wants exactly, but you're part of it for some reason. You can't believe him."

As I listened to Vincent speak I felt as though it were M. Dumont talking – only he was referring to Vincent. I was confused.

"We should probably go to class," Vincent said. He held out his hand and helped me up from the machine. He didn't let go of my hand until he had brought me out of the sub-basement.

Vincent walked me to my class. His demeanor had already morphed into its icy façade, masking the emotion he'd just displayed. I understood now. As with any armor, Vincent's icy exterior protected him from the onslaught of human judgment, ironically, extracting judgment of a different kind from those who didn't understand him. He was suffering. In my self-absorbed quest to uncover the mystery of my dreams, I had ignored his struggle.

It was too easy to pretend none of that existed.

That never-ending day did at last wane. Luke sought me out before it was time to meet in the lab. He came to my room.

"How are you?" he asked. "Any crazy dreams?" He smiled good-humoredly.

"Something's wrong with me," I answered. "I don't feel *anything*. All I can think about is the Somnium Medicus, and the program. I'm obsessed. I think I hurt Vincent too."

Luke leaned against my desk and crossed his arms, looking down at the floor. "Vincent has feelings for you. It probably doesn't take much for him to feel hurt by something you say." He looked up at me. "He's logging in with you tonight though, so I think that issue will fix itself."

"What do you mean by that?"

Luke laughed a bit oddly. "We don't always know ourselves Elena. He'll be able to hear your thoughts." Luke's expression was embarrassed. "I felt a bit foolish in your dreamscape, to be honest."

His words, though imprecise, hung acutely in the air, impressing me with meaning. Luke was too considerate to say it outright, but I knew what he was implying.

"As for your obsession…what you've experienced these last couple of months has been invasive. I felt that as well. You feel helpless, as though you've been dragged through someone else's story. You think the only ending is the one with you in the machine. I don't know Elena." Luke shook his head. "Stories can have alternate endings."

"What am I supposed to do? Abel Dumont is in my dreams now. He's like, part of my thoughts or something." I sat on the edge of my bed and leaned forward, elbows resting on my knees.

"I think we'll find our answer soon. Just don't mix up your friends with your enemies. Vincent is trying to help you. He's just not good at expressing his thoughts – or emotions."

"He's still not dreaming," I blurted. "That's *my* fault. I let the shadow monster take him. He might never get his dreams back. I have to sit in the machine too."

"So, what? You're going to punish yourself to make it even? That's not logical," Luke countered.

"None of it is logical," I mumbled. "It's just what has to happen."

Luke sighed. "It's probably not worth arguing over. I'll be on the monitor tonight, so I'll keep an eye on you guys. If anything happens, I'll pull you out."

"Thanks Luke. I don't think we would have gotten this far without you."

"I don't know about that. Make sure you save some of that gratitude for Vincent. He's the one with all the ideas."

In the lab that evening, Vincent explained what changes he had made to the weapons mod. "I augmented our weapons with additional abilities. Since we were unable to beat that monster in the basement before, this time, we'll have the ability to utilize other kinds of attacks that affect defense and armor"—

"Wait a sec. What you're describing sounds an awful lot like casting magic in a role-playing game," I interrupted.

"That's exactly what it will be like," he replied, coolly.

Vincent was different when Luke was around. It didn't take much effort on my part to notice how visibly rigid Vincent became whenever we worked with Luke on our hack plan.

"How will we know how to use it?" I asked.

"Not sure yet. You need your weapon in your hand though. I don't know how it will affect our stamina or speed either. Guess we'll find out."

Luke's expression was a little lost as Vincent and I went back and forth about the changes. He wasn't a gamer, after all.

Before we logged in, Luke came over to me and said quietly, "I'm sorry I won't be the one going in with you again. I enjoyed sharing the dream with you." He smiled, meeting my eyes with a meaningful look as he did.

I smiled back. "I'm glad you're here Luke."

Vincent walked briskly by and sat in the chair next to me. His eyes flicked between me and Luke. "Ready?" he asked me.

I nodded.

"The data didn't save when we went down into the basement last time. We'll have to start over," Vincent said. His eyes watched Luke move back to the monitor, then they rested on me. "Elena," he said quietly. "Stay with me, ok?"

"Ok," I agreed.

"Let's get that thing in the basement."

# CHAPTER 17

"Vincent?"

"I'm here," he replied, coming out of the shadows.

"This is the original dream."

Vincent nodded. "We're back where we started. We should hurry. The shadows will be coming for us."

Vincent had placed us close to the basement in the original dreamscape. We could hear the shadows rustle in the corners of the mansion, but we didn't wait for them to appear. We rushed through the dreamscape to the basement, and headed straight for the stairwell.

I felt no fear. I felt nothing, but I thought of the machine. I tried to hide my desire to find it, knowing Vincent would be aware of my feelings.

"You're not afraid," he remarked, once we'd made our way to the stairwell.

"No," I said.

"That worries me, to be honest. A little fear would be good…"

I didn't reply.

Not far ahead, a small, familiar figure lurked at the top of the stairwell.

"Vincent." I pulled his arm and whispered, "The creature is back."

Vincent drew his swords.

"Wait," I said.

We stood still and watched as the small figure crawled toward us, reaching out in desperation.

"What's wrong with it?" Vincent asked.

It screamed in pain, opening its mouth wide, and revealing a black, empty hole.

"The faces are gone," I noted. "Something happened."

I stepped forward until the creature was right at my feet. I knelt to look in its eyes.

It lifted its head and looked at me with hungry longing, yet I still felt nothing. Then the small figure sighed heavily and fell in a heap on the floor. It lay motionless.

"That was a bit...anticlimactic," Vincent commented.

"Let's go," I said.

Vincent hesitated. "You sure you're ok? You're moving so quickly."

"We don't have time to waste."

Vincent's eyes followed me as I approached the stairwell.

"Are you coming?" I asked.

"Why is the dreamscape different now? It should be the same one"– He stopped and looked at me surprised, but his expression quickly melted and was replaced with a hard-set look.

*He can hear my thoughts.*

"You're different too," he said. Then he moved ahead and proceeded to descend the stairwell.

It took effort to keep my thoughts focused on the task at hand. For the first time, it was inconvenient that Vincent knew what I was thinking. My mind was extremely preoccupied and I still didn't *feel* anything. It was unsettling. I could see it affected Vincent more than he let on.

Before long, we had passed through the foul-smelling muck and down the ancient hatch, further into the abyss of the dreamscape. Though we made the same progress as the last time we logged in together, it felt much different, as though we were watching a re-run. There was no element of suspense; we knew what would happen.

"What if it turns out the same way?" I said. "You might get taken again."

Vincent didn't reply at first. Then he said, "You sort of want that to happen though."

I couldn't think of anything to say. He was right.

We didn't speak again for some time.

"I can hear it," Vincent said quietly, as we came to the monster's lair. "Remember, we can use other abilities this time. Your weapons should be more effective."

"Sort of like we leveled up, huh?" I said, with a short laugh.

"Yeah. Let's watch each other's backs."

We plummeted further into darkness and began a fierce attack on the large, hulking shape residing in that place. Everything happened as it had before, except we cut down the shadows with greater force. Vincent's enhancements to our weapons caused them to glow in the darkness.

We rushed around the great monster and cut at its legs. Vincent leaped atop its head and drove his weapons down with such violence, the creature's head smashed to the ground. With one final shudder, the black beast cast Vincent off, so that he landed hard several meters away. Then the giant shadow lay still.

"You alright?" I asked, racing to where he lay.

He got up, slowly. "Sure. Let's move forward."

We made our way slowly to the far end of the dungeon, until we came upon an aged, wooden door. Written across the top were the words *Les Cent Ans de L'Enfant – Ésaïe 65:20.*

We looked at each other.

"Ready?" Vincent asked.

I reached my hand to the door and pulled on the bronze handle. It opened more easily than I expected it to. Beyond, we could see only white; glaring, painful white.

Once we passed through, we were met with a merciless wind. Vincent had grasped my hand as we crossed the threshold, yet now I feared we would be separated in the violence of the blinding storm.

"Vincent!"

"Hold on! Don't let go Elena!"

It was as though an unseen power had determined to separate us. One moment, I held on to Vincent's hand, and the next, he was ripped from me and carried off into the distant light. Then I fell hard on a solid surface and the wind vacated my lungs. I gasped while attempting to rid myself of the spinning, nauseating feeling which currently kept me in a state of paralysis.

At length, I pushed myself into a sitting position and studied my surroundings. Alas, I was still in the mansion. It was younger though, and everything was clean and in order.

I heard voices.

"She's ready for the next treatment. Prepare the machine."

I couldn't move in time. Two people appeared around the corner, but they didn't respond to my presence.

*They can't see me.*

Abel Dumont walked beside another individual in a lab coat. I gazed in awe at the man before me. M. Dumont was tall and young, yet his hair was almost white as snow and his eyes were pale marbles – hard and cold. He was incredibly good looking, despite his harsh demeanor, and spoke with a strong French accent.

"Watch the dosage. Last time it was difficult to wake her," he said to the person in the lab coat.

I watched them disappear again around the corner, then released the breath I held in suspense of being noticed. I stood to my feet and followed the pair, absorbing my surroundings as I did. I was indeed in the original mansion. It looked exactly as I pictured it would – everything ornately decorated with precision. Everything perfect.

I could still hear M. Dumont and his companion speak in low tones, but I was too far to distinguish their words. I followed anyway, passing with wonder through a bygone era. Suddenly, feeling had returned and I felt a strong attachment to that place. I wanted to stay forever, part of the dream. I had forgotten the present-day Academy with its modern research labs and dilapidated west wing. I had forgotten Luke on the monitor in the lab as Vincent and I dreamed.

I had forgotten Vincent.

M. Dumont led us down a stairwell to a darker place, filled with machines and lab equipment. I passed more people in lab coats, working on obscure experiments and writing lab reports.

We went even further down until we were clearly in a basement hall. We passed rooms with closed doors. I watched M. Dumont's back as he walked, wishing he would notice me. I wanted to be one of his subjects too.

At the end of the corridor, we came upon a larger room which housed the Somnium Medicus. A little girl sat still in the machine, attended to by another person in a white lab coat.

"There she is. My little *ange*," M. Dumont said, accenting the last word in French. "Are you ready for pleasanter sleep?"

The little girl, brown eyes wide and afraid, nodded. She looked with wonder at the impressive figure of M. Dumont. I sensed her trust in him: she believed he could heal her dreams.

*"Elena. Where are you?"*

For a moment, I thought I heard a voice call to me. I was too intrigued by the current scene to pay it any mind, however.

M. Dumont moved around the small laboratory, speaking in low tones to technicians, placing a hand on their shoulder as he spoke. He was good with people.

"Now my little darling, it is time to sleep," M. Dumont said, soothingly as he came next to the little girl and helped fit the helmet on her head. "The nightmare is almost over. Do not fear."

I watched the little girl's body tense as someone placed a needle in her arm. Then she relaxed and was soon asleep.

M. Dumont stood up straight and spoke curtly, "No mistakes this time. The mother is beginning to worry." He turned and walked out of the room. I followed, feeling a bit out of place; I was still armed with a katana, though I could hardly recall why.

At some point, I stopped trailing M. Dumont and began to meander without purpose through the mansion. I passed dozens of closed doors, eventually making my way upward until I came to a place that resembled an attic. Even so, there were more doors. I was overcome with curiosity and opened a door to find a small, vacant room which contained nothing but a nightstand and wire-framed cot. Each successive room looked identical to the one I'd first opened, until finally, I came to the end of the attic corridor, to the last room.

My heart thumped, pumping blood so that the sound rushed in my ears.

*Someone's in this room.*

I sensed a presence beyond the door, and with that knowledge, fresh fear filled me. It rushed upward within me and created a choking sensation in my throat, as though I were drowning. Overwhelmed by the fear, it was difficult to move, yet my hand did at last turn the knob.

The door swung inward.

In that tiny attic room lay a small child on the wire-frame cot. His hair was even whiter than M. Dumont's and his face expressed troubled sleep. He opened his eyes and sat up slowly.

*"Why are you here?"* the child said.

Though he spoke to me, he did not look in my direction, but stared at the wall in front of him so that I could not fully see his face. His voice sounded unnatural.

*"How did you get through?"* he questioned.

I realized that this small child was the only person in the mansion who had addressed me directly, though he didn't seem to be able to see me.

"Where am I?" I asked.

The child replied, *"Somewhere you do not belong unless your dreams are haunted. They take our dreams away."* His voice dropped to a whisper. *"They take our life from us as well."*

"What does that mean? I thought the Somnium Medicus healed dreams and prolonged life."

The child shook his head, then stood to his feet and turned toward me. He didn't look young, despite his short stature. His face was drawn and worn, a dwelling place for tormented eyes. His skin seemed to sag on his bones and his hair was thin and white, like someone who has reached their end.

I stepped back.

*"I am the first, but not the last. They will fill these rooms with the dying. We will live eternally in dreams."*

It was a eulogy.

*"I am the first, but not the last. They will fill these rooms with the dying. We will live eternally in dreams."*

The child's voice grew louder and echoed through the mansion. He morphed as his eyes grew wide. He stood taller.

*"I am the first, but not the last. They will fill these rooms with the dying. We will live eternally in dreams!"*

I backed away until I was in the hall again. The child followed me, growing as he came toward me. His face had become a nightmare.

I turned and ran, hearing his footsteps behind me, and the eulogy, repeated over and over again. With each repetition, fear crashed into me, almost knocking me off balance. I ran for fear of my own life, flying through the mansion.

The walls rumbled. The shadows broke through, peeling back the remnants of the past and revealing the darkened Academy.

They came at me like a tumult, savagely grabbing and clawing for me. I swung my sword in panic, vaguely aware that I was heading to the research lab.

*"Elena!"*

*Vincent.*

He called to me. I ran toward the sound of his voice.

Then at once, I passed through the doors to the research lab and stood before the Somnium Medicus. Behind me, the shadows had ceased their pursuit. They didn't need to come after me any longer. I was where they wanted me to be.

*"You made it."*

Vincent appeared from behind the machine, relief written on his face. "I worried you would never get out. I figured you would come here."

"Vincent, I was in the past...I think. I saw the original mansion and Abel Dumont. He had a little girl in the machine." I frowned. "There was a boy in the attic. Something was wrong with him. He chased me out."

Vincent came toward me and put his arms around me. "You weren't supposed to see that."

"What?" I pushed away from him.

M. Dumont looked back at me. He shook his head. "You are so persistent. Just sit in the machine and you will understand."

"What's going on? Where's Vincent?"

He sighed. "You always ask the same questions. Don't you want to know what will happen to you when you sit in the machine? Don't you want to save everyone? They are going to die if you do not have your turn."

"You're lying. The machine doesn't heal dreams or give anything back. It just takes." I moved back, toward the door to the research lab.

"You still do not understand anything. You think these small, irregular pieces make a complete picture, but you do not *know*."

The machine called to me.

"Then tell me. Tell me why I'm having these dreams. Tell me what it means," I pleaded.

M. Dumont smiled rather appealingly. "I *will* tell you. Just sit in the machine. There's a good girl. My little *ange*."

His reassuring words were like balm on a wound. This is what I had wanted in the past; I wanted him to speak to me in this manner. He would take my nightmares and replace them with something good.

"There now. Come, just a little further." He held out his hands to me.

I had already moved toward him.

He took my hands and grasped them firmly in his own, then led me to the machine. I sat down and leaned back in the seat. M. Dumont fastened my arms and legs, smiling at me all the while, speaking soothing words as though I were that little girl from the past.

He brought the helmet down on my head.

*"Elena!"*

A very brief wave of fear spiked through my body as I registered what was happening. It was quickly replaced with apathy and relief. I wouldn't have to run from the shadows any longer. I would find the truth.

M. Dumont spoke to me one last time, "There now. You will soon understand. Sleep my dear Elena."

# CHAPTER 18

My face was wet. I blinked to clear my vision and gazed up at the lab lights. More tears fell from my eyes.

"Elena." Luke came toward me, speaking quietly. "How are you feeling?"

I didn't answer right away. I still felt as if my body were tied to the machine and I still heard Abel Dumont's voice, assuring me I would soon know the truth. I wanted to go back.

I looked over at Vincent, who lay motionless beside me. Luke followed my gaze. "He should rouse soon."

"We were separated for the last half of the dream," I told him.

"Really? I wonder why he didn't wake up?" Luke said, thoughtfully. He moved back to the monitor to check on Vincent's readings. "Everything looks ok..."

Vincent stirred. "Elena," he said, eyes still closed.

"I'm here," I replied.

Vincent opened his eyes and sat up, removing the halo from his head. "Where were you? I kept seeing glimpses of you and I tried calling your name."

"I heard you. I just couldn't answer."

Vincent looked at me a bit skeptically.

We left the lab and met in Vincent's room to discuss the hack in. "We killed the monster in the basement," I began. "Well, Vincent did.

There was a door at the end of the dungeon with the French words from the book of Isaiah written on the door frame." Luke frowned as I spoke. "When we passed through the door, there was nothing but white light and a very strong wind. We tried to stay together." I paused to look over at Vincent. He was staring at the floor. "We were pulled apart. I ended up in the mansion again, but a younger version of it." I proceeded to explain my adventure in the past – or what I believed to be the past. Luke listened intently. Vincent did at some point look at me, but I couldn't tell what he was thinking.

"I ended up back in the mansion with the shadows," I concluded. I didn't mention M. Dumont or the machine.

"So you think you were watching something that already happened at one time?" Luke asked.

I nodded. "At first, yes. But that boy in the attic...that was something else."

We were quiet for a moment. Then Vincent spoke. "I saw something different." Luke and I fixed our attention on Vincent. He shifted in his seat. "I'm not sure, but it may have been that woman from the case studies. Helen – something."

"Helen Locke," I said.

Vincent continued. "She was being treating in the Somnium Medicus. That Dumont guy was there too. I didn't really hear much of anything though. I was trying to find Elena. I searched all over the mansion, and sometimes, I would catch a quick glimpse of you, but then you would vanish."

Luke spoke up. "Who do you think that boy in the attic is?"

"He said he was 'the first, but not the last.'" I shook my head. "I'm not sure what he was referring to."

"I just don't understand how you could be viewing the past," Luke said. He shook his head in disbelief. "This all keeps getting weirder."

"Maybe we need to spend some time analyzing what we know so far," I suggested. "It might help us figure out what to do next."

Luke stood up. "That's fine. I think I'll sleep on it though, if you don't mind." He said good night and left us.

Vincent stared at me.

"What?" I asked.

"You want to tell the whole story now?" His eyes expressed what he didn't say.

I sighed and leaned back on the bed, staring up at the ceiling.

"Dumont got me to sit in the machine," I confessed.

Vincent sighed almost inaudibly. "Thought so. You seemed to want me to get out of your way in the dreamscape. I knew you would end up in the machine."

"The shadows chased me there. I couldn't get away," I offered, weakly.

Vincent didn't reply. Instead, he got up from his desk and sat on the edge of the bed. He leaned back on his elbows. "We don't have to keep doing this, you know. I mean what's the point now? Your dreams will be gone. Maybe we should focus more on getting things back to normal."

I sat up and hugged my knees. "Vincent"–

He cut me off. "Yeah, I know. You're not going to stop until you get it all figured out." He laughed and shook his head. "You're the weirdest lab partner I ever had."

I smiled and nudged him with my foot. "Guess we deserve each other then."

"Nah, I think of the two of us, you got me beat. I only have the appearance of being strange. But you – with your freaky dreams and crush on a dead French scientist"–

It was my turn to interrupt. "Shut up!" I laughed. I whipped the pillow out from behind me to smack him.

Vincent caught it before it connected with his face. "Starting that again, huh?" His eyes gleamed good naturedly. "I thought we already established that I'm better at this." He yanked the pillow toward him, pulling me with it. I let go before I fell on top of him.

Instead of retaliating, Vincent swung the pillow around behind his head and leaned back on the bed. "I feel merciful tonight. And I'm too tired anyway." He yawned. It wasn't long before he had completely fallen asleep. I was actually surprised how quickly he dropped off, especially since half of his body was hanging off the bed.

I got up and leaned over him. "Vincent," I whispered, tapping his shoulder.

"Hmm?" He raised his eyebrows, but kept his eyes shut.

"Why don't you get in bed." I shook him gently.

Vincent responded by sluggishly pulling himself fully onto the bed. I put the pillow back in place and he got under the covers. Before I knew it, he was out again.

I stood, motionless for a time, watching Vincent's body rise and fall rhythmically, aware that he would wander through darkness instead of dreams. A thought struck me then: perhaps Vincent's dreams were gone because we didn't allow him to complete the process in the Somnium Medicus. It was possible that given enough time, the machine was more effective. Perhaps we hadn't found all the research data; Abel Dumont might have been successful in his research after all.

It was quite late when I left Vincent's room. Though I should have been exhausted from using the Dreamscape Program, I was oddly invigorated and awake. I went to Luke's room and knocked on the door.

"Come in," I heard him say.

He sat in bed reading. I shut the door behind me and took a seat on the end of his bed.

Luke put his book down. "I had a feeling you wouldn't go straight to bed. You didn't tell us everything that happened in your dreamscape, did you?"

I sighed. "Vincent figured that out as well."

Luke was nodding. "You sat in the machine."

"Yes. And I've been thinking…what if Vincent's dreams are gone because we didn't let him stay in the machine long enough? I want to log in again and see what happens in the machine. I want to see the process through to the end."

Luke's face expressed obvious disapproval. "I don't think that's a good idea."

"I thought you would say that. But what if there's more to Abel Dumont's research? It's possible he was successful after all and we just haven't found the data yet."

"If he was successful, we would know about it. More than likely his research was dangerous and that's why it's been 'swept under the rug' so to speak," Luke countered.

*He's probably right.*

"Let's look again," I suggested. "You said before we might find more in the library to help us. Let's go back and have a look."

Luke stared at me for a moment, as if trying to determine if I were serious. "Now?" he asked.

I nodded. "I won't be able to sleep."

He hesitated again. "Ok. I'll go with you. Is Vincent coming?"

"He's asleep already." I stood up. "I'll wait for you in the hall." I left the room so Luke could change.

A few weeks ago, I would have been too terrified to stand alone in the dark halls at night. I used to see the shadows emerge from the darkness, even when I wasn't dreaming. But now, fear had become commonplace and I was more afraid of failing to uncover the truth.

Luke's door opened and he stepped out of his room. "Let's go."

As we walked I said quietly, "In my dreamscape, there was a basement in the west wing. That's where M. Dumont conducted research."

"You want to look for it?" Luke guessed.

"We might as well, while we're at it."

"You must have been big on mystery novels as a kid," he surmised.

"I was more of a sci-fi reader, actually, although I did go through an Agatha Christie phase."

We didn't speak again until we made it to the west wing. I had an uncanny feeling that once we walked through the doors, we would step into the past again and see things as they used to be.

It was just a feeling.

"Looks like they've done more since our last visit," Luke observed.

Large, plastic, white sheets hung from the ceiling, creating a painfully eerie atmosphere in the abandoned wing. The construction crew had started demolition on some of the rooms, but the change in the place bothered me. It suddenly felt as though time were running out. We needed to solve the puzzle soon.

"Do you want to go to the library first?" Luke asked.

"Yeah. Let's start there."

As we passed each room, I noticed one of the white sheets billow slightly.

"Maybe someone left the window open," Luke said.

The movement created by the plastic sheet called to me, just as the small creature had at the top of the basement stairwell.

I stepped into the room and felt a damp draft seep from behind the plastic sheet. I pulled it aside. The stairwell it revealed yawned before us unendingly, breathing cold breath on my face.

I gasped. "Luke..."

He had been by my side all along. "Yeah. You were right," he said slowly.

"This is the place from my dream. Abel Dumont conducted research here. I wonder why it was sealed up?"

"It doesn't look very safe...the stairs are crumbling," Luke cautioned.

"We have to go down. I need to see."

He took hold of my arm. "I don't want you to get hurt."

"Luke, I'll be fine." I gently freed myself of his hold and started gingerly down the decaying stairwell. It wasn't exactly like the one in my dream, yet images from my nightmares danced behind my eyes and invoked the dormant fear that hadn't fully departed after all. The stairwell sighed wearily, blowing more damp, musty air on my face and filling my nostrils with the smell of decrepitude.

Deeper we went, into the belly of the mansion, seeking the answer to the sleeping mystery of Abel Dumont's past. At one point, the stairs had almost entirely collapsed, forcing us to move along the stone walls. But the stairwell was shallow, so I didn't fear falling as much as I feared what would meet us below. The creature from my nightmares had revived itself in my memory, and opened its mouth to absorb me into that pit of death. I willingly stepped inside.

We did at last reach the bottom of the stairs and stepped over a pile of rubble to continue further down the passageway.

"This really isn't safe," Luke warned. "The ceiling seems to be collapsing."

"Just a bit further. I know where it leads."

We wove down the tunnel and passed through what was once M. Dumont's laboratory. I could almost see the ghosts of the people who'd once worked there, wandering the place in their white lab coats.

Then finally, we came upon the large door which lead to the testing room where I'd seen Abel Dumont and the little girl.

"Be very careful Elena," Luke whispered, as I pulled open the door. It moaned on rusty hinges and moved begrudgingly, as if unwilling to allow us to see what lay beyond.

We pointed our lights inside the small room and stood aghast.

"There's another machine?" I said in shock.

It was much more worn and rusted than the one we'd found in the sub-basement of the research wing. The leather padding on the seat and arms of the chair had been chewed by rodents and the metal was a brownish color, instead of the bronze we were used to. Various tubes and metal arms stuck out from atop the machine, creating the appearance of some misshapen, metal monster. Except for a few tables and chairs, the rest of the room had been emptied of its contents, leaving the machine to corrode in solitude.

"Why two machines?" I said aloud.

"Maybe Dumont needed more than one to conduct his research?" Luke ventured.

"No. I think they were created for separate purposes."

"Why do you think that?"

I shook my head. "I just do. This might have been the machine M. Dumont was afraid to use...he sealed it up down here and made a different one."

"It's all speculation. Why don't we get out of here and search the library again?" Luke proposed.

"They *know* about it, Luke. The faculty here. They *have* to. What's going on?"

"Elena, please. Let's get out of this place. It's not safe." Luke touched my shoulder.

I allowed him to lead me out of the room, without protesting further. Then we made our way to the library. Luke picked the lock and we set out to explore the room.

As I once again entered that place from the past, I found myself inexplicably drawn to the portrait of Abel Dumont. It wasn't mere curiosity any longer — I *knew* the man. I had walked through and experienced a life lived long ago, which forged a connection between us. Even then, gazing at his portrait, I felt as though he called to me: *"Return to the machine."*

"Elena, come have a look at this," Luke said.

I met him at the other side of the room. He had managed to open one of the locked drawers in the desk and was perusing an old manuscript, not unlike the one we'd originally found.

"It's kind of scary how easily you pick locks," I remarked.

Luke was too fixated on the text before him to respond. "This is it. Abel Dumont's personal memoir."

"How can you tell?"

"It's written like a journal. This isn't merely research data — it's a personal account of his experiences."

I glanced down at the French text, written in small, precise script.

"I don't know if we can take this one. Someone might notice," Luke said, thoughtfully.

"This room doesn't seem to be in much use though," I argued.

Luke considered for a moment, but it didn't take much convincing. "We might learn something important," he reasoned.

It was quite late by the time we returned to Luke's room.

"You should get some rest," he said to me.

I sighed. "I really don't feel like sleeping."

"But I do. I have a lot going on tomorrow."

I felt guilty for having kept Luke up half the night. "Oh, right. I'm sorry Luke. I'll get out of your way."

"You're never 'in my way.' In fact, I wish you'd hang around more. I guess it pays to be a tech nerd."

I understood what he was referring to, naturally, but I pretended his meaning was lost on me.

Truthfully, I knew it would be impossible now for me to become more involved with Luke, outside of a friendship and research partnership. It had been some time since I had thought of him more as a brother than anything else. It was selfish, but I was relieved that Luke seemed to understand. As much as I had made light of my attachment to Vincent up to that point, it was in fact, very real.

Sleep completely evaded me that night. I obsessed over what would happen when I next logged into the program, and found myself seated in the Somnium Medicus. I also wondered which machine Dumont used in the dreamscape — and what the purpose of each had been.

At close to 6:00 am there was a knock on my door, interrupting my stream of thought. I pulled myself up and opened it to find Vincent standing in my doorway.

"Morning," he said. His eyes flicked across my face. "You didn't sleep."

"No."

"Can come I in?"

I stepped aside and he brushed past me. Then he leaned against my desk and shoved his hands in his pockets.

I closed the door and sat back on my bed. "What is it?"

There was a brief pause before he answered, "I had a dream."

My pulse quickened and I sat up straighter. "What was it about?"

His eyes hesitantly met mine. "You." Vincent sighed. "I was in this long hallway with doors on either side. They were shut at first, but then one of them opened at the very end of the hall and you stepped out of the room. You looked weird though – like you were old, but not wrinkled. It's hard to explain. Anyway, you started chanting something. Then the other doors opened and a bunch of old looking people stepped out and chanted with you." He paused and swallowed. "Then the dream changed and you were strapped into the machine in the lab. There was no one else around – even that Dumont guy wasn't there. I went up to you and tried to wake you, but you were lifeless and cold. Then you grabbed my hand suddenly and your eyes opened wide – it scared the crap out of me. You said, 'We should have figured it out sooner.' You gripped my arm so hard, I thought you would break it. After that, the little creature from your dream jumped out of nowhere and landed on top of the machine. It smiled at me and then it opened its mouth and devoured you and the machine all at once. I woke up after that." Vincent gave a short laugh and shook his head. "I think you infected me with your weird dreams."

I considered the dream for a moment before saying, "The first part of the dream sounds like the attic I found with the small boy that turned out to be old. He was chanting something too. Remember I told you about that? He said: '*I am the first, but not the last. They will fill these rooms with the dying. We will live eternally in dreams*'" –

Vincent cut in, "Yeah, that's what you were saying in the dream – over and over."

I nodded. "I thought so. Listen Vincent, last night, Luke and I went back to the west wing to look through the library again." I stopped for a moment, to give him a chance to react, but his expression remained unchanged. "We found an opening in the wall leading to the original basement laboratory. There was *another* machine down there."

Vincent frowned. "The same kind of machine?"

"We're not certain if it served the same purpose, or did something else entirely."

"Two machines," Vincent wondered aloud.

"I want to log in tonight and see the process through in the machine."

Now Vincent's expression did change. "No. That's not happening."

"Vincent, the dream you had was *just* a dream. It doesn't really mean anything."

His face visibly showed frustration. "How can you – of all people – say something like that? You *know* it means something. All of this means something. I'm sick of watching you get dragged around that nightmare. I can't do it anymore Elena." He huffed and bowed his head, crossing his arms in opposition to my plan.

I got up and came toward him. Then, almost cautiously, unsure of his reaction in the real world, I slid my arms around his neck.

He didn't even hesitate. He'd already uncrossed his arms and wrapped them around my waist, squeezing me as though I might disappear if he didn't cling to me. His face brushed my cheek so that I felt his breath on my neck.

"Vincent...you worry too much," I whispered lightly in his ear.

Vincent didn't waste the opportunity. He pulled back slightly and then kissed me long and passionately. I could tell he had been waiting for it.

When we broke apart, Vincent's eyes met mine and he said, "You convinced me. I guess we'll do things your way."

I laughed. "I wasn't trying to manipulate you into doing what I wanted."

He scratched his head and smirked. "Yeah, but maybe if I do what you want, you'll follow up with something else."

I pushed him away and laughed again. "Wow. Way to be subtle Miller."

186

Vincent grinned. "It's part of my charm, and it seems to be working."

I couldn't argue there.

"I should get ready for class," I said.

"Yeah. I'll see you later then." He gave me a last, appeased look as he left.

It wasn't my plan to fall for Vincent, but reflecting on what we'd experienced together, it made a lot of sense. The attraction had gradually grown over the past few weeks, to the point that it was no longer a question in my mind.

I knew for certain I cared deeply for him.

Though our attachment had formed in an unusual way — arguably with the help of the Dreamscape Program — it was more real than anything I'd ever known.

After showering, I met Sophie in the cafeteria. I hadn't spoken to her much since Luke became involved in my hack plans with Vincent, but she had been texting me regularly, wanting to know how I was doing and so forth.

We found a secluded table so we could talk more freely.

"I have something to tell you," I began, as I took a sip of coffee.

Sophie's dark eyes looked expectant. "Let me guess: you've cracked the code to the mansion and there's a secret treasure buried somewhere on campus? I'll bet the dreams are the key." She laughed.

*Not too far off.*

"It's not about the dreams," I said, smiling. "It's about Vincent."

Now I really had Sophie's attention. She sure loved gossip.

"Well..." I shrugged. "Let's just say, I can confirm a mutual interest."

*"Mutual?"* She appeared genuinely surprised. "When did this happen?"

"Don't look so shocked," I said, good naturedly. "It wasn't too difficult to predict."

"I guess not, but I thought you and Luke...it is kind of surprising that you chose Vincent over Luke after all," she admitted.

If I didn't know Sophie like I did, I might have been a little offended. It didn't matter. In fact, I sort of enjoyed the response my news generated.

"So, you object to my choice?" I raised an eyebrow and smiled, knowing Sophie would never raise any serious objections after the time Vincent had invested in helping me with my dream problem.

Sophie rolled her eyes. "Of course not. I don't know the guy, but from your description, he doesn't quite fit in with what we heard from Rachel and Julie."

I reflected on the first time I'd heard anything about Vincent Miller. According to Julie's report, he was *one of the tech nerds...an anti-social geek who needs a shower and a hair-cut. Probably a pervert too.* Only about half of that was true.

"They got some of it right," I permitted.

Sophie looked like she wanted to say something else. She played with her juice glass, turning it thoughtfully. "Whatever happened with that manuscript Luke found?"

I was quiet, unsure how much to divulge.

"Come on Elena. You're not telling me what's *really* going on. I've tried to be patient, but I'll be honest, I feel left out."

I sighed. "There's a lot. I can't tell you now though...it will take time. Can you give me until the weekend?"

Sophie contemplated, then slowly nodded. "Yeah. I can wait until then."

All that day, I replayed the details of what had recently transpired, and as the time drew near to log back into the program and face the unknown in the Somnium Medicus, I was more worried than I thought I would be. After the discovery of the second machine in the basement of the west wing, fear had resumed its prominent place in my mind. It was a stealthy, dark fear that permeated the wall of defense I had raised against the nightmares. It sought those small cracks of doubt and seeped into my inner thoughts. I feared that darkness had already found a perpetual place within me and I would carry the nightmares forever.

In the lab that evening, Vincent was very in tune with my mood.

"You're worried, aren't you," he said, as Luke worked on the computer terminal.

I breathed out deliberately. "Yeah, I guess I am."

"I'm going to find you. I'll get you out of the machine," he assured me.

There was new warmth in his tone as his eyes met mine. He didn't try to touch me though. I guessed because Luke was present.

"Let's run through the plan again," Luke said, joining us where we stood.

"I'm going to log in to see what happens when I'm in the machine," I confirmed.

"I'll find Elena and get her out of the machine," Vincent added. "If I'm unsuccessful, it's your turn," he said to Luke.

Luke nodded, in agreement, but his face expressed displeasure.

"What's wrong?" I asked him.

"I did some translating today. I should probably tell you guys before you log in, Dumont's personal journal contains some disturbing information."

"Anything about the two machines?" I questioned.

"No. But he had plenty of nightmares himself. He didn't try to use the machine initially, because he wanted to experiment on others first. It's kind of twisted actually. He was tormented by a rather unusual fear, but I couldn't properly translate the word into English. It's a very old, Germanic word for 'darkness.'" Luke shook his head. "Just be careful."

Vincent frowned. "So Dumont had nightmares, but he wasn't able to fix his own problem?"

"I don't know. I didn't read that far yet," Luke replied.

"It's not really too surprising though, right? I mean, I started researching more and trying to find a solution when the nightmares kicked in. Isn't that how people seek solutions?" I said.

Luke was quiet.

"Let's log in," Vincent said to me.

We were all rather solemn as we resumed our positions, as though the unnamed darkness had already settled over us. But it was much too late to stop. The second machine we had found in the basement and Abel Dumont's own memoir invited further inquiry into the true meaning of my recurring nightmares.

Slipping into the Dreamscape Program was like second nature that time. I practically blinked and was somewhere else – not in the machine, however. A gentle breeze and light rain confirmed I was outdoors, and a glance around brought the landscape into focus.

I was on a beach.

The sky was patched with clouds, but a pillar of sunshine broke through not far away. The waves were gentle, lapping the shore almost timidly.

I was alone.

*This is the beach I brought Vincent to last time.*

I reached behind me instinctively to find that my katana was missing.

Perhaps I didn't need it here anyway.

# CHAPTER 19

The emptiness on the beach mirrored my emotional state. In fact, it didn't take long for me to suspect that the beach itself *was* my emotional state. It was the place I always tried to find in my dreams, and when I did, I felt profound satisfaction.

As if I had come home.

Now I see how significant a thing it was that I brought Vincent there, back when we first hacked into my dreamscape. It had been warm and sunny then – the perfect beach.

Not so now.

A gloom had settled, and the longer I stood in one place, the more I felt it. I moved forward, closer to the gentle waves, intending to dispel the melancholy air.

Then, barely audible above the soft breeze came the whisper of a child's voice: *"Stay away from the water."*

Was it my imagination, or did the sky darken at those words?

The breeze picked up, whipping a piece of hair across my face. The sunny patches disappeared.

Something moved in my peripheral vision. I looked out across the water and spotted a dark shadow below the surface. It was still quite far off, but appeared to be moving rapidly toward the shore.

*I'm dreaming.*

I reminded myself again and again that it was merely a dream. Nevertheless, fear stole my breath away as I stood helpless to defend myself from the unknown shadow beneath the water.

*An unknown fear.*

I had difficulty recalling why that sounded familiar to me. On that beach, only the present mattered, and presently, the dark shape fast approaching consumed my thoughts and threatened to steal any lingering calm my nerves possessed.

I stepped backward, slowly at first, then turned and ran with all my might inland, away from the sea.

I *heard* the thing behind me. It groaned and creaked laboriously. I looked over my shoulder to see it rise out of the ocean, dripping with dark water. It kept growing, an unknown shape, black and ugly. Then it loomed over me. I stopped and faced it, expecting it to crash down on me at any moment.

The shape unfolded what appeared to be beams and walls, stretching itself out longer and wider until a structure had literally been built around me.

It was the Academy.

I continued to watch the building settle itself, still wet from the ocean. It didn't come together quite the way it should, however. I noticed dark spots in places, as though it were unfinished – like it had been patched. The dimensions were off as well. Walls slanted unnaturally and the floor bent upward and down. It made me slightly dizzy to look at.

More than anything, I felt profoundly confused. The mansion itself seemed to have been brought to me, but I couldn't understand why.

The creaking and groaning continued and the dark patches swayed as the mansion attempted to maintain its form in this manner. I realized that the dark patches were the shadows, absorbed into the building to hold it together.

I moved forward, and as I did, everything moved with me. A few more steps continued this strange phenomenon and increased my frustration and fear. It was the kind of frustration dreams often produce when we don't arrive at the outcome we seek. I was dimly aware of this, but everything around me felt so *real*. Even more real than my waking life.

It seemed to take hours to get anywhere, yet at last, I moved through the mansion and found the lab with the Somnium Medicus.

Without hesitation, I sat in the machine, hoping to return to the mansion as it should be. But as I sat in the machine, it too came alive. The straps grabbed my arms and the helmet descended on my head, almost suffocating me as it did. The panic I felt then was more intense than anything I'd ever experienced as suddenly the room filled with water. Rapidly, the water swirled around my ankles and continued to creep upward until it reached my knees.

The machine would not let go.

I understood then that the mansion was still part of the ocean and was now collapsing around me. The machine had known. It wanted me to sit there. It gripped even tighter as the water reached my waist and flooded through the doors.

I was going to drown.

With the realization that death had come for me, my body felt limp with despair. Tears filled my eyes as I thought of all the things I had wanted to do and would never complete. I contemplated even the way I held other people at arm's length, unwillingly to let anyone get too close.

I thought about Vincent.

As the water level reached my neck, I suddenly panicked. I was going to drown. Despite my efforts, I was soon enveloped completely by the cold and horrifying dark waters. I can still recall the unbearable sensation of water in my lungs as the ocean stole my breath and held me prisoner.

No, not the ocean. The machine.

The Somnium Medicus was my tormentor as it forced me to experience the worst possible scenario I could contrive.

I suddenly blinked to find that I was in my own room at the Academy. No trace of the nightmare remained, in fact it was perfectly peaceful and quiet around me. The sun gently filtered through my window as I sat up in bed.

*I must still be dreaming.*

There was no way I could have escaped the Somnium Medicus. I should have drowned, yet here I was. Then again, it wasn't possible to actually die in a dream — or at least, it shouldn't be.

My door opened and Vincent stepped through. "I finally found you. Hurry, we need to get out of here." He came toward me and helped me out of the bed.

"No, this isn't right. Why aren't you taking me out of the machine? This isn't real." I shook my head and pulled my arm away from him.

"This *is* real, and Abel Dumont will be here any moment. We are in the *lab,* can't you tell?" His face expressed impatience as he tried to make me understand.

I still didn't believe him completely, but I was afraid of getting it wrong if I refused to comply.

It was difficult to stand. My limbs were heavy and everything took a great deal of effort.

"Hurry," he said, tugging my arm so I would move more quickly.

We started to leave the room, but when I passed the mirror the reflection that looked back at me was one of someone very old and decrepit. She was haggard and ugly.

"Look at that!" I exclaimed, pointing at the mirror.

Vincent didn't even stop to turn, he kept moving without me.

I stood, frozen at the sight of the ancient person looking back at me. We were too late after all. The machine had held me and aged me to the point of no return.

Then someone else came into the room.

"Do you understand yet?" Abel Dumont asked me. He casually sat on the edge of my bed and looked at me expectantly.

"I thought you said the machine would heal my dreams..." I faltered.

He laughed gently, then looked at me, almost pityingly. "It gets worse before it gets better. Often healing requires purging. Your body is ridding itself of the fears it has clung to for so very long. This part always interests me most." He got up and wandered to the window. "To observe the fear people keep bottled up inside them — it's such a rush." He turned to look at me. "You've certainly looked better. Just be patient. It is going to get a bit more intense."

"I already faced the worst of it...drowning," I told him.

He studied me for a moment. "You think *that* was the worst? No. It begins with the most docile fear and progresses from there. There is *much* worse ahead, my dear *ange.*"

"Please don't go," I pleaded. "I just want to understand it all. We've been trying to figure out"—

Abel Dumont held up a hand to stop me. "That is the trouble with Science, my dear. We always want to 'figure out,' but I have found that some things cannot ever be known for certain. They can be experienced perhaps, but not fully explained. You must be patient now. Let the machine do what it does."

"But we read your manuscript. The machine has a life of its own."

Dumont had already vanished and left me to myself once again.

It was maddening – to be so close to the answer only to have it disappear right in front of me. I could hardly stand it.

Another glance in the mirror restored my original visage; age had vanished with Abel Dumont. Perhaps the nightmare wasn't so bad after all.

I left my room and wandered through an empty Academy, utterly void of sound. A profound awareness of the absence of anyone else filled me then, and I had difficulty overcoming the loneliness it produced. It surprised me, to find that I could stand so little time completely alone. The same panic I'd experienced while drowning returned in full force, and threatened to overcome any remaining rational thought.

In the back of my mind, I was thoroughly ashamed of my weakness. How was it possible that I relied so fully on human companionship? Perhaps my attachment to Vincent was founded only on the fear of being alone. Such thoughts plagued me as I tried to leave the nightmare and move on to the next.

It was ironic: to be so anxious for a different kind of fear. Yet I was stuck, and found that this nightmare lasted much longer than the drowning had, and it felt as though I were drowning, over and over again.

Loneliness.

Maybe that's the worst fear anyone can have.

Forced to face ourselves with no distractions; but no – I wasn't afraid of facing myself. I was afraid of being wrong. Alone, there was no one to correct me if I strayed from the path of truth. I could think what I wanted, even if it was completely erroneous, and I would always be wrong.

I could go insane, and no one would help me come back.

It was like getting on a roller coaster that never ended, thinking that way. A thrill at first, maybe, but quickly tiresome and monotonous, soon replaced with the worry that the car would detach from the rails and toss you into death.

I don't know how much time I spent circling through the Academy and thinking I had gone insane. After a while, I believed I had always been there.

Alone.

"Elena, this way," Vincent said.

He had appeared at the end of the hall without any warning.

"I know it's not you Vincent. This is part of my nightmare."

"No. This is part of the mind game Dumont is playing. He wants you to think you're being healed in the machine. It's not really happening. He trapped you here so he could steal your dream energy," Vincent explained.

"Dream energy?"

Vincent nodded as he came toward me. "That's how it works, remember? It was in the manuscript. He harnesses the dream energy and stores it in the machine. Then the machine acts as the conduit to transfer that energy to him. Elena..." Vincent now stood directly in front of me. "Abel Dumont is still alive. He's been dreaming in the machine for decades now. This place must be feeding him." He looked around warily. "We have to get you out of here."

I wanted to go with him, though I still didn't believe it was really him.

*I don't know what to believe.*

We started walking toward the lab.

"Do you think Luke will wake us soon?" I asked. "I feel like it's been a long time we've been dreaming."

"Luke? Why would he wake us?"

"He's in the lab...he's supposed to get us out after a certain time..." I started to say.

Vincent was clearly confused. "No one else is in the lab. It's just you and me." He stopped walking and looked me in the eye. "Did you tell someone what we're doing?"

"What?"

"The hack in, did you tell someone about it?"

"Vincent...Luke's been involved for almost a week, remember?" I shook my head. "I knew it. This isn't really you." I rubbed my forehead and closed my eyes, expecting Vincent to be gone when I opened them again.

He was still standing next to me, gazing at me as though he couldn't understand what I was saying.

"Let's just keep moving. I'm afraid Dumont has already drained you of too much dream energy," Vincent said. He moved forward again.

I followed, warily, knowing this wasn't real. It couldn't possibly be.

"Why aren't you armed?" I asked him.

Vincent glanced at me over his shoulder. "Why should I be? It's just you here. You wanted me to pair with your dreamscape, remember?"

"No, that's not right. *You* wanted to pair with me. There should be shadows here...we should be armed." I shook my head again, trying to clear it. "You used a weapons mod so we could fight the shadows in the program."

Vincent laughed. "That sounds pretty cool, though I doubt it would work. The Dreamscape Program isn't a game."

*Are you sure?*

We continued to walk through the halls, heading toward the research lab.

"How do you know Abel Dumont is still alive?" I asked him.

He looked back – but it wasn't Vincent.

It was Luke.

"What?" he said.

I stopped and squeezed my eyes shut. "Stop. I just want it to stop."

"What's wrong Elena?" Luke asked.

"I don't know what's going on anymore. It's all so mixed up." I rubbed my head, which had begun to ache now from trying to keep my thoughts straight. "I'm ok. Of course it keeps changing. Nightmares do that," I said.

Luke was staring at me as though I'd lost my mind. "Nightmares? What is *that* supposed to mean?"

"What? You're kidding, right? Oh, never mind. It's not really you anyway."

Luke laughed awkwardly. "Are you feeling alright? Or is this just a joke? I'm not following."

I realized then that the Academy was occupied again. Students walked by and faculty made their way to the research lab, or wherever they needed to be. Luke continued to look at me with concern. "If you're not up for the lab session, I'll let our instructor know," he offered.

"Lab session...but why are *you* here? Where's Vincent?"

"Who? Is he in your research track?"

"No. He's my lab partner."

Luke raised an eyebrow. "*I'm* your lab partner. We've been partners for two weeks now. You forgot already?" He laughed again, but this time I sensed it was forced.

"I can't go to the lab with you. I need to find Vincent."

I didn't wait for his reply. I turned and practically ran the other way, back toward the dorm. If this dream were anything like reality, Vincent would be in his room. Then again, he might have gone to the lab like everyone else. Maybe I'd made the wrong decision. I was already halfway to the dorm though, so I kept going. When I got to Vincent's room, I pounded rather violently on the door. It opened after several seconds.

"What the hell? What do you want?" Vincent asked. He appeared disheveled and sick.

*He probably has a migraine.*

"I need you," I said desperately. "I don't know what's real. Please, don't leave me anymore."

Vincent stared at me, mouth hanging open slightly. His ears turned red. "Wh-what?" he stammered.

"Please, just come with me. Help me get out of this nightmare."

He closed his mouth and set his jaw. "Funny joke." He turned and shut the door in my face.

I stood helpless, unable to think or do anything for several minutes. Tears streamed down my face as I tried to make myself accept the nightmare.

I *knew* none of it was real.

*Maybe it is just a game. How do I make it stop?*

"Vincent. Please hurry. I don't want to do this anymore," I said aloud.

There was no reply.

I blinked and was somewhere else entirely.

"And that's why...I'm sorry Elena, we have to ask you to leave," Dr. Hammond said to me.

A quick glance around informed me I was seated in his office, Dr. Belle sat nearby as Dr. Hammond addressed me.

"I'm sorry, could you repeat that please?" I asked, trying to appear as though I simply didn't hear him.

"The fact that you *hacked* into our program is a serious offense. Obviously we can't have you continue here at the Sleep Research Academy," Dr. Belle explained. "You do understand of course." Her expression, though civil, was cold and distant.

Dr. Hammond's face appeared more distressed. "I wish you'd come to me, Elena. I could have helped you work it out."

"Oh. Yes, I'm sorry. What will happen to Vincent?"

"Who?" Dr. Hammond asked.

"My lab partner — I started to say. "Ah, never "mind."

Dr. Belle and Dr. Hammond exchanged glances.

"You knew he was the one who turned you in," Dr. Belle said. "After all, he did help write the program."

A heaviness like a weight dropped onto my shoulders and my stomach hurt. Then the headache that had started a little while ago grew more intense. It was difficult to breath.

Dr. Hammond got out of his chair and came toward me. "Elena, take it easy. Everything will be fine," he assured me.

I was hyperventilating. I couldn't make myself calm down.

"Let me get something to help her," Dr. Belle said, leaving the room for a moment.

Dr. Hammond placed a hand on my shoulder and transformed into Abel Dumont. "It's not so amusing, is it? You are doing very well, I must say. I expected you would get stuck in one of the nightmare segments. That often happens and the treatment is slow. But your progress is remarkable — as I hoped it would be."

M. Dumont awarded me a rather charming smile and look of endearment. His hand moved from my shoulder to my face and he brought his own face closer to mine. Then he whispered in my ear, "Thank you for helping me, my *ange*."

CHAPTER 20

A shifting nightmare.

Just when you thought it had settled into something predictable and not so terrifying, it changed and you didn't know what to expect any longer.

Unpredictable.

Sudden changes.

As though the floor were ripped out from under you as soon as you thought you'd found a steady foothold; like getting out of debt and having to start repayment all over again. There are many ways to describe how it felt, but it wasn't pure, traditional fear. I realized that most of my life, my notions of nightmares had been solidly based on fiction: horror films and dark video games with no basis in reality.

No. Real nightmares are firmly founded in truths and possibilities.

The Somnium Medicus peeled each layer of fear — one at a time — until you had to accept the fear as not so terrifying. It forced you to face worst-case scenarios, created by the subconscious. Although one could argue this process is foreseeable, we don't really know ourselves. We live two separate lives, one awake, and one at night in sleep. When our conscious mind has control, it excels at deceiving those around us, as well as ourselves. Our true selves come alive at night, when the conscious mind has fallen into sleep and loses its control. It's a frightening thing, to be at the mercy of our subconscious, with no chance of waking if we don't like what it shows us.

I don't know how many layers of fear the machine forced me to endure. I lost track after a while. Eventually, I reached the point where Vincent and even Luke didn't appear much anymore, or if they did, they didn't seem to know who I was. I moved through several scenes from my childhood as well, but nothing I ever wish to share with anyone.

M. Dumont didn't come to me anymore. I even missed him. At least when he spoke to me, I felt as though I weren't alone.

Oddly, while I experienced each nightmare sequence, I almost grew accustomed to it. I began to look forward to what came next, though simultaneously, I wanted it to end. It was a strange sensation. Then, with a sudden yank, I was violently pulled from the nightmare prison and woke gasping and trembling in Vincent's arms.

He held me tightly as he murmured, "Breath Elena. You'll be alright."

I buried my face in his neck and clung to him like my life depended on it. "You know who I am," I whispered.

"We need to get out of here. They'll be coming for us soon," he warned, pulling me up and out of the machine.

Vincent nearly dragged me to the lab exit. He stopped to glance cautiously down the hall. "They were here a minute ago. I know they'll come back."

We staggered on together as he led us away from the lab.

"Where are we going?" I asked.

"To the library."

"What?"

"You said we needed to find a way in. That's where we're going."

I had forgotten about the library. I was glad Vincent was thinking more clearly than I at that moment.

Gradually, I was able to move on my own, but Vincent still held my arm for support. We didn't encounter shadows until we had left the research wing and entered the original portion of the mansion. Even then, there were few of them and Vincent easily cut them down.

"Why are we still in the program?" I wondered aloud.

"It hasn't really been long yet," Vincent told me.

"Feels like ages to me."

Vincent nodded. "That's how it is in the machine."

We continued further down the hall, to where the library should be.

"You never told me much about the nightmares you had in the machine," I said.

Vincent looked at me. "Do *you* feel like talking about the ones you had?"

I dropped my gaze. "No. You're right."

"It's personal. That machine knows how to extract things that you don't even know are there. It's dangerous."

"Why do you say that? I think it's a good thing to face your fears," I responded.

"But it isn't necessary. It's invasive. Our conscious mind protects us from that stuff."

We walked the rest of the way in silence, then stood still in front of the wall where the library entrance should have been.

"There's no way in," I said. "Maybe it doesn't exist in the dreamscape."

Vincent was running his hand along the wall. He pounded his fist in places and listened. "I think we can get in. Let's try breaking through."

"How are you going to do that?"

He didn't reply. Instead he demonstrated by kicking the wall with such force, pieces of the ceiling cracked and fell.

"You better get on with it then...before every shadow in the mansion comes," I warned.

"Are you well enough to cover me if they do?"

I nodded and Vincent proceeded to kick the wall.

It wasn't long before the shadows appeared. They weren't difficult to eliminate, but I was still weary from the time I'd spent in the machine and fighting was burdensome.

Then a large crash brought the wall down and dust flew up into the air. Vincent grabbed me and pulled me through the opening he'd created, before more shadows could come.

A glance around informed us that we had made it into the library, though I couldn't put my finger on what it was that had changed.

Vincent dragged one of the large arm chairs to block the hole in the wall and prevent the shadows from coming through.

I walked around the room, trying to discern what bothered me about the layout of the place. The books were as they should be, and the desk and leather chair stood just as I remembered them.

I perused the shelves, looking for the manuscript or something familiar. On closer inspection, I discovered the books were more like stage props, without titles or even words on the pages.

"Come here Elena," Vincent called. He stood staring at something on the desk.

"What is it?" I came up beside him.

A cold sensation crept down my neck and shoulders as I read the words etched into the desk: *"THE CHILD IS DEAD."*

"What does that mean?" I managed to say.

"I don't know...it sounds twisted though."

"Maybe we shouldn't be here..." I said.

"Something is wrong with this room," Vincent muttered. He looked around, frowning as he did.

"I noticed it too"– I started to agree, then stopped. "Wait, you've never been in this room before. How do you know something is wrong?"

Vincent shrugged. "It just looks off, doesn't it?"

I was wary. I suppose the unending nightmares I experienced in the Somnium Medicus had taken a toll. I still didn't completely trust this wasn't one of them.

"It's almost as if the whole room is staged," Vincent observed. He walked around once more, feeling along the walls again. "Here. There's a crack in the wall," he told me.

I couldn't tear my eyes from the strange writing on the desk. I hardly heard what Vincent said.

"Elena..."

When I turned, it was Luke, not Vincent who called to me.

*I knew it.*

"Where's Vincent?" I asked.

Luke frowned. "He's sleeping. You wanted to go back to the library, remember?"

Panicked, I looked back at the desk to find that the writing had disappeared. The whole in the wall was gone as well.

"Not again," I groaned. I fell into the desk chair and covered my face with my hands.

"What's the matter?" Luke came to where I sat and placed a hand on my shoulder.

"I hate this. I just want to get out of here," I said.

"Ok, let's go. We don't need to stay here anymore."

"No. It's the program. I'm stuck in the program," I told him.

"I know. That's why we're doing this — to find a way to solve the nightmares."

"You don't get it. *This* is the nightmare."

Luke was silent. I didn't bother to look at him as I tried to regain my composure.

*It's a game.*

The thought had been occurring with growing intensity; perhaps I had it all wrong from the start. The puzzle of my recurring dreams was not a nightmare sequence triggered by my logging into the program. It was part of a larger story — a game. Abel Dumont's game.

"I'm through with this," I said aloud, standing to my feet.

Luke watched me in silence.

Nothing changed.

"I said — this is over. I'm getting out of here," I announced. With that, I rushed out of the library, down the hall to Vincent's room. I stopped and calmed myself before knocking. It was a few moments before he opened the door.

"Sorry, guess I fell asleep, huh," he said. He yawned.

"Vincent...I want to go to the lab."

"We can't hack in again tonight. I'll get you out of the machine tomorrow."

"No. I'm in the machine *now*. I need to undo this. Give me your keycard." I held out my hand.

Vincent sighed. "Just a sec." He picked up the keycard from his dresser and handed it to me. "I'll come with you," he suggested.

"That's ok. I'm going by myself."

Vincent's face looked troubled. "That's not a good idea."

"I'll be fine."

I turned and almost ran to the research wing. I couldn't say I had a clear plan in mind, but I thought if I did something unexpected, I could break the cycle and emerge from the nightmares. I had never been to the lab by myself at night; never tried to log into the program when no one was around.

It was time to do it alone.

*The real Vincent would have followed me.*

The lab was empty and cold, like a tomb undisturbed. The machinery hummed soothingly, somehow creating comfort in the solitude.

I didn't waste time. I quickly prepared the program and logged in.

Darkness hit me like a door slammed in my face. My body jolted in response.

Then, as if I were pulled back on a giant sling shot, I catapulted forward. Rapidly I traveled, centering my mind on a single thought: *The Child of a Hundred Years.*

I repeated it over and over, willing myself nearer to the source of those words – to the beginning.

Then suddenly, I stopped and the darkness lifted. I blinked several times until the scene around me came into focus. At first, there were white blobs and unfamiliar sounds. But a voice addressed me and made everything clear when it said, "It's over, my dear *ange.*"

My hands were small. My feet didn't even reach the floor.

*I'm a child.*

"She's fully awake," someone said.

Abel Dumont, young and handsome, smiled and knelt in front of me. "Come my sweet one. Would you like to visit my special library?" His words were soft and full of warmth.

I nodded obediently, but couldn't bring myself to speak.

M. Dumont took my hand and led me from the Somnium Medicus and the underground lab, upstairs. He didn't speak as we walked, but he continued to hold my hand until we reached the library door. He took a key from his suit pocket and unlocked the door.

"Come, there is a special chair in here just for you," he said.

A small fire glowed in the hearth, creating subtle warmth in the room. M. Dumont had me sit in a chair just my size, near enough to the fire so that I could enjoy it dance.

He circled the room and returned with a large, leather-bound book. Then he sat near me.

"Do you know why we have nightmares?" he asked.

I shook my head.

"Let me tell you a story." He didn't even open the book, but rested his hand on the cover as he recited from memory, "Long ago, when people didn't understand the visions they saw at night while they slept, they sought protection from an ancient race. The name is so old, no one remembers what they were called, but one name for them is *Somnium Custos,* or Dream Guardian.

These beings lived high on a mountain top. They watched over the towns and villages, viewing the dreams of the people. You see, these creatures themselves never dream. They lived to protect people – especially children – from the terrors of night. Children have the worst nightmares, my dear. That is because their subconscious has not yet been tempered by reality – but I digress."

He paused, and smiled at me. Then he continued, "There was a child in one of those villages who fell into sleep one night and had a terrible nightmare. This child saw the Dream Guardians descend from the mountain and devour his village. He awoke in the morning and tried to warn his parents. Sadly, they did not listen.

It wasn't long before a prophet visited the village and pronounced judgment on them for their sins. You see, the people of the village had begun to worship the Dream Guardians and create small statues in honor to them. They were denounced as pagan and a plague fell upon them.

The boy understood that the Dream Guardians did not seek to protect them after all. They wanted to devour the people and absorb the energy from their dreams so that they could live as long as they liked. This boy alone was protected from the plague, because he did not worship the Dream Guardians; he wanted to stop them."

Abel Dumont sighed and patted the book on his lap. "Alas, the Dream Guardians did come down one night, when the people were weak from the plague and asleep. They consumed the village, and though the boy tried to flee with his life, they overcame him as well. Those Dream Guardians did not protect the people – they *created* the nightmare.

Even so, they did live long from the dream energy they had absorbed. But they did not consider the death they would have to carry with them; the death of the people. And because they had consumed the boy while he was awake and not helpless in sleep, he lived on inside them, and was at last able to defeat them from within."

M. Dumont put the book aside and looked at me seriously. "My dear child, nightmares are not something we should seek to eliminate.

They are messages to us, warning us of things to come. We can change our fate if we would but listen. Do you still wish to make them stop?"

My heart pounded hard as he spoke. I didn't know how to answer. All along I had thought Abel Dumont to have some devious purpose, yet now he spoke kindly, and offered me a choice.

With difficulty, I said to him, "Are there any Dream Guardians left? Did you capture one in the machine?"

His face appeared troubled at my response. "Why do you ask such a question?"

"There's one in the machine," I said again. "You're going to hurt people if you continue to use it."

My words came out differently than I intended. They sounded childish.

M. Dumont rose to his feet and paced the room. He looked at me once more and his expression became wary. "What did you see?"

"There's a child in the attic," I told him. "Who is he?"

He shook his head. "There is no attic. What are you talking about little one?"

"The Child of a Hundred Years. *'I am the first, but not the last. They will fill these rooms with the dying. We will live eternally in dreams,'*" I quoted.

He was thoughtful. "Why don't we take a break. You must be tired after your session in the Somnium Medicus." He resumed his pleasant demeanor and helped me out of the chair.

I didn't speak again. I allowed him to lead me to a clean, comfortable guest room where he left me to rest. A woman came by to check on me. She stroked my forehead and said soothing things.

Then I was alone, trapped in a child's body.

# CHAPTER 21

I stayed very still for a long time, almost holding my breath, afraid to move. Someone might come back to check on me. I pretended to sleep. Then, when I could no longer hear footsteps or voices, I tossed the covers aside and placed my small feet on the floor.

The mansion had grown quiet and dark with evening shadows. With shorter legs, it took a long time to pass through the hall. I scurried along, praying no one would pass me as I made my way through the house. Then at the far end of the hall, I reached a door. I opened it to find a stairwell leading up to the attic.

*So he lied.*

The stairs were quite steep and I had to pull myself up each new step by the wooden bannister along the wall. My footsteps stirred up dust, which filled my nostrils. It was that hot, dry dust that accumulates in well-sealed attics. I'd forgotten my slippers, so my bare feet became rather dirty.

At the top of the stairs, I looked down the hall at the rows of doors, one on either side. I had made it.

Knowing what I would find at the end of the hall, my heart gave way to fear. The boy was there – the old, decrepit, strange boy I'd found ages ago when I defeated the monster in the basement with Vincent. But now *that* felt like the dream, and *this* the reality. Had I always been a child? Did Elena exist, or had I traveled to her from here and merely visited her life for a time?

I couldn't remember.

Padding along the attic hall, my heart grew heavier with childlike fear and each door I passed promised unfathomable terror.

Then finally, I reached the end of the hall – the last door. My tiny hand reached forward to grasp the knob and turn. I expected to see the cot with the boy resting there. Instead the room was empty but for a large, ornate mirror, and staring back at me was a face, hideous and old, despite childlike features. She gasped and screeched at me, mimicking my every move.

Another figure appeared in the mirror behind me.

*The boy.*

"Do you understand yet? Do you remember?" he asked.

I was crying. "What? I don't know! What's wrong with me?"

The boy looked at me with compassion. "It's me Elena. Don't you recognize me?"

"I don't know who you are!" I yelled back, stepping away.

"You still don't remember," he said sadly. "You think this is a dream, don't you?"

"It *is* a dream! This is the nightmare created by the machine. The Somnium Medicus is playing with me. I can't stand it anymore!" I moaned. I fell to my knees and cried into my hands, a pitiful, childish cry.

The boy watched me. Through the cracks in my fingers, I saw his reflection in the mirror. He was waiting for me to finish crying. I didn't want to know the truth. I wanted to prolong the tears so I could keep believing that it was all a terrible nightmare.

He placed a hand on my shoulder. "It's me Elena. Vincent," he whispered.

I shook my head again. "No. This can't be."

He crouched beside me, his hand still resting on my shoulder. "We're trapped here. Our only chance of escape is to go back. We need to return or we'll be stuck here forever. The Dream Guardians still live in the machine. We need to defeat them."

My head ached more than ever. "No. I still...don't know." I breathed out a sigh.

"Give it a minute. It will come back to you," he encouraged. "It's not hopeless. We still have a chance."

As if a spell had been broken with his words, the memories rushed back to me, mercilessly flooding my mind.

It was almost painful.

"You remember now, don't you?" he asked.

I nodded. "We were absorbed by the Dream Guardians. They took our village – only you and I survived."

Vincent nodded. "We weren't sick with the plague, so we didn't die. They've been feeding on our energy ever since."

"Abel Dumont...he knows everything. He trapped the Dream Guardians in the machine," I continued.

"He didn't mean to. The Dream Guardians had traveled to other people's dreams. They began to feed on nightmares, so Abel Dumont gathered the people he suspected were being attacked by the Dream Guardians. He was able to absorb them into the machine."

"Then the shadows..."

Vincent nodded again. "That's what remains of them, once they pass on. You could say that the shadows are the remnants of old nightmares."

"What about the small figure and the monster in the machine?"

Vincent sat beside me and hugged his knees. "The Somnium Medicus began to leak or something. It stopped working properly and began to *create* nightmares. Abel Dumont shut it away and stopped using it when he thought his purpose had been accomplished. That small figure was a shadow of the guardians. Dumont sought to get rid of them." Vincent looked at me. "But I think he knew it wasn't over. The machine in the basement...it still contained the energy of the Dream Guardians. They were waiting for a chance to come back."

"Then the purpose of the other machine..."

"The one in the basement contains the remains of the Dream Guardian. Dumont shut it away, trying to bury the ancient nightmare. The first machine had the ability to prolong life with the dream energy it absorbed. The second machine only temporarily recalibrated dreams. It wasn't as effective as the first."

"So, the Dreamscape Program is built on Dumont's idea?"

"Yes," Vincent agreed. "The program borrowed from Abel Dumont's original prototype. They didn't mean to do it, but the

Academy somehow tapped into the energy the Dream Guardians had been feeding on for centuries. It was the only way the program worked."

"But how did the program erase people's dreams to begin with?" I asked.

Vincent looked thoughtful. "The Dream Guardians took everything with them. It would seem Abel Dumont's plan was incomplete. He couldn't get the Dream Guardians out of people's dreams without removing everything."

I was quiet for a moment, as the random pieces of the puzzle continued to settle into a coherent pattern in my mind.

"What about Elena?" I asked.

"Elena is a strong dreamer. She stumbled onto the never-ending cycle the Dreamscape Program used to keep it going. Actually, you could argue that's what *makes* the program work. She didn't understand it at first, but when she and Vincent hacked into the program together, they merged with us. We were able to use them to move around once again. Except"– He stopped and put his hand to his forehand for a moment. "They didn't understand what the program was meant for. It's all bits and pieces to them. They kept moving through the same loop without any progress. That's why you had to get in the machine."

"What about Abel Dumont?"

Vincent shrugged. "Somehow, he allowed himself to get absorbed by the Dream Guardians so he too could continue to fight them from within the program. He's been reaching out to us, trying to help us remember."

"But he told me a story, and he made it sound as though the boy had defeated the Dream Guardians," I said.

Vincent shook his head. "It wasn't just a boy. It was both of us, remember?"

I nodded slowly. "We had both been warned in our dreams. No one listened."

"Abel Dumont thought he could harness the power of dreams to prolong life. It started out that way, but then he realized that there were people who needed help; whose lives were in danger from their nightmares. The Dream Guardians still lived in our darkest fears."

"But Vincent, it's the fear that makes them live," I corrected.

He nodded. "I know. You could say that when we give way to fear, we also give life to evil."

"I don't want to die," I said suddenly.

His eyes once again filled with compassion for me. "We have to, especially if Elena and Vincent are to live. If we continue this way, *they* will cease. You *must* die."

"I'm afraid," I whispered.

"And that's why the Dream Guardians come after you. We can't keep this cycle up any longer. I'm tired." He sighed, and his shoulders sagged in dismay.

"So what do we do now?"

"We can't do anything in this form. We need to get back to Elena and Vincent. I followed you here, because I couldn't wake you from the machine. But I think my time is almost up. Luke will come looking for you soon."

"Are we going to forget again?"

"Maybe. We must act quickly."

It was still difficult to understand exactly what had happened. I was Elena, and yet I was the girl from that ancient village – she and the boy had lived so long they forgot their own names. Vincent and I were merged with them. Somehow, Vincent seemed to understand more clearly.

We devised a plan. I must have still been in the Somnium Medicus within the program and Vincent had been unable to find me. The boy said he would merge with Luke once he entered the program. We would go to the source of the nightmares and defeat the remaining Dream Guardians. Vincent seemed to think we needed to use the two machines to bring an end to the cycle.

It turned out the program had created a memory of what used to be, using Abel Dumont's own consciousness. The dreams I'd had outside of the program were a part of those contrived memories. Even Abel Dumont appearing to me in my dreams had been a subconscious act planted by the program.

I sat with the boy a little while, once we'd discussed our plan. "When will we disappear?" I asked him.

He got up and walked toward the mirror, reaching out to his reflection. "Look at us. There's almost nothing left. We'll use the last of our strength to help Vincent and Elena – or Luke and Elena –

destroy the Dream Guardians. We will fade with them." He turned to look at me. "Do not fear death. It will be welcome after this eternal torment we've endured, suffering in this endless nightmare."

I nodded, sadly. Though I knew Elena would survive, I feared for the ancient girl. She was, after all, still a girl. She was afraid and helpless.

Vincent held out a hand to me. "Let's go Elena."

As I took hold of his hand, the attic vanished. We moved through darkness until his hand too disappeared and I was left alone once again.

Then my eyes opened.

"My dear *ange*. You have returned."

Abel Dumont's face peered down into my own. His hand felt my pulse and touched my forehead. He nodded, satisfied.

"I remember," I said, my voice horse. "The girl from the village...I remember."

M. Dumont frowned. "Girl?"

"The little boy and girl...they've been trapped by the Dream Guardians for centuries. They want to destroy the Dream Guradians."

M. Dumont's face darkened. "What is this? What do you know of the Dream Guardians?"

I was suddenly confused. "*You* told me about them."

He shook his head. "It was not I."

"Fine – the memory was fake, just like the rest of this," I started to say.

Abel Dumont looked up suddenly as someone entered the lab.

*Luke.*

"Let's go Elena," he said calmly. His eyes were fixed on the figure of Abel Dumont beside me."

"He's not our enemy. He's trying to help us," I explained.

Luke raised an eyebrow. "Let go of her," he demanded, addressing Abel Dumont.

An intense pressure gripped my head, as though it were clamped in a vice. I cried out in pain.

Luke rushed forward, drawing his weapons as he did. The painful grip released me then and I watched a hideous, dark form endeavor to swallow Luke. I looked down at myself and saw that I was attached to the machine by a number of tubes and straps. My arms were thin and pale, like the life had been slowly drained from my body. I tried in vain to free myself as Luke fought the black monster in the lab.

Then at last, Luke managed to fell the creature. He came toward me, breathing heavily. "I finally found you," he said, relieved.

Quickly, he released me from the machine. I could hardly move on my own, I was so weakened.

"Slowly. You'll be fine," he said, reassuringly.

"Vincent?" I managed to say.

"He had to log out of the program. I came in to find you. When I got here, that creature had latched onto you and was trying to suck the life out of you or something. Thank God I made it in time." Luke gently lifted me from the chair and carried me out of the lab.

"Luke...did the boy merge with you? Do you know what needs to happen?"

Luke was quiet for a moment, his face appeared troubled. "Elena...I don't understand it, but I have memories that don't belong to me. We should get out of this program now."

# CHAPTER 22

Luke moved quickly down the hall and into a small, dark room in the research wing. He placed me gently in a chair and barricaded the door against intruders. Then he came over to where I sat and began checking me to be sure I was ok.

"You know this isn't real-life, right?" I said, half kidding.

Luke didn't stop examining me. "It's habit — but just to be sure..." He felt my pulse and frowned. "You're in rough shape Elena."

I sighed and laughed weakly. "It's no wonder. I was stuck in that machine for ages."

Luke shook his head. "It shouldn't have had this effect on you. We'll wait it out here until we leave the program. Shouldn't be long now."

"Luke...about those memories. It's going to be difficult to explain, but you should know what's going on." I spent a few minutes describing some of my experience in the machine.

Luke listened attentively, but when I finished speaking he said, "Maybe we should discuss this when we're not in the program..."

I frowned. He didn't seem to understand the urgency behind the situation. I wondered if the boy hadn't been successful in merging with Luke.

Then the lights went out suddenly and we were yanked from each other without warning. I opened my eyes to a bright ceiling and the dull hum of machinery. Vincent's face appeared.

"You ok?" he asked, concerned.

"Yeah. Luke got me out of the machine," I told him.

He was visibly relieved. "Thank God."

We were all a bit dazed as we left the lab. It had felt like we'd spent an eternity there.

"Why don't you guys come to my room tonight?" Luke suggested. "There's something I want to discuss."

We followed Luke obediently to his room. Vincent exchanged a look with me once and I felt as though we could almost read each other's thoughts, even then. Without speaking, I knew he remembered what had taken place in the program.

Luke offered us something to drink as we settled into his room. There was something in his air that made me a little apprehensive, and I had the feeling what he was about to say would be unpleasant.

He began by saying, "I think we should stop using the program."

Vincent and I stared at him in disbelief, but neither of us spoke.

He breathed out a sigh. "Elena told me what happened in there. It strikes a cord with what I read in Abel Dumont's personal memoir, but..." Luke sat on his bed and fidgeted slightly. He looked up at us. "This isn't going to end well if we continue."

"Luke, why don't you just explain?" I offered.

"It's difficult. I suppose I don't completely understand myself," he admitted. "Up to this point, we've believed Abel Dumont to be some kind of crazed, villainous scientist, out to suck the life force from helpless patients." He stood up again and paced a little. "But when I read about the darkness in his dreams, I began to think something else was going on."

I nodded. "We know this already." Vincent and I looked at each other. "The two children from the village"—

Luke interrupted. "They don't exist. They can't. Abel Dumont was too thorough in his manuscript and other writings to have left out a detail like that. Don't you see?"

"He didn't know about it until too late," I started to say.

Luke looked impatient. "It's all wrong. Something just doesn't make sense about it all."

Vincent chimed in, "Beside the fact that some weird Dream Guardians lived centuries ago and have somehow managed to live inside a machine?" He laughed. "None of it makes sense. It never has."

"No. That's not the point. We're not seeing something here. It's bugging me."

I was tired. "In any case, we can talk about it more tomorrow, can't we?" I asked.

Luke sighed. "You two won't give up. This isn't why we're here."

"We can't stop now Luke," I said. "We need to finish what we started."

"Are you still having the nightmares?" Luke asked me. His eyes fixed on my face meaningfully.

"Not exactly..."

"But there's more to this," Vincent argued. "We're too involved now."

Luke gave Vincent a rather hard look then which I found surprising. It quickly vanished as he said, "I understand. I've been an outsider all this time when you think about it. But don't forget, I've been reading Abel Dumont's writings first hand. I'm closer to it all than you think." He gave me another look that seemed to hold greater meaning than his words expressed.

I wondered at Luke's strange behavior. It was almost as though he were trying to tell me something he couldn't say aloud — at least, not in front of Vincent. I was frustrated with him for not seeing what Vincent and I did about the situation. Clearly, he didn't fully comprehend the program's versatility and legacy. Though I thought this consciously, something vaguely ominous nagged at me from the back of my mind, but I wasn't sure why.

"There's just something not right about all of this." Luke shook his head and fell into thoughtful silence.

"Luke, we'll talk more about it tomorrow," I said.

He looked at both of us in turn before saying, "Don't do anything without me. Please." His sincere expression was effective. Vincent fidgeted a little, uncomfortably, and I nodded seriously in reply. We left Luke's room in silence, but Vincent motioned for me to follow him so we could speak more freely.

"What was that all about?" Vincent asked, once we'd closed the door to his room.

I shook my head. "I'm not sure..."

"I never wanted that guy involved," Vincent grumbled to himself. He plopped down in front of his computer and stared at it absently. "He's probably right though."

"Right about what exactly?"

"Everything. But he knows something he won't tell us."

*He sensed it too.*

Vincent glanced at me. "He doesn't want *me* to know it, that's for sure. He'll probably end up telling you if you ask him. I have a feeling..." He stopped abruptly.

"What?"

"No, never mind. I don't want to speculate any further."

I sighed, frustrated. "You and I both know the purpose of the program."

"Are you sure about that? I thought I was, but I'm not anymore. As much as I hate to agree with him, Luke has pointed out several things that just don't add up."

"So what then? We stop using it like he said?"

Vincent replied slowly, "No, not exactly."

"He'll know if we try to use it on our own. And what's the point anyway?"

"What happened when Luke got you out of the machine?" Vincent asked suddenly.

I sat down slowly on his bed and frowned thoughtfully. "I thought I was with Abel Dumont, but then Luke started yelling at him to get away from me. It turned out to be a shadow or monster of some kind. Luke defeated it and pulled me out of the machine. Then we waited in a small room to wake from the program."

Vincent leaned back and looked at the ceiling. "Before you and I were – those old kids – what happened?"

I sighed. "It's going to take a while."

Vincent watched me, expectantly.

I divulged the details of my experience, beginning with the beach. Several times as I spoke, I found it necessary to swallow unwelcome emotion in order to relay everything accurately. Vincent didn't interrupt. I did leave out anything having to do with my childhood, only because it seemed irrelevant. Maybe I'd share it with him someday – then again, maybe not.

"Abel Dumont came to you while you were in the machine?" Vincent asked when I'd finished.

I nodded.

"See, this is what I don't understand: it's as if the guy is bi-polar or has an evil twin." He shook his head. "And what did he mean when he thanked you for helping him? What was he referring to?"

I shrugged wearily. "I know as much as you do."

Vincent continued to look thoughtful.

I asked him then, "What was the machine like for you?"

His gaze fell. "Just a bunch of nightmares and fear mashed up. It changed a lot, like you described."

"Are you going to *tell* me about it?"

Vincent made eye contact with me then and held my gaze for a moment before saying, "I will sometime."

"So, we don't know what's going on," I summed up.

"I'll admit, I feel like we've gotten further from finding the answer. The whole thing with those kids and the Dream Guardians...it seemed to explain so much, but now that we're not in the program, and based on what Luke said..." he stopped abruptly. "Wait a sec." He turned then and began typing on his computer rapidly for a few minutes. I knew better than to interrupt until he'd finished.

At length, Vincent sat back in his chair and stared at the computer screen. "I have an idea." He turned to me. "Can you give me some time Elena? Damn. I've been so stupid, but I think I know what's happening. I just need a little time."

I was puzzled. Vincent's face expressed both excitement and relief as I nodded and stood to leave. He lost no time returning to his task. I closed the door to his room and made my way back to my own room.

For once, I felt left out. Luke and Vincent had discovered something that was completely lost on me. I was annoyed with myself for my inability to uncover what they seemed to have found in all this.

Frustrated as I was, I soon fell into heavy, peaceful sleep. I awoke ages later, afraid I would be late for class, but a glance at the clock informed me that I had plenty of time to get ready for classes that morning. I was confused. I couldn't have gotten more than four hours of sleep, yet I felt more refreshed than I had in months. I wondered if the Somnium Medicus had really been so successful in healing my dreams. Perhaps Abel Dumont had been right – it gets worse before it gets better.

I went through my day with surprising calm. Almost as if life had returned to normal. Yet vaguely, in the back of my mind there remained that nagging sensation – we were missing something. *I* had missed something.

I didn't see Vincent or Luke until after the dinner hour. Luke invited both of us to his room so we could continue discussing our theories. While Vincent and I were full of energy, Luke appeared weary and tense. He must have spent a great deal of time translating the documents we'd acquired.

"Who wants to go first?" Luke asked, as we settled into his room. There were papers and books everywhere, so that it was a bit of a challenge to find somewhere to sit.

"I think Elena should," Vincent said.

I shook my head and sighed. "I have nothing. I don't understand what's been happening."

"Sure you do. Why not tell us the part before anyone else got involved?" Luke encouraged.

"Ok," I agreed. "Let's see...it began with the first lab session. I logged into the program and immediately found myself in the Academy with the shadows. I felt very afraid of death, especially seeing those dead faces on the walls. Then in the basement, the small figure tried to beckon me down." I continued: "I had a conversation with Sophie and Julie one day and they were talking about Vincent. They mentioned he worked on the Dreamscape Program, which gave me the idea to ask him for help." I smiled at the memory. "You agreed to help me, but only if you could be part of the dream as well," I said, looking at Vincent.

Luke eyed Vincent silently.

"The dreams persisted, though they changed a little at times. Vincent was in them occasionally. And once I used the weapons mod, that was added to my dreams as well." I stopped. "There isn't any point going on really. Vincent knows what happened once we started working together. I've told you most of it already too Luke."

Luke nodded slowly.

"I'll go next," Vincent offered. "I had an idea last night that I decided to explore a bit more. We've had lots of theories about what the Dreamscape Program really does, but no concrete proof." He paused and scratched his head, then continued reluctantly, "I think the real problem is the hack program itself."

Luke nodded in agreement, as though he'd already known.

"There's something wrong with it – or rather, I think I screwed up. It doesn't just give us the ability to be lucid." He sighed. "Somehow, the hack program creates what we expect. It pre-empts what we think we'll find and makes it so we do..."

"You're kidding, right? So, what's been the point of all this?" I said, incredulous.

"Exactly," Luke said. "There isn't any point. At least, not anymore."

I sighed. "What about the original nightmares?"

Luke looked at Vincent, who shrugged and said, "That's all I got."

"Ok. I guess it's my turn then," Luke said. "Elena, we know that when you first logged in to the program, it didn't calibrate well to your brain. That initial login tripped a circuit, so to speak, that made it so you kept dreaming the same thing over and over – with little, but some variation. When you and Vincent began the process of joining in your dreamscape, it must have reset things and your dreams went back to – at least, a semi-normal state. Would you agree?"

I thought back to when we logged in together and realized that although I still had strange dreams after that point, they were not of the recurring nature the original nightmares had been. I nodded, hesitantly.

Luke wore a satisfied expression. "It's been like a game all along. A game that hack program created. The only problem is, the hack program works like a drug: the brain keeps wanting more of it and isn't satisfied until you have another login experience. That's why you have to stop using it."

"What about when Vincent got stuck inside the program?" I asked.

Vincent answered, "That was the program doing what it does. We expected I was stuck inside the machine, and so I was."

"So everything with Abel Dumont and the manuscript..." I began.

"Think back to when you started dreaming about Abel Dumont: you had already seen his portrait in the library and found the manuscript. The program then created a 'game' for you based on what you expected to find," Luke explained.

"Ok. So the hack program didn't do what we thought it would. What about the original dream? What does it mean?" I pressed.

Luke shrugged. "Probably nothing. Perhaps you were anxious about your experience here at the Academy. Maybe you watched something that influenced your dreams. Who knows?"

I frowned, altogether frustrated and unsatisfied with the explanations thrown at me. The feeling that something still wasn't right continued to tug at my intuition until it was almost unbearable, but I kept quiet then. Despite Vincent and Luke's reasoning, I felt there were too many pieces that didn't fit. I wished that I could read the documents Luke had gathered for myself.

"What else have you read in Abel Dumont's memoirs?" I asked Luke.

Luke's expression grew thoughtful. "He was a troubled man. His research turned into a dangerous obsession at some point and even endangered some of his patient's lives. That's why there's nothing on his research — it didn't matter. His process of 'healing dreams' backfired greatly and his patients sued as a result."

I stood up. "Well, that's that I guess."

"I'm sorry Elena. I know it's disappointing," Luke sympathized.

I laughed ruefully. "I just feel foolish I guess. It doesn't matter."

Vincent got up and we left the room together. "I'm sorry Elena," he said as we walked the halls.

I looked at him and smiled. "You did accomplish what I asked you to. It just wasn't what we expected. Don't worry about it." I slipped an arm around his waist and he placed his arm on my shoulder. "Anyway, you can admit now that it was all just a ploy to get closer to me."

Vincent smirked. "Well, since you figured it out, there's no sense denying it."

# CHAPTER 23

Two weeks passed.

Vincent and I stopped hacking into the Dreamscape Program at night and Luke kept his distance. Life returned to normal and so did my dreams.

I'd been successful in extracting Vincent from his solitude and he even frequented the cafeteria with me now. He told me he didn't mind being around other people, as long as I was one of them.

Vincent and I sat with Evan, Alex, and Sophie at dinner one Friday. Once the initial shock of my relationship with Vincent had worn off, Evan and Alex began to develop something of a friendship with him. They approached him cautiously at first, unsure of what to expect, but soon found a common ground in their avid video game playing.

That evening, Evan and Vincent argued over something related to an online game they had been playing. Their discussion was somewhat heated, though I sensed Evan took it more seriously than Vincent did.

Alex nudged me. "You better keep an eye on him," he said, nodding to Vincent. "Evan might steal him away from you."

I laughed. "He's certainly welcome to try it."

"I don't think anything could get in the way of those two," Sophie said, referring to me and Vincent. Sophie had wanted to know everything about my hack-in experiences, so I filled her in on our conclusions beforehand. She was fully aware of the strong bond Vincent and I shared and she had accepted it without question.

Vincent looked at me once during his chat with Evan and rolled his eyes. He grinned, obviously enjoying himself immensely. I reveled in the satisfaction of having successfully merged my anti-social, tech nerd boyfriend into my friend group. Turns out, it kind of matters whether your friends like who you're dating.

We had finished our meal, but Evan refused to let up. "Well, I guess we can settle this later," he said to Vincent, as we got up to leave.

Vincent smiled. "Not tonight man. I have other plans." He glanced over at me and I returned the smile.

Evan reddened slightly. Alex clapped a hand on his shoulder. "Let's go out tonight. You've been holed up in your room too much lately. Don't wanna turn out like him." He jerked a thumb at Vincent.

Vincent raised an eyebrow and shrugged. "He'd be so lucky," he returned. He took my hand and led me out of the cafeteria. Once we were out of ear shot he said to me, "You ready for tonight?"

"Yeah. I can hardly wait," I replied.

"I'm surprised you were able to wait *this* long."

Several hours later saw us sneaking into the lab one last time.

"Are you sure he doesn't know?" I asked Vincent, as we prepared to log in.

Vincent nodded. "He really thinks we bought it. Let's finish it for good this time."

I nodded, still worried.

Vincent laid a hand on my arm. "We owe it to them," he said.

"We certainly do," I agreed.

We had waited until Luke was off campus for work at the hospital so he couldn't interfere, before hacking in one last time.

Vincent figured it out before I did. I was skeptical at first, assuming that perhaps Vincent just wanted to believe Luke had betrayed us. Yet once he presented me with the evidence of Luke's tampering, I understood.

It hadn't started out that way. I believe Luke genuinely wanted to help, but the possibility that the program did more than we expected was too tempting. Little by little, Luke rewrote the hack program to fool us. Therefore, Vincent's discovery that the hack program was at fault was in fact true, only it wasn't because Vincent had made a mistake. Luke had changed the coding, so cleverly, that Vincent admitted he was at first unsure whether it really was his fault or not. But Luke had underestimated Vincent's thoroughness. Naturally, once Vincent stumbled on the error, he wouldn't rest until he found the solution.

We weren't sure of Luke's plan, but guessed that he intended to present the hack program as his own, possibly as a modification to the Dreamscape Program. Luke was much more connected to the Academy and the faculty respected his obvious talent. It should have been that way for Vincent, but for his anti-social behavior. In this case, charisma would win. Luke must have known that we wouldn't dare try to take credit for the program, once he had submitted it to the faculty. It would have forced us to confess everything.

So, he tampered with the program and attempted to convince us we had gotten everything wrong. How could we argue? He had access to all the original documents and Abel Dumont's history.

We believed what we experienced in the Dreamscape Program was true, despite Luke's attempt to deceive us. The task weighed heavily on both of us; we wanted to set things right again.

"You know if we do this, there's a chance we'll damage the Dreamscape Program itself," Vincent had said to me. "The coding is looped — reliant on that pattern you've been dreaming. By abolishing it, we will more than likely introduce a virus into the Dreamscape Program." Vincent sighed. "Luke might even implicate us. He knows everything."

"It needs to be done. It's worse if we leave it unfinished like this."

Vincent agreed.

I had felt the urgency when I was last in the program. Evil was rising and would eventually spill over into the rest of the Dreamscape Program. The Dream Guardians themselves might even once again be unleashed, and Abel Dumont's plan would then fail utterly. We needed to act soon.

Preparations were made and we logged in to my original dream, equipped with the weapons mod. Immediately, memories rushed up to greet me and I sensed they belonged to the girl from the ancient village. I felt her urgency and fear — she thought I wouldn't come back.

There was something else there too.

The mansion had already begun to decay quite rapidly. The walls oozed a black, foul smelling substance and the shadow creatures had merged with the structure, as if to hold it together.

"This isn't good," Vincent warned. "We might be too late."

"Let's hurry," I said.

"I don't like the thought of splitting up," Vincent said.

"We have to in order to use the two machines. I'll go to the lab. You take the one in the west wing."

Reluctantly, we parted ways. I used my weapon more as a means of cutting a path through the shadows hanging from the ceiling and walls. They no longer attacked as they used to, but made half-hearted attempts to grab me as I passed through. I was afraid. The fear of death had by then so overwhelmed me that it was difficult to move forward on my own. I wanted it to end.

I reached the lab and gazed through the glass enclosure. There, seated on the Somnium Medicus as though it were a throne, was Abel Dumont. He stared directly into my eyes and smiled maliciously.

"Do come in," he said. The lab doors opened and I passed through them.

"I need to sit in the machine," I told him.

He sighed and leaned his head back, like I'd asked a great favor of him. "You *stupid* child," he murmured. "You got it all backwards. I should have known when you stumbled into my dreamscape that it would be nothing but trouble. I thought perhaps you would help me, but now you've gone and sided with *them*."

"Who do you mean?" I asked slowly.

"Those disgusting children. They are not what they seem — nothing is here. You never understood." He shook his head. "You must go. I will take care of things now."

I moved toward him, determined to sit in the machine. His face expressed mild amusement at my attempt to be defiant.

"Listen here sweet one, I am master of the program. You will never take it from me. Those children have been scheming for decades against me, but look how I've trapped them here!" His faded blue eyes flashed triumphantly. As I neared where he sat, I saw that he too had aged tremendously. His already pale hair had turned whiter than snow and almost glowed on his head. His skin was now practically translucent.

"You're ill," I stated. "Let us end it, please."

"You do not understand," he groaned.

"I know we don't, but this cycle must end. It has caused so much pain for all of you. Let us stop it, please."

To my great surprise, Abel Dumont suddenly collapsed in a fit of sobs. He fell to the floor and pounded dramatically on the ground, yelling and flailing uncontrollably. "I should have been able to do it! Why couldn't I do it?" he wailed again and again.

I was moved to pity. This man had tried to find the key to eternal life and instead, he had opened a world of evil. The dreamscape he had created for himself was purgatory.

I knelt beside him and placed a hand on his shoulder. "I know I don't understand, but please let us put a stop to it. You've been so afraid of death...but it must come. It always does."

He lifted his eyes to mine and I saw that he too appeared as a child. Perhaps we all become this way near the end – afraid to move beyond the curtain of death and into the unknown behind it. We fear darkness and separation from those we love. Gazing into his eyes, everything snapped into place with such clarity. I knew. This was the world Abel Dumont had created in his obsession for prolonged life. The mythology of the Dream Guardians had become his reality and his consciousness was trapped here now, as he fought a never-ending war.

This is what fueled the Dreamscape Program.

"Don't worry," I whispered. "We'll fix it."

I stood up and sat in the Somnium Medicus, one last time. The machine woke to my presence and seemed almost to meld with my body. The mansion shook and the ceiling began to crumble. Abel Dumont had vanished.

I brought the helmet down on my head and closed my eyes, thinking only of waking from the nightmare. I felt Vincent's mind touch my own and knew he too had found the machine. We were linked together then, by some unseen force – just like the first time we logged in together lucidly.

The mansion collapsed around me as I allowed the machine to absorb my life energy. The ancient girl – whether she existed or not – cried out as she was ripped from me in that instant.

Then everything went white.

CHAPTER 24

"Did it work?" I asked, as Vincent and I woke sluggishly from the program.

"I don't know," Vincent replied.

We had been thrown out; tossed from the program. In fact, I think the program itself stopped working. A quick check, and Vincent confirmed my suspicions.

"This is a mess," he mumbled, working at the computer terminal. "Oh boy."

I came to where he stood and watched him pull up several screens of code. "What happened?" I asked.

"Just what I thought might happen. The program was built around that dream loop. Now that it's gone, the program is corrupt." He sighed unsteadily. "How are we going to explain this?"

We hadn't exactly planned what to do if this kind of thing were to happen. We could certainly feign innocence, but I worried Luke would tell the faculty what had really happened. As if to answer that worry, Luke appeared in the doorway of the lab. He came up to where Vincent and I stood. Vincent stopped typing and set his jaw.

"I just received a text message from a hospital in France," Luke explained. "Abel Dumont passed away."

I was dumbfounded. "He was still alive all this time?"

Luke replied, "If you could call it life. He was hooked up to a machine for life support. I'm told he had them log him into the Dreamscape Program permanently. Seems he managed to prolong his life after all. The program helped him conquer a fatal illness." Luke came around and glanced at the computer terminal. "You guys sure created a mess."

We didn't respond. What could we say?

"I knew it wasn't over, even though I tried to get you two to stop. You were clever though, waiting as long as you did. So, you didn't realize that you'd be ending Abel Dumont's life?" Luke asked.

I shook my head. "Not until we logged in just now. I met Abel Dumont in the program. He was afraid to die, but his dreamscape was collapsing and it couldn't go on like that."

Luke sighed. "Why couldn't you just let him die naturally?"

I couldn't answer Luke's question. Perhaps what Vincent and I had done was wrong, but we were driven to complete the task that seemed to have been given to us. Not only that — I knew Abel Dumont wasn't alone when he died. If nothing else, I was with him at the end.

"Well what now?" Vincent asked.

"Nothing. There's a chance they won't find out it was you two," Luke said. "Dr. Belle knew Abel Dumont was logged into the program. In fact, they knew it wouldn't work without him. Word will get out that he passed away and they'll know that's why the program no longer works."

"That's it then?" I said.

Luke shrugged. "I didn't come up with the idea. It was ludicrous to begin with."

Vincent and I stood dumbly, too shocked to speak. Had it been pointless after all? I kept telling myself what we'd done had been necessary, but now, after everything, I wondered if perhaps we shouldn't have interfered to begin with.

"Listen, this is why I tried to get you guys to stop. Maybe I should have been more upfront about it...I just didn't think you'd listen. You were too convinced you needed to 'fix' everything." Luke looked at me, pointedly.

"This is so stupid. Why would they create a program that only works if a dying man is hooked up to it?" Vincent muttered, angrily.

"It's what he wanted," Luke explained. "You could argue that Abel Dumont and the program *needed* each other to exist. The Academy saw it as a great opportunity to advance their research."

Vincent made a noise like he was still highly irritated. "I'm gonna get something to drink," he said to me. "I'll be in my room."

Once Luke and I were alone, Luke's expression softened. "I'm sorry for deceiving you."

"I guess I still don't understand why you wouldn't just tell us something like that. We thought you wanted to take credit for the hack program."

Luke's eyes met the floor. "I think I was upset with you for...you know. I started to hate Vincent after a while and I couldn't stand being in the same room with the two of you anymore." He rubbed his neck nervously. "I knew for a long time, what was really going on. It was all in his memoirs, I lied to you about that. The man had sort of lost it though. Maybe I felt sorry for him."

"I understand. I felt that way too."

The weekend seemed to go on forever. Then Monday morning, we received an email notice that lab had been cancelled for the day. Our normal classes carried on as usual. It got out that the program was experiencing technical difficulties, but that didn't hinder research and lectures.

Then Thursday morning, I received an email from Dr. Belle, asking me to meet with her in her office that afternoon.

I feared the worst.

Dr. Belle's office was as neat as the last time I met with her. She greeted me with the same neutral expression and asked me some mundane questions about my research before saying, "There's something I've been wanting to talk to you about Elena."

With effort, I managed to control my nerves and calmly listen to what she had to say.

"Several weeks ago – maybe almost two months now – you came to me, asking about Monsieur Dumont."

"Yes."

She gave me a thin smile. "I have a confession to make. I told you he had already passed away, but that wasn't altogether true. We received news late Friday night he had died." She paused, apparently giving her news time to sink in. I wasn't sure how to react, so I didn't.

"That doesn't surprise you?" she asked. Then, not waiting for a reply she said, "You're experience with the Dreamscape Program has not been such a pleasant one, has it?"

I managed to say, "It's been fine."

She smiled, wryly. "No...recurring dreams then?"

I shrugged, innocently.

"Elena, we have access to all the students' dream records. Dr. Hammond was concerned for you. He watched your dreams and saw that you were having the same nightmare over and over. He was waiting for you to come to him with your problem. However, it would seem you had help from other sources." She looked at me, meaningfully.

*So, they knew.*

"Naturally, in most cases, we would put a stop to the unauthorized use of the program. But you two seemed to be getting on so well, and we were interested in where your independent research would take you. I suppose now we know."

I listened with mounting dismay as I waited for my nightmare to come true: I was going to be expelled.

It was then a great surprise when she said, "We would like your help Elena. I've discussed your issue with other faculty members and we're all in agreement. We would like you and Vincent to reconstruct the program." She leaned back in her chair and clasped her hands together. "We've already approached Luke Phillips about writing a true history for Abel Dumont and he's agreed to help us. We believe it's time to share this man's legacy."

I was conflicted. The methods employed to make the Dreamscape Program work in the first place seemed unethical, and it came as a shock that the faculty had been aware of my actions all along.

"I'll consider it," I said, standing to my feet.

She rose with me. "Please do."

I left her office, annoyed and distressed.

Vincent was waiting for me at the end of the hall. "You look like you just woke up from a bad dream," he commented.

I frowned in reply. "They knew all along. They want us to help reconstruct the Dreamscape Program."

"Like hell they do!" Vincent exclaimed.

"Quiet!" I said. I took his hand and led him away from the faculty wing. "This is bad. What if we refuse and they press charges or something?" I was worried.

"On the basis of what?"

"Tampering with their technology, unlawful whatever. I don't know! This is not good." Then I told him, "Luke is going to help them compile Abel Dumont's legacy."

"It's like they're using us now. This place sucks." He rolled his eyes and huffed.

"Maybe we shouldn't look at it from that perspective. We did 'break' the program. It's sort of logical that we be asked to fix it – or rather, you're the one they really need. I'm just being asked as a courtesy."

We walked together, until we had left the building and been greeted with a subdued afternoon sun. It was a mild day with little wind.

"Fine. I guess we should do it then. Don't want to end up on their blacklist." He was obviously unhappy. But Vincent didn't like feeling forced to do something.

The process of 'fixing' the Dreamscape Program was tedious. The entire tech program had been tasked with cleaning up the system and rewriting parts of the code.

The truth about what had taken place wasn't revealed all at once. Yet little by little over time, the story was pieced together in the form of a research document. Luke and I collaborated on a paper discussing Abel Dumont's dream theories and subsequent research. The one area we struggled to explain was the Dream Guardians. I believed the two children to have really existed in the program, despite Abel Dumont's apparent aversion to them in the end. Luke disagreed. He stuck to his theory that what we'd experienced was all part of Abel Dumont's delusion inside the program. It was a point of contention for some time, until at last, we agreed to explain each theory as possibilities, instead of concrete fact. The theories surrounding the ancient Dream Guardians were compiled in a separate document.

Even after it was all over, I sometimes watched that first nightmare, analyzing each part and trying to understand what it meant. According to Abel Dumont, I was in *his* dreamscape. Therefore, the images were most significant to him, which is why I had difficulty understanding them. I spent some time studying the dead faces on the walls, and managed to find old photos of the patients Abel Dumont had treated. They were the same. Some of those people had indeed died, possibly as a result of Abel Dumont's treatments. The few who survived the treatment lived to be quite old. Helen Locke for example had only recently passed away, and not from any kind of disease, but natural causes.

That mystery was solved.

Much of the rest I already knew. The small figure that had so frequently visited me in my dreamscape was supposedly what remained of one of the Dream Guardians. When it opened its mouth to reveal the dead faces, I knew it had absorbed those people and devoured their dreams. The shadows were remnants of the nightmares.

Vincent and I couldn't explain how sitting in the two machines had wiped the nightmare away. We thought perhaps our joined effort to wake was enough to rid Abel Dumont of his nightmares and release him from the program. In the end, we were uncertain what Abel Dumont hoped to achieve. Perhaps he remained in the program and used his machine again and again, attempting to prolong his life. It seemed as if this created a distortion in his dreamscape, diluting it and further corrupting his nightmares. That's what Luke thought, anyway.

Strangely, Vincent's migraines never returned, and since using the Somnium Medicus inside the program, I've hardly ever been sick or had trouble sleeping. It's possible these anomalies were nothing more than a "pseudo-effect." We believed the Somnium Medicus to have healed us, and our bodies yielded to that belief. I for one think we were really healed.

Several weeks later, the Dreamscape Program was restored. It came as no surprise to me that Vincent was the one who got it to work again. He created a new, artificial loop for the program to feed on, using his own hack program.

"If anyone ever stumbles into that nightmare, they'll be scared half to death," he joked, referring to the loop he'd created. Oddly, the program needed to be fed an endless dream of its own in order to work.

I was nervous when lab sessions were resumed. It was the first time I would log back into the Dreamscape Program since it had stopped working and I kept imagining the nightmares would begin again. I contemplated making some excuse to get out of lab, but Vincent insisted everything would be fine.

"It would be nice to see one of your *real* dreams," he said.

I placed the halo on my head and leaned back in the lab chair nervously.

"You forgot to set your parameters," Vincent said, ironically. He did it for me, meeting my eyes with a suppressed smile on his face. Then as he sat in his own chair and prepared to log in, he turned to me and said, "Sweet dreams."

# EPILOGUE

*(Excerpt from the memoirs of Abel Dumont)*

*I fear death.*

*For many years now I have had the same dream — a haunting, dire dream that gives me no rest. I am forced to look upon evil and I see myself dying as an old, decrepit man. But I believe I have finally found a way out of the nightmare — a way to prolong my own life.*

*It will not be an easy task. Though there are many who suffer from night terrors, few are willing to try the experimental technology I've assembled, which is still in the developmental phase. It is necessary that I find strong dreamers. I need their ability to dream, for the purpose of my plan.*

*I know what I am doing. Some of my colleagues have denounced my science, saying that it treads on the unnatural; that it plays at God. They are foolish. I know I can accomplish what the ancient texts describe. Too long has this wondrous secret remained hidden from humanity. Imagine! It is locked away in our dreams. I must uncover it at any cost.*

*There is one other thing I fear: that the evil in my nightmares consume me and I will die anyway. It must not be so. I will elude Death; yes, and bring life to others. I will not go down the path of darkness. I will make my own path.*

*Acknowledgements*

I would like to thank my parents for raising me to know God, who gives us the ability to dream. Without dreams, I would never write. I would also like to thank my older brother for sharing his dreams with me when we were children, and for inspiring me to be creative. Also, my sister for reading through my original manuscript and giving me the criticism I needed to make this story better. I thank my husband for his support in my writing journey, and his willingness to provide ideas to help my stories along.

A special thank you to my high school teachers for their influence. Years later, I remembered your lessons while writing this story!

Lastly, thanks to all my friends who have read my work and encouraged me along the way. You know who you are! I'm forever grateful.

Made in the USA
Middletown, DE
25 May 2021